what lies between us

A Novel

ALSO BY NAYOMI MUNAWEERA

Island of a Thousand Mirrors

what lies between us

A Novel

NAYOMI MUNAWEERA

Perera Hussein Publishing House
COLOMBO

Published by the Perera Hussein Publishing House, 2023
www.pererahussein.com
First printed, 2016, reprinted 2019

ISBN: 978-955-8897-27-0

For sale in Sri Lanka only

First published by St. Martin's Press, New York 2016

Printed and bound by Thomson Press

 To offset the environmental pollution caused by printing books, the Perera-Hussein Publishing House grows trees in Puttalam, Sri Lanka's semi-arid zone.

To Whit.

You and I have always shared a love of words.

But (always) there are only three words that matter.

You will leave behind everything you love
most dearly, and this is the arrow
the bow of exile first lets fly.

—DANTE ALIGHIERI, *The Divine Comedy*

PROLOGUE

A child is nourished upon her mother's blood. If it is a time of star-
vation in the village, the crops lean, the riverbed dry, a mother takes
what food there is and gives it to her child. She denies herself, mor-
tifies her flesh, suffers in silence rather than let her child feel the
smallest discomfort. All creatures abide by this law. This is the way
of nature. To be otherwise is to be unnatural, to be a monster, out-
side the pale.

In a region stretching from the Himalayas to Japan lives an animal
called the moon bear. It is named for the luminous sickle moon glow-
ing in the midst of its midnight chest. The moon bear is the genetic
originator of every bear on the planet; it is the great ursine ancestor,
content to wander within its secret realms. It lives in the treetops,
climbing high to huff at that celestial orb by which it is claimed. It
lives on a fairy diet of acorns, honey, termites, cherries, and mush-
rooms; it is a peaceable citizen of these wild and lonely places.

The moon bear is not just ancient and magnificent, it is also in possession of something treasured by humans. In Chinese medicine the moon bear's bile is believed to remove heat from the body, curing tragic ailments of the liver and the eye. A kilogram of bear bile is valued at half the price of that other, shinier human obsession: gold.

Thousands of moon bears are captured and stuffed into small "crush cages." In these devices they are unable to stand upright or turn around. They may be kept in this condition for decades. Periodically each bear's stomach is slit and into the incision is inserted a tube that drains the precious health-giving liquid. Human beings ingest the bile and swear by this tonic for their various and painful afflictions.

Some years ago, at a Chinese bile farm, a mother moon bear did something thought to be outside the realm of her animal nature. Hearing her cub crying from inside a nearby crush cage, she broke through her own iron bars. The terrified men cowered, but she did not maul them. Instead, she reached for her cub, pulled it to her, and strangled it. Then she smashed her head against the wall until she died.

Why do I tell this story? Only because it tells us everything we need to know about the nature of love between a mother and a child.

part one

one

The walls of my cell are painted an industrial white. They must think the color is soothing. Where I come from, it connotes absence, death, and loneliness.

People write to me. Mothers, mostly; they spew venom. That's not surprising. I have done the unthinkable. I have parted the veil and crossed into that other unseen country. They hate me because I am the worst thing possible. I am the bad mother.

But here's a secret: in America there are no good mothers. They simply don't exist. Always, there are a thousand ways to fail at this singularly important job. There are failures of the body and failures of the heart. The woman who is unable to breastfeed is a failure. The woman who screams for the epidural is a failure. The woman who picks her child up late knows from the teacher's cutting glance that she is a failure. The woman who shares her bed with her baby has failed. The woman who steels herself and puts on noise-canceling earphones to erase the screaming of her child in the next room has failed just as spectacularly. They must all hang their heads in guilt and shame because they haven't done it perfectly, and motherhood is, if anything, the assumption of perfection.

Then too, motherhood is broken because in this place, to be a good mother is to give yourself completely. It is to erase yourself. This is what I refused to do. So they shudder when they hear my name, but inwardly they smile because they have not failed in the way I have.

There are others who write. Men who find the grotesque act I have committed titillating. They send propositions and proposals of marriage that I tear up into scraps of white that match the walls of my cell. I hate their unknown, unseen faces. They remind me that in this country, celebrity is courted no matter the cause. The fact that strangers have heard your name and know the secrets of your life is supposed to be pleasing.

I never wanted this macabre interest, this unsettling notoriety. I never asked for it. I would have preferred to have been locked up and forgotten. Instead, I have become a known thing. My name, the one I had before, is gone. Instead I am named by the act I have committed. To be named thus is to be pinned down onto the corkboard with a needle piercing one's abdomen and a curl of paper underneath with one's genus and species on it in slanted writing. I have been named, and therefore you think you know my story, why I did what I did. To this I object. Perhaps this narrative is a way to undo your knowing, to say the truth is somewhere else entirely, and I will tell it in my own voice, in my own time.

And so, as all stories must open, in the beginning, when I was the child and not yet the mother . . .

Birth. My face was pressed against the bones of Amma's pelvis, stuck there, so that instead of slipping out, I was bound like a lost fish in a too-narrow stream. It wasn't until the midwife, tiring of my mother's screams, reached in with her forceps, grabbed the side of my head, and wrenched me out that I was born and Amma was born into motherhood, both of us gasping from the effort of transformation.

For three months after, there was a hornlike protrusion on the left side of my head. It subsided eventually, but for those months my parents were alarmed. "We didn't know if it would ever go away. I didn't know what sort of child I had given birth to. You were the strangest creature. A little monster," Amma admitted. "But then the swelling went down and you were our perfect little girl."

After that, the doctor looked at my mother's slimness, her girlish frame, and said, "No more. Only this one. Any more will wreck you." She had wanted scores of children filling the grand old house. She had wanted so many to love her. The love of an entire army she had created herself. She rubbed her nose against mine and said, "Only you to love me. So you must love me double, triple, quadruple hard. Do you see?" I nodded. She kissed me on the forehead, searched my eyes. I was blissful in the sun of her love, my entire being turned like a flower toward her heat.

Yes, I could love her more. I could love her enough to fill up the hole all those brothers and sisters had left by never coming.

I was born in Sri Lanka, a green island in the midst of the endless Indian Ocean. I grew up in Kandy, the hill city of the Buddhists. A city held high like a gem in the setting of the island. Maha Nuwara, meaning the great city, is the name of Kandy in Sinhala. Or even Kande Ude Rata, the land on top of the mountain. It is the last capital of the Lankan kings before the British came to "domesticate and civilize," to build railroads and scallop the hills into acres of fragrant tea. In their un-sinuous tongue, Kande Ude Rata collapses, folds into itself, and emerges as Kandy. But not candy sweet in the mouth, because this place has a certain history.

In the capital Colombo's National Museum in a dusty glass case lies the sari blouse of one of the last noblewomen of the Kandyan Kingdom. Splotches of faded red stain the moldering fabric of each shoulder. The last Kandyan king was fighting the British when his trusted adviser too turned against him. Enraged, the king summoned his adviser's wife. His men ripped her golden earrings out of her flesh, so she bled down onto this blouse. They beheaded her children and placed the heads into a giant mortar. They gave her a huge pestle, the kind village women use to pound rice, and forced her to smash the heads of her children. Then they tied her to a rock and threw her into Kandy Lake as the king watched in triumph from the balcony of the temple palace. Soon after, the British conquered Kandy and took over the island for centuries.

This is the history of what we do to one another. This is the story of what it means to be both a child of a mother and a child of history.

The house I grow up in is big and old. It has belonged to my father's family for generations. It has rooms full of ebony furniture, waxed, polished red floors, white latticework that drips from the eaves like lace, and dark wooden steps that lead to my little bedroom upstairs. A wrought-iron balcony hangs outside my window under a tumble of creeping plants. If I stand on its tiny platform just over the red-tiled roof of the first floor, I can see our sweeping emerald lawns leading down to the rushing river. Along the bank a line of massive trees stretches upward toward the monsoon clouds.

In the living room is a small, slightly moldy taxidermied leopard. There are very much alive dogs in the house, but the leopard is my infant obsession. This is because the leopard lets me ride him, while the dogs do not. Amma says I should call him Bagheera, for Kipling's black leopard, but the name Kaa, for Kipling's Indian rock python, is what I choose. The sound is easier and there is something slithery in his yellow marble eyes. Exactly between these eyes is the neat bullet hole that my father's father put there. The hunting guns are locked away in a chest in my father's study, but the leopard is here as evidence of their presence.

A formal portrait of my grandparents hangs above the leopard. My mustachioed grandfather is in a three-piece suit, my grandmother in a Kandyan osari over a Victorian blouse, ruffled and buttoned against the tropical heat. My father is a boy in short trousers, the only child of the five my grandmother gave birth to to have survived the ravages of malaria.

The house is a kingdom divided into dominions, inside and outside, and ruled over by the keepers of my childhood, Samson and Sita. In the kitchen, Sita shuffles about in her cotton sari, her feet bare. She has been with my father's family since he was a baby. She and her sister came as young girls. Her sister was my father's ayah, while Sita set up court in this kitchen, which she has never left.

Samson is Sita's nephew. His mother has returned to the village down south they came from so long ago, but Samson stays to wrestle our garden. Once a week he cuts the lawn, balancing on his heels, sarong pulled up along his thighs. He swipes the machete back and forth as he makes his crab-legged way across the grass. His skin shines like wet eggplant, and at his throat a silver amulet flashes in the sun. "Inside this. All my luck!" he says. He has pulled it open before to show me what it holds, a tightly rolled scroll of minuscule Sinhala script, a prayer of protection bought by his mother from the village temple at a great price. She believes it will keep him safe from the malevolent influences, the karmic attachments that prey upon the good-hearted.

I am eight years old, tiny and spindly, and Samson is my very best friend. After school I race to throw off my uniform, kick away my shoes, slip into a housedress and Bata slippers, and escape into the garden. The red hibiscus flower nodding its head, yellow pistil extended like a wiry five-forked snake tongue; the curl of ferns; the overhead squawk of parrots—these are the wonders that welcome me home.

Samson speaks to me in Sinhala. He says, "Ah, Baby Madame. Home already? Come!" He swings me onto his shoulders. My thighs grip the sides of his throat, my legs hook behind his back. I reach both hands up into the guava tree to catch the orbs that are swollen and about to split, a wet pink edge in their jade skins. I grab, twist, and pull. The branches bounce and the birds rise, squawking in loud outrage. His arm reaches up to steady me. When my pockets are bulging he gently places me on the ground.

I bite into sun-warmed guava, that familiar sweet tang, small gemlike seeds crunching between my teeth. Samson is cutting away dead leaves from orchids suspended in baskets from the tree trunks.

I ask, "Why do they call these flowers Kandyan dancers?"

I already know why. These small yellow orchids are named for the dancers of this region because with petal and stamen the flowers imitate perfectly the headdresses and the sarongs, the drums and white shell necklaces that the twirling dancers wear. But I ask because I want to hear him talk and also because I want to show off what I have learned in school. I want to show how much more I know even now at eight years old because I have gone to school and he has only ever been a servant in our house.

He says, "This is the name. No? What else can we call them but their name?"

"No! I mean, did they call the flowers after the dancers or the dancers after the flowers?"

"You are the one who goes to school, Baby Madame. How could Samson know these things? Ask your teachers? Ask someone who knows these big-big things." A perfect yellow flower loosens its grip, tumbles to the grass. He stoops and picks it up between thumb and forefinger as gently as if it were a wounded insect, places it on his palm, and holds it out to me. I tug the rubber band at the end of my plait loose and settle the flower there.

He says, "Come, Baby Madame. I need your small fingers to work in the pond today." We walk over and he sits on the edge while I kick off my rubber slippers, hike up my dress around my thighs, and slip into the water. My feet in the mud, I reach into the water up to my armpits, follow the fibrous stalks of the lotus plants down to their main stem. I pull so the plants tear loose, the mud releasing the roots reluctantly. The koi come to investigate this curiosity in their midst. Their silver, orange-streaked quickness flashes all about me, their mouths coming up to nibble at whatever they can find, shins, calves, fingers. I work my way across the cool muddy water, throw the too-fast-growing lotuses onto the bank, where a mound of uprooted leaves, stems, and unfurled flowers lie open to the sky. Samson gathers the beautiful debris. He will burn it with the evening's other rubbish.

Other days I am the watcher and he the worker. I squat on the bank with a bucket as Samson wades in. He spreads his fingers wide to catch yards of gelatinous strands studded with shiny beadlike eggs, then returns to deposit these offerings in the bucket, which turn quickly into a shuddering viscous mass. Waist-high in the deepest part of the pond, he says, "Bloody buggers. Laying eggs everywhere. Pond is chockablock full already."

I say, "In France people eat them."

Astonishment on his face. "What? No, Baby Madame, don't tell lies. Who would eat these ugly buggers? What is there to eat?"

"Yes they do. Our teacher said. They eat the legs."

He stares at the water between his own legs and says, "No. Can't be. Legs are so thin. Nothing there to eat . . . Maybe the fat stomach, no?"

"No. The legs. She said."

He shakes his head. "Those people must be very poor. I might be poor like that if I wasn't with your family." A little nod acknowledges all the years he has lived with us—all my life, all his much longer life. "But even if I was on the street I wouldn't eat these buggers."

"But they are a delicacy there. In France."

"Shall we try, Baby Madame? We can catch them and give Sita to make a badum. Badum of frog."

"No!"

"That's what Baby will eat tonight. Just like the people in Fran-see. Fried frog curry with rice." He raises his arms, trailing streams of jelly in the air; he looks like a tentacled creature rising from the depths and shakes his fists so the water sparkles, lands on my bare thighs. Our laughter echoes across the pond.

In the monsoon months, the gardens are a different place, the ground sodden, the pond swollen. The sky lights up in the midst of dark stormy days as if a mighty photographer is taking pictures of our little piece of earth. It isn't unusual to come upon a flash of silver and gold, a koi flapping on the wet grass, swept out of the pond by the onslaught of rain. The river is dangerous at this time. It rushes by, carrying all manner of things—furniture, quickly rolling trees with beseeching arms held out to the sky, drowned animals. It is a boiling, heaving mass. The banks could crumble inward, the ground falling away under your feet. We all know this; in these months we keep away from the garden and the river.

Evenings in the living room, the brass cutwork lamp throws a parade of shadows on every surface. My father reads student papers; he is a professor of history at the University of Peradeniya and always has this stack of work to bury himself in. I read books in English. Stories of boarding schools and midnight feasts featuring foods I've never tasted, but yearn desperately for. I read about children who have to put on scarves and mittens and hats to go outside and wish I too had a pair of mittens. What would they look like covering my small hands? What would they feel like? How exciting to live in a snowy place and eat crunchy red apples and chocolate digestive biscuits. How exotic, how enticing. How boring my life is in comparison.

Here then are my father and I, each of us wrapped in these other worlds. My father is reading about some atrocity of the raj, shaking his head now and then, sharing out bits and pieces with us. This is how, of course, I first heard of the Lankan lady mashing up her children's heads. My father is denouncing colonialization and the history of imperialism while I, thoroughly colonialized by the very books he had approved for me, secretly dream of some other more desirable and colder childhood. But a third person is with us, and it is her presence that brings us all together.

My mother sits and stares at a page in a Mills & Boon novel. Sometimes she sighs loudly, declaratively. Sometimes she leaps up, puts on music, grabs my hands, sends my book flying, says, "Come, child! Dance." Anxiety and joy flood through me in equal measure. Joy at her closeness, anxiety at the thought of what my ungraceful feet are doing under me.

She holds me, her hands on my haunches, pushing them one way and then the other. "Like this, like this, sway your body, move, child. Don't be so stiff. Move around." My elegant, beautiful mother. I can read the messages in the arch of her supple, fluid body: "How is this my child? So different from me, so stiff and so serious?" I can't tell her that I am not serious. That it is only this unexpected closeness to her that is making me awkward and gawky. In the garden with Samson, in the kitchen with Sita, I can dance mad baila like an undulating dervish. I can lose myself and be just a whirl of motion. I can be silly and unfettered and ridiculous. But here with her, I am tongue-tied and thick-footed.

Her hands push me away. Quick footsteps. The bedroom door slams, reverberating through the house. My father looks up from his papers and says, "Your mother is delicate. We need to treat her carefully. You understand this, don't you? The need for care."

Of course I do. She is my mother. I know better than anyone that she must be handled with diligence, like all things precious and dangerous.

Sometimes on the weekends when I wander down to the kitchen, she is already there. She says, "We don't need Sita today. I sent her to the market. I'll make you breakfast myself." I sit at the table and watch. She talks fast, her housecoat wrapped over her nightdress, her hair pulled into a gushing ponytail on the very top of her head, cascading down in an inky waterfall to her elbows. She says, "I'll make pancakes. The way you like. Thin. Crispy like an appa." Her fingers crack eggs on the rim of the bowl, slide them in with one quick motion. "Just the way you like."

I watch this mother, the one that appears sometimes. She is demonstrative, coming over to hug me, so I open my nostrils wide to inhale her scent—like nothing else, the smell of this woman. She pushes a bowl at me. "Here, you whip the eggs." She heats oil, tilts the pan to coat it. Pours the batter onto the hot oil and swirls it so that the thinnest of crepes emerge. She flips these onto a plate, sprinkles sugar granules on the hot surface, squeezes a lemon over it, rolls up the little package, and passes the plate to me. I love the sweetness and the bite of the lemon, the hot delicious crepe. She watches me with hungry eyes. She never eats while I do. Watching me is enough for her, she says.

This too happens. I'm playing outside her locked door, waiting and wishing for her. I'm being careful, but somehow the big doll slips from my fingers, falls banging on the wooden floors. Her bedroom door whacks open and she comes for me. The clutch of her fingers around my upper arm is like a tourniquet. Her face close to mine, she hisses, "I told you to be quiet. I need to rest. I *need* to sleep. Migraine is splitting my head apart. You *need* to be silent. Do. You. Understand." Important information is being transmitted. Yes, I understand. I must not make noise. I must be quiet; I must let her rest. By the age of seven I have learned the lesson of silence perfectly.

In every house on this island, in a frame as extravagant or as meager as the family's fortunes can afford, is the talisman of the wedding portrait. Without this photograph the house cannot stand.

The wedding photograph of my parents is in a heavy gold frame poised in the center of the living room wall. It shows my mother enwrapped in a Kandyan osari, her eyes huge, the gleam of lipstick on those virgin lips. Her neck is weighed down by the seven concentric gold necklaces that go from encircling her throat to dangling at her waist. Her hair is bisected by a ruler-straight part, on one side of it an ornament in the shape of a dazzling sunburst and on the other a curved crescent moon.

Next to her, my young father-to-be wears the costume of the Kandyan kings. In later decades it will become fashionable for all young grooms to don these garments, but during this period, the early 1970s, they are still reserved exclusively for the old Kandyan families. So he wears it not as fashion but as a marker of a certain heritage, a certain history. Here on his feet are the curved slippers, and above that, the various complicated sarongs. One's eyes move upward to the maroon matador jacket studded at the shoulders with sequined lions. On his head is a tricornered crown, itself topped with a small golden bodhi tree. The only costume in the world perhaps where the male's outshines the female's.

They don't look at each other, these two. They face the camera and barely touch. They are not smiling; smiles were not requisite in those days. This is one of the only photographs that has survived, so it remains here large on the wall. If my mother had had another, she would have replaced this one, but she doesn't, so it is the one that endures.

When Amma is in a bright mood she tells me how matches are made. We are Sinhalese Buddhists, and this is how it has always worked. When a son comes of age, a mother makes inquiries. The matchmaker comes to the house wearing his cleanest white sarong and swinging his black umbrella, sheaves of astrological charts and photographs of girls in his battered briefcase. He sits in the best chair and makes his pronouncements. "The Kalutara

Ratnasomas have four daughters of marriageable age. No sons. The mother must have very bad karma. The eldest girl is ready and they are eager to find a boy for her so that they can also start looking for the younger three."

When he leaves, the women of the family gather to compare the girls he has suggested. Beauty, lineage, docility, and culinary skills—these are the subjects of comparison. And then a girl is chosen. For a doctor son, an engineer son, a mother can expect a pretty, fair-skinned daughter-in-law from a good family. For a son who drinks or who is lame, who shouts so the neighbors can hear, a dark girl or one who has done badly at her O levels will do. A dowry of course changes everything. A father will collect money for years to marry off a daughter. A father of many daughters is an unlucky man: he will work tirelessly, and after his girls are married off, will have nothing to show for it.

Everybody knows that happiness in marriage is not expected. It is a possibility, of course, but it is not the reason one gets married. If it happens, one is lucky, but marriages are arranged for many reasons—financial, social, as a calming agent on the hot tempers of young men and the possible waywardness of young girls. Happiness is hoped for but is never an expected consequence.

Amma says, "We didn't do it like that. We broke the rules." I can tell she is both proud of and ashamed about this. They had been on an up-country bus. My father, a young man on his way to the university; Amma, a girl of unknown pedigree, certainly not someone his parents if they had been alive would have approved of. He had seen her, her bare arm snaking up out of her sari blouse sleeve to hold on to the swaying strap of that bus, which moved like a boat. She was willowy in her printed sari, her feet in leather sandals, the toenails painted the lightest blush of pink. He had looked at these toes and then dared to look at her face, and she had not looked away, as almost any other young woman would have done. Instead she had held his gaze for the briefest moment, and he had been snagged on that glance.

She says, "He had a nice shirt. I knew he was a Peradeniya boy, and that was all the difference." She continues, "He passed me notes after that. On the bus. He was so nervous. He didn't even need to take the bus. He had the car. But that one day it had broken down and he had taken the bus, and from then on, every day he took the bus and I was there."

He'd had his friends make inquiries. They learned that she was poor. Her sister and she were living with relatives after the parents had been lost in some typhoid complication. Her dowry was meager. What she did have was beauty, and for my father, who owned this house by the river, whose own parents had died, and even more important, who was rich enough to do as he pleased—including studying something as useless as history, getting a doctorate in it, and then teaching it at the university—this was enough.

They saw each other on the bus for months. He passed her notes that declared his undying passion, slipping them into the open mouth of the shopping bag at her feet or into the cheap unclasped bag under her armpit. She never responded either in

word or through letters of her own. She never even looked at him
again. That initial meeting of his gaze, that was all she could de-
clare. After that everything was up to him. "A girl can't be cheap,"
she says. "You have to maintain yourself. Do you understand?
You have to keep your pride. Without that, a girl is nothing."

They met formally thrice before they were married. He went to
her relatives' small, battered house and was fussed over and served
weak tea and plain cake on two occasions. Once he had escorted
her to the cinema, where a thin, sweating aunt had sat between
them and they had watched the earnest Professor Higgins labor
over the guttersnipe Eliza Doolittle's vowels before falling in
love with her. The young professor sat in the dark and wondered
if he could enact a similar metamorphosis with the girl who sat
on the other side of the thin aunt. Meanwhile, the girl was rigid
with terror and excitement at the spectacle of the moving giants
above her. It was her very first movie. She was seventeen years
old, and her suitor was twenty-nine.

After the movie they went for falooda and Chinese rolls. The
thin aunt had gone off to the bathroom and the young man had
realized that what he had seen in her eyes when she first met his
gaze on the bus had not been passion or rebellion but desperation. It was frightening to realize this, but it did nothing to as-
suage his desire. He was hooked.

They were engaged and her relations were jubilant. Most incredible, this bridegroom had not asked about dowry, had not
mentioned the requisite plots of land, refrigerators, or houses that

were usually expected. His own family was livid. An extensive collection of aunts and uncles and cousins and assorted jetsam of the far-flung family refused to come to the wedding. There were only the groom's colleagues and their wives. On the bride's side, only her older sister, some of her badly dressed family, and a few of her young school friends, shy around the older people. It was a truncated and odd assortment in a country where extravagant weddings are a national pastime. And then even in this small gathering, all around the couple, a hum of gossip.

One professor's wife bows her head close to another's, says, "Do you know? They met on a *bus*?"

The other takes a shocked suck of air. "What? Can't be."

"It's true. I heard from Sujatha's son."

"These modern girls. They'll do anything to catch a good one."

"Yes men. Can you imagine if his parents were alive to see?"

"They must be turning in their graves. Such a good old Kandyan family."

"Yes. What to do? The world is not what it was. All the old rules are broken."

They, the newlyweds, heard the whispers and ignored them. They ran out to his car in a hail of rice. No more buses for them. Then they were alone. They were not used to each other's scents or tastes. The bride had only ever shared a bed with her older sister. They had never kissed or held hands. But this was normal and natural. For it to be otherwise would have been unthinkable. In this place and time, one did not dip a toe into marriage; one plunged into it, fully dressed.

There is only one other wedding picture in the house. It sits on my mother's dressing table, and when she sees me looking at it, she says, "I was just a child. Only seventeen. And I had you the next year. You were with us from the very beginning. It was always the three of us." She considers the picture and tells me the story yet again. "Only those two photographs. The photographer went out and got drunk after the wedding. Got in a fight and destroyed his camera. All the rolls were ruined. I cried for a week when they told me. Thank god, at least Aruna Uncle had a camera. Otherwise even these two we wouldn't have."

Beneath the glass of its frame, the photograph still shows off its cobwebbed crinkles. I had been small, maybe four or five. I had awoken in the middle of the night to loud voices. I had slipped out of my narrow bed and gone to stand in the hallway that led to their bedroom. I saw his arm raised and this photograph in its previous frame hurled across the room. Heard the crash of it against the wall. He saw me then. He came to the door, put his finger to his lips. *Shh,* he was saying, I must be quiet. I must be good and go back to bed. He closed the door.

Later either he or she had taken the picture, unfurled it, and put it in a new frame. It was something I learned then. That you could take the crumpled remains of something destroyed and smooth them into newness. You could pretend certain things weren't happening even when you had seen or felt them. Everything done can be denied.

Sometimes at twilight she goes out to stand at the line of trees by the river's edge. She watches the dark water flow by her bare feet.

I watch from a window. I know my father is watching her from a different window in his study. His hand is curled around a glass of arrack. He will drink for hours and then he will fall asleep in his chair. I have found him there, his head lolling on the student papers, the empty glass dropped from his nerveless fingers onto the floor, making a pungent puddle by his bare feet. I don't wake him. I have done this before and he had looked at me with some terrible warning in his eyes, so now I always let him be.

Now from our separate windows, we watch her. She does not belong to us, but to some other state, some other mood, and even if we called to her, she would ignore us or stare back at the house, past us in the windows as if we did not exist. When the sun drops as suddenly as a shot bird, all we can see are her earrings, jagged lines of silver that dart from the tips of her earlobes to the silhouette of her rounded shoulders. We watch these lightning flashes until they too disappear.

two

She bakes cakes; she sings songs. She sews clothes for herself and for me and my dolls on her Singer. Matching outfits in the same fabric—a long yellow maxi for her, a mini for me, and a tiny replica for my doll. She is bright; she is beaming. She is just like the mother in my English storybooks.

But some mornings I wake to muffled shouting across the hall. I pull the single sheet over my head and pretend it is only the roar of the ocean, which I have seen on trips to Colombo.

Later my father tells Samson, "Keep an eye on Madame today. Okay, Samson? She's resting."

"Yes sir."

He drives me to school. Hours later, I come back in a trishaw with my friend Puime, who lives nearby. Samson greets me at the gate, takes my bag. I say, "Did Amma come out?"

He says, "No, Baby Madame, not today."

I go and sit against her door, my knees folded under me, an ear pressed to the wood. I hear nothing. No rustling of clothes, no whisper of pages, not even the sound of a body turning in bed. For hours I wait to hear the slightest sound, the merest whisper of evidence that she is inside. Crying, shouting, raging—anything rather than this haunted silence.

Later I open the door and go in as quietly as I can, moving as sly as a cat. She lies in the bed, her eyes following the spokes of sunlight that move across the wall. I climb onto the bed, take the hand that lies clenched over the coverlet, ease open the fingers. She clutches my hand like she is drowning, won't look at me.

We stay like this for a long time and then her head whips across the pillow, her gaze narrowing on me. "Why do you always *look* at me like that?"

My heart racing, I shrug.

"Honestly, child, what is wrong with you? Sometimes I feel like you will eat me up. It's frightening."

I look away. How do tell her I am afraid she will disappear? That one day I will push against the door, come in on my cat feet, and find no sign of her. They will tell me that she never existed. That I never had a mother. It is the most terrifying thing I can think.

On good days she leaves her room as soon as my father's car has pulled away and goes down to the garden with Samson. When I don't have to go to school, I follow along, quiet as a shadow. I listen to them speaking in Sinhala, a language she never uses with my father. Samson says, "Look, Madame, the double-petaled hibiscus has flowered." Her face dips to the blossoms, deep red and frilled like one of her dresses. The stamens leave golden stains on her nose. They stay there because he cannot reach out and dust them off as I can, or as my father can.

She sits on the wicker chair under the shade of spreading trees and arranges lush bouquets of frangipani, jasmine, and orchids, giant crab claws curving over the other blossoms. Samson brings her a silver tray of tea and sandwiches and waits to hear her instructions: the new flowers she wants planted, the number of coconuts he must scale the trees for.

She waves her slender arm and says, "Samson, don't you see? There, in the guava tree. The birds are eating all the fruit." Samson says, "Yes, Madame," and runs to chase the birds away while she watches keen as a hawk.

She does not believe in safety. Catastrophe is always around the corner. It is clear in the sharpness with which she looks at me if I sneeze or cough. The sudden fear sparking in her voice like a match lit in a dark room. "Are you getting sick? Are you feeling hot? Come here." The back of her cool hand against my throat, her palm cupping my forehead. If I go to the toilet at night, I creep silent along the wall, afraid to turn on the light, feeling my way with my bare toes. She calls out in the dark: "Is that you? Where are you going?" Her voice urgent, afraid, wide awake.

She is afraid of *as vaha*, evil eye. *As* meaning eye and *vaha* meaning poison. The poison that drips from covetous eyes. She believes that people envy the good fortune that has brought her to this house, saved her from whatever horrors there were before. The as vaha can bring ill fortune, sickness, and death, so once a year she takes me to a temple where a Hindu priest sits bare-chested, ash on his forehead. He takes the small green limes we have brought and holds each one up to my forehead one by one. He slices them in two with his silver lime cutter. Fifty limes, cut one by one. He intones the verses that will splash acid juice in the eyes of all those who envy our good luck.

We don't tell Thatha about these trips. He is Buddhist in a lazy way, but he will not like this. He will say that she is polluting her Buddhism with these Hindu rituals and superstitions. So the lime-cutting trips are a secret held tight between Amma and me.

In the morning before school I am tugging my hair into sections for braids. The rules are strict. The part in the hair must be straight as a ruler and the hair must be pulled away from our faces, secured at the ends with the blue ribbons that along with the blue tie on the white uniform are emblematic of our school.

Amma comes in quietly, takes the comb from me, glides it through my hair, the teeth a gentle rasp against my skull, her hands careful. There is a slight tug as she sections the hair, inter-twines the shanks. I close my eyes and imagine that this is always so. We are like this for a long, quiet time. She says, "I think that's good." A kiss on the top of my head. "That looks nice, right?" We survey her work in the mirror. My plaits are perfect, so much better than what I can usually manage alone. I say, "Yes, Amma. That's very nice. Thank you." She breathes a sigh of relief, pats my head, goes off. Some loveliness blooms.

Thatha's dogs, Punch and Judy, were named for the puppets that were popular in his childhood. They lie at his feet watching his face with the devotion of lovers, waiting for instruction from this god. There is devotion too in the way he speaks to them. A certain tone of voice that makes these enormous, snarl-snouted dogs writhe with delight when he pauses with his hand on their heads. When he is home, they have no eyes for anyone else. But there are always students waiting, lectures to be written, books to be read, so often the dogs must make do with me. When he is not home, they are my constant companions. I throw stones, which they dash to retrieve. They come back panting, drop saliva-covered, river-smooth rocks at my feet to be thrown again and again.

In a corner of the garden is the well. Its mouth sinks down into the river through some long, secret drop. When the cousins come for school holidays we look over the edge, feel the cool breath of hidden water, peer down into the deep darkness with no end. We drop stones to hear them splash minutes later, shiver to imagine what it would be like to fall, to hurl ourselves into the cold water, to look up and see that perfect circle of light.

On the hottest days when everything is sticky and sweating and the cousins are far away in their boarding schools and Amma is closed up in her darkened room, I make Samson go down to the well with me. I take off my sandals and stand on the soft earth in my cotton housedress. Samson throws the bucket into the depths; we hear it clanging as it falls. He draws it up arm over arm, cold water sloshing over the lip, and says, "Ready, Baby?" I stand there, arms crossed over my shoulders in the fierce beating sunlight, tensed and ready for the chill. And even though I know it is coming, when the icy water spills down over me I jump, looking up through that veil of silver water into the sunlit world. The water is electric, alive. It sets me ablaze, it is so cold. Through chattering teeth I say, "Again, again, again!" He hauls up the bucket, pours the water slowly over my upturned head and shivering body. He does it over and over until finally he says, "Okay, Baby Madame. Enough now. Samson has so much to do and your Amma will be up soon."

I lie flat, spread-eagled on the grass, soaking wet, my dress clinging to me. The red of it has turned a wet maroon. But minute by minute it is pulling free of my skin, the breeze is taking it, the sun is smashing down, and quickly I am dry again, sand dry, the only hint of wetness, like a secret, in the depths of my braids.

In the evenings, Sita brings dishes to the table. Red rice on a platter with a small tea saucer to serve it, the curries in their various bowls, fried beetroot, crackling papadams, a fiery chicken curry. The ceiling fan stirs the air methodically. We gather under it, an assortment of whatever relations have come that night. A clatter of spoons as we serve curries onto the rice. Gathered around the table, we sink our fingers in the food, smashing together rice, silver-skinned fish, fried potatoes, coconut sambol, making perfect bite-size balls, a bit of every delicious thing. The heat of the air, the heat on our tongues, a scorchingly delicate, almost unbearable pleasure.

My mother keeps a sharp eye on every plate, serves whatever is missing before recipients have realized they are low on rice or curry. It is important that everyone be treated well. She has won over my father's family with patience and generosity. But she knows their allegiance is paper-thin and she must be solicitous so that they will not go away bearing tales that she is still that girl he met on the bus.

After dinner, chairs are scraped away and a dance floor is created. Music on the stereo. Boney M. or ABBA. Everyone is singing, "Brown girl in the ring, tra la la la la. There's a brown girl in the ring, tra la la la la la . . . She looks like a sugar in a plum, plum, plum," and then inevitably the baila music starts. Sinhala lyrics on top of old creole Portuguese rhythms. Women hitch saris up to their knees, pretend to be the coy Surangani waiting for her fisherman. They sway around men who channel the fisherman with the freshest catch. A shuffling and swaying of hips as they circle each other, arms hooking, skipping and swaying, eyes and hands flirting. My father refuses to join. But he smiles and claps us on. My mother grabs my hands and sways with me around and around in a riotous circle until I am sure that I am that girl, the "brown girl in the ring . . . like a sugar in the plum." All of us singing the words to songs as we've done hundreds of times.

Later there are long ambling gossips that last through the night. The women stay in the parlor. The men drift out onto the lawn to settle themselves in chairs and nurse their glasses of arrack in the midnight breeze. Their faces are blurred and indistinct in the dark. The smoke rises from mosquito coils. The frogs in the pond sing long and loud. I sit in the hammock-like curve of my father's sarong at his feet, half asleep but listening as they talk, the ebb and flow of voices washing over me. They discuss the situation in the country, the skyrocketing price of everything, the Tamil trouble gathering in the North.

A sudden plunge into darkness in the house behind us, loud *aw*s and *oh*s from the women. The electricity has gone off again. Samson is shouted for and comes slowly, his face lit by candles. The talk continues, the darkness pushing closer until we see one another only as silhouettes. Long drowsy hours of half-lit talking and drinking. And then with the suddenness of a threat, the lights jump on. I had been cradled and almost rocked to sleep in the low sling of my father's sarong.

He says, "Ahaaaa, still here? Go to sleep. Go-go. Quickly before I give you a swift slap." But his voice is laughing. I leave them then, my hand in Sita's as she leads me to my bed. Behind me, that close knot of men still talking and laughing as dawn comes.

I am ten years old and cast in a school play. It is based on a collection of Kipling's stories. I am the evil old Crocodile who snaps onto the trunk of the Elephant's Child and pulls and pulls until the Elephant's Child's once tiny piglike snout is long and sinuous. Onstage under the lights I preen in a costume Amma has labored over on her Singer for weeks. It is the most fantastic of her creations, made of a green bodysuit replete with scales, a long swishing tail waggling behind, a row of white teeth through which I look out upon the delectable Elephant's Child as he approaches my forest pool. I love this. I feel seen. A tingling joy runs through me as I bellow my duplicitous reptilian lines.

Afterward there is applause, and as I come offstage, looking for my parents, Thatha catches me in a bear hug, says, "So good, so good. You were wonderful."

I say, "Really?"

"Yes! Perfect, excellent."

He says, "Okay, come, let's take a photo. Stand here, pose like this. With your friends, now." We pose, all of us in our costumes. Rikki-Tikki-Tavi, Shere Khan, Kaa, Crocodile, Elephant's Child. My arms are around Shivanthi and Puime's shoulders. Thatha is beaming, clicking and clicking. Amma says, "We need to go. Now." I turn to her, wanting to hear everything he has said, but in her voice. She says nothing.

He says, "Come on. Just a few more. Almost done."

She walks by him, and with a heart-sickening crash, Thatha's beloved camera is dashed on the floor, the film curling and exposed, lenses broken, small cogs rolling under women's saris. People stare and whisper. Thatha's face breaks and then reassembles even as he bends to pick up the various pieces, muttering, "An accident. That was an accident," then out loud to anyone who was near and had seen, "An accident, she walked by and it must have caught on her sari. My fault, really. Must be more careful."

She waits for us in the car. The look on her face, imperial. He says, "What the hell was that?"

"What? The camera?"

"Yes, the bloody camera, of course. What else?"

"Well, you should take pictures of the rest of us too."

"Why wouldn't I take pictures of her? It's a big day for her."

"The way you treat her. Don't be sorry when she gets a big head. Spoiled rotten. It's only a school play. What will you do when she attains age? When she gets married? Rent the bloody Grand Oriental Hotel?"

In the backseat, I peer out from between the rows of white teeth and hold on to the tip of my emerald tail and know that I must be even quieter, even more still.

I read *Alice in Wonderland* obsessively. Not because I like it. All those panicked, devious animals, the uncontrollable growings and shrinkings that suggest one's body is never quite one's own. When the Queen of Hearts shouts and demands obedience, it feels real and close. When everyone scampers to obey her orders, when the soldiers paint each white rose red so that she is appeased and satisfied, I understand the threat of the cold blade slicing through their necks. They are waiting to hear her words "Off with their heads!" I too am waiting for the cold steel of her disapproval to drop. In these days I too live in the kingdom of the Queen of Hearts.

I go into the kitchen to find Sita. She is stirring red rice in a pot, rinsing the dust out of it. She watches me from the corner of her eye as I drift about the kitchen. She says, "What happened?"

"Nothing."

She shrugs her shoulders, slowly pours the water out of her pot, not looking at me. I say, "I hate her. She broke Thatha's camera. And he didn't even do anything. He was just taking pictures of me."

She doesn't look at me when she says, "Your mother. She doesn't mean it, you know. She's had a hard life."

"She hates me."

She sighs, turns to me, wipes her hands, says, "Okay, come with me."

She takes me into her little room; unlike Samson's, this one is inside. She sits on the sagging bed and puts her arm around me. She says, "Your mother came to this house very young. She doesn't have any people, you know. Her parents, they died when she and her sister were small. Then her sister went abroad to America. It's difficult to be alone in the world."

I say, "She's not alone. She has Thatha." I don't say the other person she has: me.

She pulls me into the circle of her arms. "Yes. But your Thatha is from a different world. His people are different. They are rich people. Your mother's people were poor like me, like Samson. It's hard for her to fit into this life. To be the big Madame."

I lean into her. "What was it like? Before I was born?"

"We came here together. My sister and I. From a village down south. We came to work for your father's parents. We were young then. My sister had Samson, and then your father was born and she was his ayah. So they were brought up together. But your father is the master now. And Samson is Samson, you see?"

I don't see anything, but I nod so she will continue.

"And then your father grew up and married your mother, and then you were born." She tweaks my nose, grabs my face, and inhales each side of my face, a fierce and potent kiss.

The lotus has risen in the pond again, taking over the water, so the koi must circle the stems. I am not supposed to trim them alone, and anyway it's no fun without Samson. I go to his small shedlike room at the back of the house and I can hear him inside muttering to himself. I have never been inside, but now I say his name and enter his small, enclosed space. He is sitting on his bed; it's bright outside, but inside there are deep shadows. There are posters of film stars on the walls. The place smells like him, as if he has been shut up here for weeks, his sweat permeating everything. I sit on the bed next to him. His face is in his hands, his hair in porcupine quills as if he has run his hands through it. Between his fingers and in a broken voice he says, "Baby Madame, you shouldn't come here."

I put my small hand on his rounded back. "What is it, Samson? What happened?"

He jumps up away from my touch, but there is nowhere to go in that small space. He says, "My mother, Baby Madame. They say she is very sick. I don't know what to do. Your Amma. I can't ask her for leave again. I went to the village last month, and she said if I asked again I should go but not come back." He shakes his head as if to clear it. He turns and looks at me, says, "You should go. If someone sees you in my place, it won't be good." And knowing somehow that he is right, that I shouldn't be found here, I leave that claustrophobic space, my lungs filling with air as I step outside as if I had been holding my breath the whole time.

Later in the week, Amma slaps her palm against the table. "Where the hell is Samson? This floor is filthy." She turns to me. "Make yourself useful. Find him."

I race through the garden down to his tiny room. I know before I enter that it is empty. In the kitchen Sita is crying, wiping the tears with the edge of her sari. She says, "That stupid boy. He went without telling her. Now all hell will come down on our heads."

The lotus grows so thick in the pond that the fish rise close to the skin of the water, their scales dull, their movements sluggish. The guavas drop from the tree until the ground under it is sludgy. I miss Samson as much as the garden does. No one to cavort with on the grass or at the river's edge. No one to pour buckets of silver well water over my head. I sit in the kitchen and sigh until Sita sends me away. Two weeks after he is gone, the news comes to us that his mother has died. Now Sita too must go for the funeral. My mother sits and stares at the river. She does not talk to us and we keep out of her way.

It's two months later and I am sitting next to her when he comes back. We look up and there he is, thinner than before, sparse as if he has not eaten well since he left. There is something new in the way he walks, flat-footed, as if careful to walk anchored so that some rage will not lift him aloft and carry him away. Amma says, "Well, what the hell happened to you? Why didn't you just ask me if you could go?"

He looks at the floor and says, "Sorry, Madame."

"I would have let you go if I knew Kusuma was dying. She looked after my husband when he was small, after all. We would have let you go." But something in his eye tells me he doesn't believe this.

She raises her hand, says, "Okay, you can go back to the garden now. It's running riot. You'll have to work hard to get it in hand."

But he stands there so that she cannot go on reading her newspaper, sipping her tea. She must instead look up at him, and then through gritted teeth he says, "You think you own us? You think that just because we are your servants, you own us?"

My mother's hard laugh is loud. "What, Samson, have you turned into a communist? My goodness, what a speech." Her eyes turn down to her newspaper. "Get out, Samson, go before I get very angry and throw you out. Your people have been with the family for a long time. But I don't need to keep you. I could throw you out at any time. And there are no jobs for people like you out there. Don't forget that." He leaves then and she pets my hair, says, "Servants, one has to know how to deal with them. Otherwise they can go out of control, no?" I nod. Yes, whatever she says, I agree with.

I had missed Samson while he was gone. But now I see a new quality quivering in his eyes, something frustrated and dark. He cuts the grass or tends the plants in silence and refuses to play with me. Now there are no walks in the garden, no wading thigh-high into the pond, no gathering of frog's eggs. His face is stormy, and when I dare ask about the trip to the village, he says, "What's to tell? We had the funeral. We burnt my mother. By the time I went, that's all there was to do," and turns away.

One day after hours of silence he says quietly, "Baby Madame, do you know how they train the wild elephant?"

I'm delighted that he's talking to me again. "No, Samson."

"They tie a big log to its leg when it's small. It pulls and pulls, but the log will not move. It fights so hard. But at some time it will give up, and then later, when it is very much bigger than the little men who control it, they will not need that log. It will re-member the weight on its leg and it will not fight. It will just remember the weight. Do you understand?"

I don't. I stand there waiting and he says, "Samson is like that elephant. Maybe I could have done something else. Maybe had a trishaw or a small shop? A wife. A woman of my own. Maybe children. Something. So now I'm like that elephant. Even my mother I couldn't see before she died. I went out to see if I could have a life away from your family, but there was nothing. Not even a job. I almost starved."

He turns and walks away from me, and I am suddenly and irrevocably shattered by loneliness.

three

Another photo on the wall. Three rows of girls, the tall ones in the back, the short ones sitting in front with crossed ankles, hands on knees. Our teacher, Sister Angelica, is poised in the very center, her hands held together, her hair hidden under the nun's habit. Around her so many hunched shoulders, thin bodies, white short-sleeved shirts bisected by the dark blue school tie. School-girls with identical postures, the glint of glasses, short hair or plaits, skirts hanging to our knees, many shades of brown skin. Here I am in the second row. Hair middle-parted, braids running down to my waist. Weak-tea-colored skin, which is fair enough that the girls laugh and call me *sudhi*, white girl. Big eyes and a pointed chin, angular lines I share with every other girl in this picture. None of us smiling. This is not a smiling moment. This is a serious moment. We are being educated. We are good girls of good families going to a good school, and it is all very, very serious.

. . .

Yet when the school bell rings, it releases a mad dash of school-girls spilling out of the old building like birds fleeing a python. I walk out of the school gate with my arm around Puime. She and I have been best friends since we were tiny. All around us, girls chatter and squeal. We gather around the bunis man's stand, reaching out for steaming seeni sambol buns. We pull apart the soft sweet bread to reveal the nests of fried onions within. We stuff these bits into our mouths, sucking air in through puckered lips to cool our burning tongues, chase it all down with a rainbow of fizzy-colored drinks—Portello, Fanta, Sprite.

Across the street, boys are walking home in twos or threes, arms around each other. My cousin Gehan raises a hand, a quick wave before he is swallowed into the gaggle of schoolboys.

Dishani, quick-witted, all-seeing, demands, "Who is that? Your boyfriend?"

I swat her shoulder. "Just go men, you know who that is."

"I don't know. Must be your boyfriend, no?"

Puime flips the end of her braid across her top lip, adopts a gruff boy voice, and says, "Look at me! I'm her boyfriend. I want to kiss her like this." She comes close to me, her eyes squinting; under her held-up braid, her mouth is puckered.

"Oh yes, I lorrrve you, darrrling. Let me kiss you, my lorrve." Holding the braid mustache in place she puts her other hand on her hip, her legs wide as a Bollywood hero's.

I jut out my own hip, raise a hand to ruffle my hair and a teasing finger to beckon her closer. Our audience hoots and calls. I purse my lips, and when she closes her eyes and stretches forward for the kiss, I rip off a piece of the last seeni sambol bun, stuff a large chunk of it into her fast-approaching lips. Her eyes pop open. She has to chew, laughing, tears streaming down her face. Girls all around me are cackling.

I say, "What? You wanted hot-hot kissing. No?"

Through a mouthful of bun, flapping her hands, we can make out the words "Aney, aiyyyoooo, my moufth is burning!"

Afterward we walk to the three-wheeler stand together, her arm around my shoulder. She picks up her braid again, puts it to her lip. "I'll be your boyfriend anytime."

I say, "Let's get ices."

The ice man sells vanilla ice cream in small plastic tubs with flat wooden spoons. It melts instantly. When the ice cream is done, I bite the spoon for the crunch of it against my teeth, sucking the last vestiges of sweetness out of the splintered wood.

On school holidays the various cousins released from their boarding schools gather at our house. It is the *maha-gedara*, the ancestral house of my father's family, and so this is the place they all return to. In the garden, the girl cousins are baking chocolate cakes, and as the mistress of the house I am the big boss. I tell Sonali where to get the choicest mud, and the sisters Kavya and Saakya where to gather flowers. They come back with these various treasures, buckets of rich river mud, sprays of jasmine and pink bougainvillea darkening to orange in the scoops of their skirts. We pat and shape multitiered cakes with florid flower decorations rising from our hands.

On the riverbank the boy cousins shed their shirts, clamber up the trees leaning over the water, leap high into the air, and drop like fishing birds into the river. Neck-deep, they climb onto each other's narrow shoulders and fling themselves into the liquid again and again with the desperation of the long-deprived. They swim and splash. They cavort like baby elephants. Their voices carry into the high bright vault of the sky as they throw their heads back to spray silver arcs from their dark streaming hair.

At night in our various beds, we are all awakened by the sudden death of the ceiling fans. Electricity cut, sudden power failure. The air is thick and hot. It is hard to breathe. We drift out of our sweltering rooms. Amma presides as Samson drags the mattresses one by one out onto the verandah. The night air is warm but stirred by a river breeze. Cousins lie down in rows, whispering, poking with elbows and knees, causing a barely contained delirious giggling at even the thought of being tickled. Amma's sharp voice rises. "Go to sleep. Now. All of you. Otherwise I will call the parents and you can all go home tomorrow and sleep in your own houses." We fall silent, lie there until the queen of the night soothes us into perfumed sleep.

In the midst of these cousin-mad days, Samson and I alone near the pond come upon a pile of squirming commas, tiny specks of curling life and a foamy substance in the midst of smashed leaves.

He looks up into the tree. "Tree frogs. The nest should land in the water, but it has fallen to the side. The tadpoles are drying out."

I squat immediately. "Help me, Samson." I am scooping tiny lives onto a stick, flicking them into the pond even as the sun is drying them into hard curls. With a sigh he bends to help.

We work diligently and I ask a question that has been tugging at me. "Why do we call you Samson?"

He doesn't reply, so I continue, "The religious studies teacher told us about that man in the Bible. But he had long hair and was Christian. You're not Christian. So why?"

His hands pause suddenly. He says, "When we were small . . . your Thatha and I. My mother was his ayah, you know. We grew up together. When we were small we used to play together, and I was bigger than him even though we were the same age. I would lift him up and carry him on my back like I do with you. He said I was very strong, so he gave me this name, and then everyone called me that. Your Thatha named me."

"But what's your other name? Your real name?"

He shakes his head. "I don't know. I don't remember. No one has called me it since I was a child, and it has gone away."

We work in silence.

He says, "I am Samson, but who is Delilah?"

Amma calls through the garden, summoning the cousins in for tea. He raises his face to her voice. The last of the surviving tree-frog tadpoles squirm off into the pond, revived at the kiss of cool water.

• • •

Another memory from around this time. A game of hide-and-seek. Kavya and I hiding behind the hibiscus bushes, trying to keep the hysterical laughter, the utter fear and delight of being found, from bursting through our mouths. When Saakya draws close, we fling ourselves from our spot, run like gazelles, Punch and Judy gamboling at our heels. I feel a sharp pain in the fleshy pad of my foot and see a thin trickle of blood where a thorn has pierced and entered the skin. I sit on the grass, raise my foot to my face, and try to squeeze the thorn out between my thumbnails. Panic throbs through my veins; it is one of Amma's rules that we are not to run around the garden without shoes on. "Samson," I gasp to Saakya, "get him, he'll know what to do."

When he comes, he squats in front of me and says, "Let me see." He rests my foot on his thigh. "Let's see. Yes, there"—his fingers poking, prodding—"there, see, a thorn has gone in. Have to dig it out." He picks me up. "Stay here," he says to the others, who are waiting, watching me, their fallen comrade, carried away.

In his dark little room he lays me on his bed. I have not been inside since the day I found him crying for his mother. Now the smell overwhelms me again, his sweat amplified. He opens a box. Inside I glimpse various things my mother has been missing, a set of curved tweezers she has searched for for weeks, a package of German-made safety pins that she uses for her saris (they work better than the Chinese ones), a cheap sari broach, some hairpins with a few of her long black hairs still caught in them. He takes a safety pin out of the package, flicks open a lighter. He holds the pin in the flame, turning it this way and that. "Okay, come here." He sits on the bed and lifts me onto his lap, the pale underside of my foot raised in his fist. I hold my breath and try to pull away, but he is too strong. I am held like a small powerless bird. The sharp point pierces my skin, pushes down like an excavation through layers of me. I cry, loud gasping sobs, but he will not release my foot. "There it is. I have it." The splinter revealed in the bed of my unearthed flesh. Then the tweezers. "Don't move, Baby Madame. Almost I have it." His face so near mine, focused in concentration. A quick movement and the thorn is held aloft in the grip of the curved silver tweezers. Ignoring my quiet sobbing, he holds a cloth gently against the skin of my foot, onto which a single tear of blood is spreading. I am crying and exhausted, not sure but also aware that under me he is rocking in the strangest way, in a motion that I had not been aware of before. A sort of fog descends, a white cloud, it's hard to see through it. My father's face. He would save me. A fierce grasping and a gasp, and then he releases me and smooths down the back of my dress. In a strange, strangled voice, he says, "Okay, go now." I know suddenly that this is not the first time I have felt his exhale, a kind of motion I can't describe. I walk out into the bright sunlight, my foot screaming as if it has been torn open. It is three weeks after my eleventh birthday.

four

Thatha and I sit at the river's edge. It is the tail end of the vacations, and this finality has given the boy cousins a sort of glimmering mania. We watch them climb into the trees, thrust into the air, and drop into the water over and over. He must see something in my face because he suddenly asks, "Do you want me to teach you?"

I say, "To swim? In the river?" He smiles at the rising excitement in my voice, says, "No, in the pond with the frogs. Of course in the river. Go and get your swimsuit on."

We walk into the river. It licks at my toes, then my knees and thighs. He pulls me in, his hands under my body holding me. The water feels purely alive. I am a small toy tugged this way and that, harboring terrified visions of water closing over my head and blocking off the sky. I cling to his shoulders and he says, "Shh, shh . . . It's okay, I have you. I won't let you go."

He says it again and again over the course of weeks until slowly the terror recedes. His hands are lighter and lighter under my body until it seems he is holding me up only by the tip of his finger, my own moving limbs making me somehow magically aloft. He says, "Yes. There you are. Just like that," and then his hand slips away and I am borne up, moving in the water, joyous. It is alive and I am alive with it, and then immediately I am falling, swallowing river water, drowning, dying, everything exploding, but his hands reach in and pluck me out. He laughs at my coughing, my spluttering face. He says, "You have it. Just do that a hundred more times and you'll have it."

Amma stands at the shore, hands on the hips of her sari. "Aiyo, be careful, be careful."

He is laughing, saying, "Come on! I'll teach you too."

"You must be mad. What shall I wear ah? A small-small bikini like a sudhi woman?"

"Wear anything. Wear a sarong like a village girl if you like. Just come. I'll teach you."

"Don't be crazy. I'm not ready to die."

I stand on a rock in the middle of the water. The sun beating down on my shoulders, the river parting around my tiny island, dashing silver droplets onto my feet and legs. I listen to the banter flowing like sweet honey between them. I can taste it. The sound of my parents' mingled laughter. The most beautiful sound in the world. I am willing to do anything to hear this sound again and again.

• • •

We swim together, my green one-piece bathing suit tight against my body. The dogs wait for us on the bank, their tongues lolling. Somewhere I know Samson is hiding and watching us. But I know this with only a corner of my mind. In the river with my father, I am safe. He holds me up against the tug and flow and then slowly lets me go as if the water is a bed that moves and rolls. I dive down to the sandy bed, see smooth stones, my father's legs magnified, silver bubbles caught in the hairs. Some terror rises into my throat and immediately slips away.

We swim every day. Downstream, women bathe and men cast fishing nets. Our swimming for pleasure is rare and precious. This is an island of people who don't know how to swim, who are suspicious of the rivers and of the sea. My father defies this fear. It is his greatest legacy to me.

Shorts! My American aunt Mallini, my mother's sister, who got married to a rich man and moved abroad a long time ago and who now lives in California, a place that I know from the song we all sing about a mysterious hotel, has sent a box as she does every three months or so. Shoes, lipsticks, and cast-off purses for my mother. Books and clothes for me from her daughter, Dharshi, who is only a few months older than me. And shorts! I've never had a pair of shorts before. I pull them on, look at the reflection, my legs long and exposed from the middle of my thigh down.

My mother says, "Okay, but only here. Only in the house. Not out on the street where anyone can see. I won't have people say-ing vulgar things about you."

There are other magic objects in these boxes that come smell-ing of abroad, magazines from America called *Tiger Beat* and *Teen Beat*. Amma doesn't like these, but she lets me have them because they are from her sister and therefore must be safe. I hurry to my room and pore over the boys with big hair and eyeliner, read ev-ery article about makeup and clothes and haircuts over and over. I take them to school hidden at the very bottom of my bag, and all the girls gather together to pore over these pictures, rushing to hide them under textbooks when someone raises the alarm that a teacher is near. They make me special, linked to something glamorous. At home I keep them in a box under my bed, pushed as far back as I can. They are precious, evidence of some other magical but faraway world.

I am at Puime's house. We are doing math problems at her table when I get up to go to the bathroom and she furrows her brow and says, "What's that? Did you sit on something?" And then her expression changes and she says, "Oh my gosh! Look, you've at-tained." I twist around and there it is, on the back of my white school uniform like a small blooming red frangipani. I know what is happening. Amma has described blood flowing, pain, pads, the whole thing. There are older girls at school who have gone through this, so I'm not scared. I walk stiffly into Puime's bathroom and lock myself in. I'm not some village girl whose mother never warned her, but I still panic when I see the thick blood. I stuff my white handkerchief between my legs, twist around to wash it off the back of my uniform, and wait. I feel my pulse burning. It had to happen at Puime's house. Even now her mother will be calling all the other women to tell them that I have become a big girl. They will all look at me differently now.

Puime's mother calls Amma, and she is at the door very soon. She hugs me tight and whispers, "You're a big girl now." There's such excitement in her voice. She says, "No one can see you. If a man sees you, it will be bad luck." She throws a white sheet over my head. I can't breathe well, but she holds me tight. Her strong, slim arm is around my shoulders and she says in my ear, "Hush, girl, hush, shh. We'll be home soon, very soon."

She leads me out of Puime's house, thanking them as we walk, my steps stumbling and hesitant. We go out to the car, where my father, embarrassed, nods at me. We get in the back, she and I, and she pushes my head down against her lap, my arms around her waist, so that I am hidden under the sheet as we drive through the churning streets.

At home Amma closes me away in my room for the traditional seven days. She hangs her thickest saris across the windows so that no man's lust or woman's envy can find me. She rubs my back. She tells me stories of the village, tells me how dangerous I am, how if a man sees me at this moment when my first blood is coming, even my own father, I can make him vulnerable to demonic possession. I can cause calamitous karmic shifts within my own fate. I listen to her, but I am also bored sitting here alone, missing school. I reread every book I own, go through my pile of American magazines over and over.

In the mornings when Amma takes away my soiled pads, she says, "In the old days, we had to use cloths and take them to the river, wash them in the water. How things have changed! Now we have maxi pads. No mess, no fuss. Just use and throw away." She unfolds one for me like a flower, hands it to me with a flourish. "No one has to stoop in the river washing away blood. Now everything is modern." I understand how happy she is to be the mother of a grown-up girl. When she leaves the room, it is with a dance in her step. She brings me trays of food, roti with eggplant and potato curries, nothing fiery, nothing with garlic or onions that could awaken desire and lust. She watches while I eat.

I'm not supposed to bathe during this time, so I become used to the scent of my body, like some small rooting animal alone in the dark. I wonder what is happening in the world. Has Puime gotten a new cassette? Has she invited someone else to come and dance around her room with her? Has the boy she has been in love with for the last three months, Suresh, talked to her? Is Thatha even now down at the river swimming, missing me? When Amma comes, I beg her to let me out, but she says, "Don't be silly. You have to stay here until you are finished bleeding and can be bathed properly."

I say that this is old-fashioned, not all families follow these traditions anymore. I tell her that I am missing schoolwork; my exams are coming soon. But she is adamant; she is doing the best possible thing for me. She will secure my future, my chastity and marriage to a good boy from a good family. She says, "If you aren't properly looked after now, no man will take you for his wife. You will stay here with us until you are old and dried up. All alone without a husband or children." She strokes my hair and says, "You don't want that, do you?" and I have to shake my head.

On the fourth day, I can't stand it anymore. I go to the window and tug aside Amma's old red sari. A blade of sunlight falls onto my face and across the room. I stretch my arms overhead and look out onto the garden, down the sloping lawns and to the river. There with his back to me is Samson, and even as I am pulling the sari back, he turns as if pulled by my gaze and looks straight at me and his hand goes to his gaped mouth. I twitch the sari down, blocking out sunlight and his shocked face. I stand there, heart throbbing. What have I done? What demons have I called forth? What pollution have I allowed to pass from me to him? I walk to the bed, sit down carefully. I have unraveled all of Amma's plans, all of Thatha's trust. It feels as if someone has pierced my skin, pulled back the plunger on a syringe full of shame and shot it deep into me. When shame reaches and floods my heart, I know I have done what cannot be undone.

I try to forget his eyes. The old fog descends. Everything is cloudy.

On the seventh day, Amma wakes me at dawn, says, "Come, come. Quickly, it is your auspicious time. Come before we miss it." I get up, bleary-eyed, dry-mouthed. She leads me outside, her arm holding my elbow. The nerves in my toes are alive, feeling cautiously along the ground, trying not to stumble. She leads me to the well, and I stand there blinded in the pink-lit dawn. The dhobi woman is there, an old woman with breasts like wrinkled fruit in her sari blouse but smiling as if it were her wedding day.

Amma gives her a package: my uniform, my destroyed panties, the small gold earrings, everything I was wearing when the blood first came.

The dhobi woman has filled a tub with well water, floating jasmine, cloves, and sticks of cinnamon. She pulls my nightdress over my head and pushes me down into a crouch. I wrap my arms around my knees. Her clawed fingers undo the ends of my plaits and rake the hair down my back. She fills a small earthen pot, pours it slowly over my head. The shock of cold water is electric against my skin. Jasmine flowers cascade onto my head, tumble down my back, land in the groove between my thighs and on my small breasts. I open my nostrils wide to catch their scent. The dhobi woman moves my head this way and that, scrubbing my scalp with expensive-smelling shampoo. She pulls me up to standing, soaps each of my limbs until every inch of me is covered in frothy white suds. She washes away the suds in streams of water. I am reborn, embraced by the light, the old woman's hands, and my mother's smile.

Amma takes me into her bedroom. I sit on the bed as she pulls out sari after sari. They are silver and bottle green, peacock blue, and every shade of gold. They throw light onto the ceiling and the walls from the reflection of their sequins, crystals, and embroidery, so the room feels like a treasure cave. She says, "All of these will be yours when you get married. I've been collecting them for you. Look at this one. It was the first your father ever bought for me." She pulls out a sari of faded ivory with a pattern of fine ebony swirls. She shakes her head. "That man. No taste at all." But the way she fingers the material tells me there is some small tenderness in the memory.

She looks straight at me and says, "You have to be careful from now on. People will make up ugly stories. If they see you with a boy. Even if you are just talking to him. Even a cousin. You have to be very, very careful. You are a big girl now, and your reputation is your responsibility. Do you understand?" I nod. She goes on. "You have to guard yourself carefully. You must make us proud. You know that, don't you?" I nod again. I agree with whatever she says, this beautiful and loving mother. I'd do anything for her. The memory of Samson turning to look straight at me jabs like a thorn. Shame flushes through me while I smile at her. She holds my face in her hands like a flower, brushes my cheeks with the pads of her thumbs, kisses my forehead with the tenderest lips.

At my attaining age party I wear a white dress with a full skirt and puffed sleeves that Amma has made for me. I pull it over my head and it falls perfectly into place around my body. It billows around my legs when I twirl for Puime in my room. We talk and talk. She tells me everything I have missed. Suresh has still not even looked at her. But she doesn't really care because a much nicer boy has started going to the boys' school, and anyway he has much better hair than Suresh.

When I come out, people hug me and kiss my cheeks. Amma and Thatha are beaming. No one can say Amma hasn't done everything the proper way for me. We have dinner, and then I slice into a cake covered in pink-icing roses that tumble down onto the mirrored platter, hold up a piece so that Amma and then Thatha can take a bite. They feed me too, pride and love glistening in their eyes.

Later Puime and I sit with the women as the men go outside. We drink lime juice or Fanta, and the women tell stories of calamity. There are misfortunes of the financial, emotional, or physical sort. But the most important are the disasters of love.

A woman begins: "Have you heard about the Somarathna girl?"

The rest of them lean in, hungry for the tale. "No men, I knew something must have happened with that one. We haven't seen her for months, and she was always a little wild, isn't it? Always people were saying this and that about that one."

Another chimes in. "Suddenly there was a proposal and a wedding. I didn't even have time to get a proper sari done. Fancy reception at the Galle Face Hotel." She sniffs so that we all know she thinks the family was putting on airs, continues, "But I always thought something funny was behind it. Aiyo, give us the details, will you? What happened?"

The first woman arches her eyebrow. "I can't tell anything. The mother swore me to secrecy. Absolute"—she puts a manicured finger to her lips—"secrecy."

A chorus of disappointment. "Aney, please."

"Come on, you know we won't tell *anyone*."

"That girl is like a daughter to me."

"Yes men, we'll protect her reputation no matter what. After all, they are my relatives on the father's side."

She flaps her hands at them, says, "Okay, okay! But don't breathe a word of this, okay? Any of you. It has to stay within these four walls." She points at each wall around us to emphasize the secrecy that everyone knows will not be maintained. She says, "I know the whole story. The mother came to me for help. Here's the thing. The girl was carrying on with that good-for-nothing, jobless, no-degree, next-door fellow. And by the time the parents found out, they were in a hotel and the deed was done. Two months later, no periods."

Delighted, shocked gasps; a collective fluttering of hands to bosoms and throats. Someone says, "And then what?"

"The mother and I had to take her to a clinic. They covered it up. That's why they married her off so quickly and all. Before the proposed family found out anything the papers were signed, the poruwa built. That mother-in-law must be kicking herself. No white sheet at the homecoming, isn't it? Who knows if she can even conceive after what that doctor did."

Tongue-clicking noises of disapproval, eyes rolled toward the heavens.

"These modern-day girls, what to do?"

"In my time we couldn't even look at boys."

"My mother would have beaten me to death. Home and school and back again. That was it. Now they are going wild. One has to be so careful with girls. I never let my Shalini anywhere near that one. Cheap girls like that only ruin the others."

They stop suddenly, remembering Puime and me with our ears open wide in their midst. I know the girl they are talking about. What happened to her? I know it has something to do with what has just happened to me, which is called "falling off the jambu tree," for the bright red fruit of the jambu. It has to do with boys and maybe even something to do with what happens to me when Samson catches me alone, something bad and secret for which only a girl is responsible, for which a girl always has to pay. I know that these women will not keep the secret. By tomorrow, the girl's reputation will be dust. Even her marriage will not protect her from the barbs of gossip. Shame is female; shame is the price I must pay for this body. The fabric of my white dress is suddenly cloying.

Amma says, "Why don't you two go to your room." We slip out. Climbing the stairs, Puime whispers, "God, when I grow up, I'm going to drink arrack in the garden with the men. I'm not going to sit around drinking lime juice and gossiping about *every single* person."

I nod. I feel as though I have watched an execution.

After school we go to Puime's house. In the kitchen her mother is wearing just a sari blouse and her father's old sarong, her hair pulled into a messy bun at the nape of her neck. She is fleshy, rounded, jiggly, and maternal in a way I long for. She grabs Puime, gives her a loud sucking kiss on the forehead, and then turns to kiss me on both cheeks.

Puime groans and wrinkles her nose. "Ammie, what are you wearing?"

"What? You don't like it?"

"Is that Thatha's old sarong?"

"Yes, child, why can't I use it? Waste not, want not, isn't it?"

She pours batter into the small curved hopper pan, turns it deftly so that the liquid coats the rounded surface, breaks an egg into the middle of it, says, "Sit and eat. Now while they're still hot-hot. Otherwise it's useless. Here, have with this seeni sambol, a little bit of kata sambol."

She flips delicate pancake-like hoppers with the bright yellow egg onto the middle of our plates, the edges delicate, the middle thick and slightly sour sweet. We break off the crispy lace ends to scoop up the sweet, burning onion sambol.

She says, "So . . . how was school today?" in a singsong voice.

"Ammie, the same, school is always the same."

"Come on, can't be exactly the same."

She turns her attention to me. "What about you? How was school for you? Since my one won't tell her mother a single word."

"Good. Aunty, it was good. We had a speaker at assembly today."

"Ah, see, *something* happened. At least you can talk, unlike my one. Takes a hundred and one times before she tells me anything."

I nod along to her chatter. I wish my mother did these things. I can't imagine her in the kitchen making hoppers, barefoot in a sarong and a sari blouse. Even when she makes pancakes for me, it is different. She's tighter, contained and serious.

Later, in her room, both of us lying on her bed, our braids falling off the edge, Puime says, "My god. My mother is such a disaster. I wish she was like yours, always so elegant and polished, no?"

"Mmm-hmmm. But yours makes the best hoppers. I wish mine did that."

"Why do you need her to make hoppers? You have Sita for that. A mother should be cool, calm, and collected like yours. That's how I'm going to be when I'm a mother. Not sweating and wearing my husband's old sarongs."

"No way. When I'm a mother, I'll be just like yours." The words leap through my mouth, and with them an instant flush of guilt. How Amma would hate to hear me say this. What an ungrateful daughter I am. And maybe Puime feels a like guilt because we go quiet, both of us staring up at the ceiling fan doing its slow revolutions.

I have a childhood brimful of river swimming and schoolgirl friendship. We eat papayas split open to reveal ruby flesh and small black seeds like obsidian pearls. I pick anthuriums, like flattened red hearts spiked by golden stamens; masses of frangipani, like bridal bouquets spreading their luxuriant perfume; small bell-shaped pink bougainvillea flowers frothing over the garden walls. The monsoon breaks over our heads and makes us splash in the street, joyous at the swift scent of wetted earth. Our uniform hems, shoes, and socks are soaked before the three-wheeler man rushes up and waves us in, drives us pell-mell through the suddenly flooded streets toward home. Carved jade geckos on the tops of doors bob up and down like miniature dinosaurs doing push-ups, darting out their heads for the grains of rice we hold stuck on the ends of sticks for them. In August, elephants trudge up the roads that lead to Kandy, a mountain of grass on their backs for their lunches, mahouts at their sides. They gather in the city for the annual Perahera, the procession of the Buddha's tooth through the streets that grants the city its sacred stature. We have the beauty of Kandy Lake and the royal palaces and the Temple of the Tooth. I have friends, school, books, and cousins; it is a childhood brimming over. But also here are some things you should know about this place in these years.

A civil war rages in the North and the East. These are the years when the military and the Tamil Tigers fight over ownership and land and belonging. These are the years of burning in the streets, when crowded buses are blown up by suicide bombers, when people necklace others in tires and set them alight. When driving in the night a family can be stopped and asked if they are Tamil or Sinhala. If they give the wrong answer, if they are Tamil facing a Sinhala mob or Sinhala facing Tiger cadres, they can be pulled out of their car and dragged in the dust by the back of their shirts, the women hauled away into darker corners.

Now here, in this other place so many years later, where I am locked up in my white cell, they ask me about it, my various doctors and lawyers. They think that maybe growing up in a war-torn land planted this splinter of rage in me, like a needle hidden in my bloodstream. They think that all these years later, it was this long-embedded splinter of repressed trauma that pierced the muscle of my heart and made me do this thing. "PTSD," they say.

I remember walking to school with Puime once, seeing schoolboys rushing by, going the wrong way, *away* from school. She calls out, "What happened?"

A tall boy says, "The Tigers have closed the university. There are signs hanging up on the gates. If anyone goes, they will be killed." We see stricken faces hurrying home.

She says, "We should go home."

I say, "But I have a math exam."

"And I have drama practice. But I don't think that matters now." She was right. We learned that none of the normal cadences of life were important. We learned to go home, close the gates and the windows, and stay inside the house. In these days that sometimes slid into weeks, there was nothing to do but wait. The waiting itself was a sort of occupation we all shared. The shops were closed, the university was shut and then open and then shut and then open until everyone involved lost their bearings. Whole generations of students were blown off their life courses, rendered jobless, unmoored by direction or occupation. My father raged about the incessant closing of the university. "How are we supposed to work like this?" he asked us over and over and took refuge in his ever-present glass of arrack. But beyond this, we knew we had it easy, since elsewhere in the country, blood was flowing. I never witnessed a bus bombing, I never lost a friend or a relative, and so to me the war in our country seemed far away.

We saw the reports nightly on television, of course. We saw the rising body counts, the footage of bloody mayhem caused by suicide bombs, the maps showing the Tigers or the army always moving back and forth over the landscape of the North and the

East like voracious enemy locust tribes. But mostly it was happening to people we did not know.

The war was just something we lived with. There was no other choice. We even made jokes about it because that was the only way to survive. And because of this, I laugh at the doctors and lawyers now when they tell me I have PTSD. If I have PTSD, then the entire island must have it. The only ones who don't have it are the lucky dead. So the war is not my excuse. The war happened to other people. I leave the story of that other, bigger war for some other teller.

But there is something else. There *was* a war, just not the one they are thinking of. In the shadow of that greater war, there was another smaller one. It was enacted within my body and between my bones. It took the small, delicate creation that I was, smashed it with a hammer, and set it upside down. All my pieces fell in the wrong order. I was separated from myself, and empty, echoing spaces were opened in me for a darker inhabitant. No one knew, no one suspected. And yet even this smaller war is not my excuse. My sin is only and ever my own.

five

Our books and sheets of homework are spread across the living room table when Puime looks at me from under her lashes. I can tell she wants to say something, so I say, "What?"

She shrugs, then says, "I don't know . . . I shouldn't say. But why does he look at you like that?"

"Who?" My heart is jumping in my throat. I keep my eyes on the page.

"You know who."

"Like what?"

"Just strange."

"Strange like what?" I grip my pencil to keep my fingers steady.

She says, "Just strange, you know. Strange." And then she looks away and is asking me if the five needs to be carried or if the ellipsis means it will be divided later, and I attend to her question.

Later that night just before I fall asleep, I remember this moment. It is startling because someone else has sensed the other and impossible world I live in. Someone else has sensed what is happening to me. But how can I tell her? I have no words.

Sometimes nothing happens for months. I do not have to start at each sound; I do not have to run for cover if I hear him behind me. Some mysterious cease-fire and he is just my old friend Samson. I am diligent, but in these times he is nice, gathering guavas and avocados for me, pointing out the fishing birds in the trees. These kinds of things do not happen to girls like me. I am from a good family. I go to a good school. I have an Amma. So how can this be happening in my own home? It is unimaginable.

When I'm sure I have only dreamed everything, I am grabbed. My body held tight. A lurching against me. Hands fumbling on my chest, rubbing against my nipples. Fingers across my mouth. A throat against my nape. He rubs against my skin, and there down below I can feel it smashing up against my flesh, grinding against my buttocks. His fingers under my uniform, on the bare skin of my buttocks, moving to the cloth of my underwear; pressure against that part of me that has become bad, the source of all corruption. Fingers groping and entering sacred space. He takes my hand and forces the fingers open, puts it there around him, his large fingers wrapped around mine, moving. I can feel his rage. Something transferring from him to me. I know that I will never again be alone in my body. A grunt, and my hand is sticky. He sags against me and I think of grabbing the hand that rests on my shoulder and putting it in my mouth and crushing my teeth down until I taste red. I don't do it. I am always too afraid of what will happen after that.

He holds me against him as his breath calms. He whispers against my hair, "Don't tell. Don't tell. Your Amma will leave." His voice is almost weeping. I stagger away. I go into the bathroom, bend my head. I vomit every single time.

I stop going down to the river. Thatha tries to persuade me to go, but I say I have too much homework. I miss the glide of the river over my skin. But it is so much better to give up these things than to think of Samson hidden and watching. I stop wearing my American shorts. I put them in a bottom drawer until Puime says, "What happened to your shorts? You never wear them anymore."

"Do you want them?"

Her eyes narrow in surprise. "What? Really? You don't want them?"

"No, I'm sick of them. You take them."

Glee in her voice. "Really? But your aunt sent them *from America.*"

I brush away the words, as if shorts from America are an everyday occurrence. "No, I don't want them. They barely fit anyway. You take them."

"Okay!"

I pull them out of the bottom drawer; with them, the memory of his hand, huge and tight around my bare thigh. I swallow hard and throw them at her head. She catches them, laughing. "I can't wait to wear these! Amma will have a fit."

• • •

I go from his clutch to sitting at my desk at school, and it is like being in another world where what happens to me at home is impossible. Someone says, "What is that? What happened to you?" She points at the bruise on my arm, just above the elbow and therefore not hidden like the others by my uniform. I rub it and shrug. "Nothing. Just bumped it somewhere."

In the bathroom I undress fast, bathe quickly, never pausing to look. My body doesn't belong to me anymore. There is a fog around it, that white cloud settling. So I never see the bruised flesh, the imprint of his fingers.

I push my table against my door every night. He has never come inside at night. But he *could* come. At any time he could come. Something has started happening inside my skin. Sprouting from my shamed heart, a dark, fibrous waterweed grows and spreads along the nerves of my body. It reaches to every far capillary and vein, turning them green, the green of algae or stagnant water. I am covered, choked up, clogged on the inside. I know that if I am cut, I would not bleed red, but instead, a rotted putrid green.

One thing helps. I keep a small fruit knife under my pillow, stolen from under Sita's watchful eye. When I feel too filled up, I press its point against the skin on my wrist. I press until a single point of red rises. It's always a relief, that glowing ruby bead when I had expected a necrotic green gush. It brings a rush of safety, a hum of quiet. I can sit back, fall asleep even. I know this:

I have magic skin. When I pierce it, it quivers like a million metal filings rearranged by a magnet. Always this to calm me, to take me away.

When I bring my school report home, Amma looks at it, then at me with enraged eyes. "What is this nonsense? You were always so good at math! And reading. What are these ridiculous scores? What the hell has happened?"

I shake my head. "I don't know, Amma." One foot rubbing against the top of the other. Can't she see what I've become? I can't concentrate in school. There is a hum in my head, a sort of heaviness and buzz that makes it impossible to pay attention. My body is always awake, wide stark awake and waiting for danger, but my head is clouded. It's hard to pay attention to the teachers. It's hard to pay attention to the other girls. Everything they do seems stupid now. As if they live some other life very far away from mine.

"Is it some boy? Is that it? My god, if you've taken up with some boy, if you're going to bring shame to us, I swear I will wring your neck myself."

Her words pound into my skull. I look down at my feet and say, "No, Amma, no boy."

Her eyes cut through me. "Then what is it? What is distracting you so badly?" She gets up, moves toward my room; already I can tell what she is thinking. "No, Amma, please, no," I gasp.

In my room, she rips open drawers, spills clothes and books until she finds what she is looking for deep under my bed. My treasure trove of American magazines. My *Tiger Beats* and *Teen Beats* and *Teen Vogues*. Sent from America, precious as gems. She rips them up in big dramatic moves, causing whirlwinds of pages, great flurries of decapitated, de-limbed rock stars and actresses. Bits fly from her open hands, taken up by the ceiling fan, throwing a maelstrom of paper in the room. She says, "This is what you spend your time on? Nonsense? This is what you are doing instead of studying?"

I run out of the room and down the stairs, burst into my father's study where he is nursing his arrack and his student papers. Behind him on the wall, his parents in their old-fashioned clothes above the chest that holds the old hunting rifles. He has been locked in here for hours, slowly sipping his drink, pouring another and another and another. I say, "Thatha! Amma is tearing up my things. Make her stop."

He swirls the amber liquid, stares into its depths. His voice is blurred. "Why is she doing this?"

"I don't know. She . . . she says she wants me to study more."

He tips his head back, hands steepled around the glass as if praying. "Maybe it is time to put away childish things. Exams are coming soon. Time to concentrate, no?"

He does not rise; he does not come. He will not intervene. He will say nothing to her as she says nothing to him. She will look away and he will drink his arrack. They will watch each other from a distance like a cobra and a mongoose and say nothing.

I run upstairs again. Samson stands outside my door. Amma comes out of the room, says, "Samson, Baby Madame has made a mess in her room, go and bring everything out. Put it on the fire with the evening's trash." I watch as Samson comes out of the room, his arms filled, his eyes apologetic. In the garden he unloads his arms into the fire that swirls and hisses and leaps into the twilight, the scent of burning fruit and vegetable matter, and with it the magazines I have hoarded like gold. I stand there, my face heated from the fire. My chest is locked, but I don't cry in front of them.

Later that night, my face buried in my wet pillow, the quietest scraping at the door. Samson's whisper: "Baby Madame?" I am instantly rigid with fear. Will he come into my room even? I have pushed the desk across it as I always do, but is he strong enough to push it aside? Am I not safe even here? If I scream, will my parents hear? He says through the door, "One book. This one was left. You keep."

And then pushed under the door like a talisman, corners burnt, flaking, a single magazine, Duran Duran, big-haired, defiantly eyelinered on the cover. I take it, ease back the burned edges. I will find a better hiding place for it. They won't take this one thing.

Months later Amma must have felt something, seen something, because she comes to me one day as I am studying and says, "Darling."

"Yes, Amma."

"Listen, my love. This is important."

Her eyes try to hold my gaze, but I look down at my page. The letters are suddenly moving like ants, defying their letter-ness and falling into the chaos of insect-ness. I move my pencil over the paper, try to ignore her shadow falling over my page.

She grabs my wrist, shakes it, my pencil still gripped inside my fist making faint scrawls over the number ants. She sits and stares at my face. "Has anything ever happened?"

"Like what, Amma?"

"With boys, with a man? Has anyone done anything?"

"Done what?"

"Like . . . anything strange. Anything you don't like?"

I look down again. "No, Amma."

"Oh, good. That's good." The words sigh out. Relief washing over her features, her ringed fingers moving through my hair. She bends and kisses me in relief. "Good, good. I'll just go and order some tea then."

I go to my room. I lie on top of the bed, careful not to disturb the sheet. I am shaking, suddenly freezing as if plunged into the river's depth. I pull the sheet over me. My teeth are still chattering.

I should have told her. She had asked and I had lied. I had wanted to see her face relax into softness the way it did.

At school I've heard the older girls saying that a girl who goes with a man is like a chewed-up piece of bubble gum. No one will want her again. No one chews used bubble gum. You just throw it away.

I *should* be thrown away. Because here is the most terrible and secret thing. If I go to him, it is easier. Then I know when it will happen and how quickly it will be over and I don't have to live with my heart in my throat. I don't have to jump at every sound and have fear grasp me around the neck. It is manageable. In this way I can keep a part of myself. I can fly away into the sky while he is ripping me up. In this way the terror does not rush upon me like a wave, carrying me under, drowning me. In this way I can stay aloft, my head above the water, breathing.

But even worse than this, sometimes when he runs his fingers through my hair, his nails against my scalp making me both wide, tingling awake and sleepy, I don't want it to stop. And then the most evil thing in the world happens. Sometimes he presses his finger very lightly against me there, in the center of me, in the place no one must ever touch, and it feels like I am melting, like I am sweetly and softly dying.

And then alone in my bed I remember how it felt. I rub against the bunched-up bedclothes, against my fingers, and it is nice and I like it.

SIX

What happened in those last few weeks? It was the season of waiting for water. The monsoon clouds gathered like a herd of elephants, they stamped with sporadic, faraway thunder, they split the sky with light, but they did not break. The earth was parched and dusty. There was a snapping static in the air; the birds, too exhausted to flit through the relentlessly burning skies, stayed hidden in the trees. We could hear them, but they did not show themselves. The dogs lay in the shade, their great pink tongues hanging out. The pond had shrunk so that what water was left gathered still and stagnant, the fish clustered thickly together. The lotuses that had floated on the surface kissing the mirrored sky now stood high and lifeless in the heated air. The river was at a crawl, the high banks exposed like gums in a rotted mouth. We waited—people, animals, the earth itself. Everything held its breath for the deluge.

. . .

The heat is so oppressive that I sleepwalk to school and back home. It is a few weeks to my fourteenth birthday, but no one has talked about what will happen. Amma has always thrown me a party. There has always been a cake with my name on it flooded with pink- and white-icing roses. The quietness around this birthday can only mean that big plans are being made. I'm thinking about who she might have invited when Samson grabs my wrist, takes me stumbling along the side wall to his room, pushes his bulk against me, pinning me against the wall. I float up and into the sky with the wheeling, calling birds as he fumbles at my uniform. A noise, a movement at the door. Over his shoulder, my mother's eyes. I break past her, run. Behind me, her shattered cry, the sound of her palms landing on his skin, his begging voice.

I run into my room, every artery and capillary of my body full of jagged ice. I close the door and sit shaking on my bed. They will throw me out. I will be without family, without people. I see it over and over: my mother instantly understanding, shame and pain crumpling her face. She must have suspected; that's why she came to his room. I lie on my back, staring at the ceiling, my fingers clutching and releasing the sheets. A beast sits on my chest pushing out all the air, making it impossible to inhale. I will choke here alone.

I reach under my pillow. I push the shining edge against my wrist. A line of red on my skin, blood welling onto the fabric of a white handkerchief. Outside, the blinding sunshine is choked, darkness drops, the elephantine clouds open, and water falls in torrents. The day is vanquished; it is suddenly monsoon-created midnight. I can hear the river's answering roar. Instantly it has gone from a slow crawl to a frothing, boiling cauldron. I run to the window and open it; the monsoon drenches my face. I watch the garden being punished, the trees whipped like cowering dogs.

And then with a sickening drop in my stomach I realize I have left my small black Bata slippers that fit only me in his room when I ran. If they are found there, there will be no way to protest, no way to say that it didn't happen, it never happened, my mother did not see what she saw. I stop with my ear to the door, hear nothing but the thunder. I open it gently, glide down the dark staircase. In the living room Amma and Thatha are at war.

Amma shouting, "I saw it! With my own eyes. How can you say I didn't?"

"It didn't happen. You're crazy to even think such a thing."

"Stop drinking! Stop hiding!" The sound of his glass dashed and broken on the ground.

I slip out into the garden and am immediately soaked, gusts of wind and rain battering me, sticking my clothes to my skin. I run, the mud pulling at my feet with every step. I stand outside his door and hear no trace of Samson. Maybe he is already gone. I walk inside. The single bulb is switched off, the darkness hanging like a curtain. My eyes adjust slowly.

The snuffling of a dog and Judy lopes into the room, licks my muddy calf, and looks up at me, questioning. I freeze as my father comes in, shines a light straight at me. My hands move up to shield my eyes. I can smell the arrack on his breath. In his other hand, a long and pointed shadow.

"What are you doing here?"

"Thatha."

We sense some small movement in a corner of the dark room. My father's eye is drawn away from me. He says, "Go back to the house."

I stumble outside into the punishing rain. I stand there and I hear them shouting. Thatha's voice. Samson's voice. How similar they are. Barely distinguishable. And then the thunder shakes the earth, and under it something else, something almost as loud as I run back into the house.

I slip up the stairs, leaving puddles of water in my wake. In my room, I drop my clothes in a sodden pile, pull on my night-gown, crawl into bed. I pull the sheet over me and lay there, my arms around my knees, hugging myself as tight as I can, making myself as small as I can.

I wait for the light and what it might bring.

But I must have fallen asleep, because this is what I dream. In the thrashing, lashing storm, Thatha paces the bank of the river, screaming into the wind and the rain as if there are demons set loose in him. He is incoherent, confused, and yet also deadly sure of one fact. He has failed. He has not provided the one thing the father of a daughter must provide: protection. He climbs the tree that curves over the river. Water runs along the planes of his face, drags at his clothes. The branches are as slippery as stripped bone under his fingers and bare grasping toes. He steps out onto the dark branches, the river rushing, hissing somewhere far under him; he can hear its roar more than see its sinuous hurry. For a moment he is still. Listening for a voice to call him back, a voice to release him. My voice. When it does not come, he steps out. I see his body in the air, the moment at which he is airborne and it is unclear whether he will sprout wings and lift into the storm or drop like a stone. When he drops, I hear a gasp as if the monsoon, the trees, the river itself is shocked. The swollen waters close over his head.

seven

When I wake, the storm has passed. The day is sparkling, the sky draped in clouds, filigreed in sunlight. I wait with my heart in my mouth for someone to come, for the shouting to begin, but instead all is quiet. I stand with my ear pressed to the door, but no voice comes through. Hours later I go downstairs very quietly and find Amma sobbing in a chair. Thatha is missing. He went out last night in the storm and has not come back. No one knows where he is. Samson too is missing.

In the evening a search party is sent out. They find my father's body three days later. Two policemen come to tell us they have found him. My mother sits with her face dry but every part of her shaking. Sita behind her, strokes her hair, whispers in her ear, tries to make her go to her room, not hear what is being said. But Amma wants to hear everything these men say. She wants to know the exact extent of the damage done to our lives.

The policemen say words that sink somewhere beneath our skins. They say that my father's body was found in the river, that he must have fallen in sometime during the night. They say that despite the storm and the river's raging surface, in its depth, all was quiet. He had sunk deeper and deeper until he came to rest on the soft riverbed. They say that when the gases started to accumulate in his muscles and his tissues, he rose. He was found a quarter mile from our house, lodged in tree roots. Village women coming for their daily bath had found him. They will keep him at the police station until the funeral, they say. He is in no condition to be looked at.

The doctor comes. He takes my mother to her room and gives her pills; she falls into a wild, disturbed sleep, Sita at her side. Relatives come and fill up the living room. Uncles unroll sleeping mats on the floor, aunties take over the kitchen. I go to my room, where none of them come looking for me. They think I am with Amma, and Sita must think I am with the aunties.

A sound, an eerie hum like static electricity buzzes in my ears, a dizzying sense of the world's getting bigger and bigger while I have no footing or purchase in it. I stumble around the darkened upstairs, where the relatives do not venture. I stare at the walls, at all the things in this house that are no longer familiar. The mirrors look like pools of dark water. If I touch the surface of one with the tip of a finger, the flatness will undulate and open and suck me under until nothing is left but a flurry of silver bubbles bursting to the surface.

Here is the wedding photo. Sita must have moved it out of their bedroom. The cobwebbed creases stand raised and white as lightning, slashing my father and mother in a thousand different ways.

In the living room the dogs lie with their heads between their paws, refusing to eat, refusing to get up. When the coffin is brought to the house Judy finally stands, the fur rising like quills on her ruff. She points her snout to the sky and howls. She has never made this sound before. It makes the small hairs all over my body alert, makes my internal organs cold. My mother raises her brittle face to say, "Shut that damn dog up. People will think we are killing it." But we don't need to kill Judy because she is killing herself. I try to coax her to eat. I put the plate of rice and meat that my father has always fed his dogs in front of her, but she ignores it. I sit on the floor and mix the food into fist-size balls, hold them before her grizzled snout. She turns her head away. She lies there, pure misery in her eyes, a broken heart, her ribs suddenly visible. I lie on the floor with her and put my arms around her and my head against her chest. I hear the breath coming in great gasping sighs, the wheeze of her lungs.

We mourn together. She had been my father's creature so purely. Without him, there is no more reason for her. The next day is the funeral. When I wake in the morning, Judy is gone. "She died in the night," Sita says, her hand soft on my shoulder. Now only Punch follows at my heels.

• • •

I stand with my arms raised over my head, not daring to move as Amma tucks and pins the swirling white fabric around me. I try to keep as still as possible because her hands are trembling. She is trying hard to contain herself, and also we are in a rush because the car is coming for us and already we are late. When the safety pin jabs hard into my hip, I gasp as the blood splotches and spreads quickly on the white sari. She sits on the bed, holds her face in her hand, says, "Oh my god, I'm so sorry. I'm sorry, my girl. I'm so sorry." But there is no time. She stares at the bloodstain spreading at my hip. The white is ruined. She pulls saris out of the almirah onto the bed, shaking her head, discarding each one. "No, no, no! What are you going to wear?" She has no other white mourning sari. "This one," she says. "It'll have to do. It's a little pink. Never mind. It'll do." Later at the funeral I feel the eyes of the relatives sliding up and down me, taking in the pink blush of my sari.

I catch fragments: "The father's funeral and the daughter is wearing pink? Really? What do they think this is? A wedding?" I feel the undercurrents of shock and outrage, backs turned to us by everyone—the relatives, my father's colleagues at the university, his young students bereaved at the loss of their favorite professor. Very subtly, even as we are encased in the "So sad, so sorry for your loss, such a tragedy," in the long line of condolences, we are minute by minute becoming outcasts, the strands that have held us firmly in place being cut one by one.

Earlier the funeral director had come to the house and said,

"He won't look like he did in life. He will look very different. There was a lot of . . . damage. It is better to remember him as he was before. It's better that you don't see him." And my mother had acquiesced. So he lies inside a closed casket, around it wreaths of lilies and orchids, which send their perfume drifting into the air.

They slide him into the crematory fire. It will take hours, they say, until the fire reduces him to a pile of ash, and then more hours until he is cooled down enough to take home. We wait, and when the attendant hands my mother the urn, her face is startled. "It's still warm," she says in wonder. "Yes, madam, this is how it is." My mother places the urn at her hip, reaches out her hand for mine, and we leave this place together.

This is what it feels like: we had all been on a train traveling together toward an unknown destination on a trip that stretched into the far reaches of time. And then abruptly and without warning, my father had stepped off that train. He had simply gotten off the ride, with no forewarning or explanation. He left us to plunge forward into the future with no sense of direction or purpose.

I refuse to go back to school. There will be so much whispering behind my back, so many questioning looks. I won't be able to stand it. We have a girl with divorced parents in our class; she lives alone with her mother and no one has ever let her forget how different she is from the rest of us. My own othering will be worse. Forever I will be that tragic girl whose father drowned during the monsoon season. I will be a reminder of bad luck, inauspicious omens. All those limes cut over me by the Hindu monk, they have not kept away misfortune. This is a place where people do not forget or forgive bad luck easily.

I wander the house and the garden, Punch at my heels, he too looking lost and bewildered. I sit by the river and stare into the rushing water. I imagine my father's body falling. An accident, they say. The storm had been so fierce, he had not seen the river; he had fallen in from the bank. But I know that's not how it happened. When the monsoon comes as it does every afternoon, I sit at my window and watch water punishing the world.

The policemen look for Samson. They want to question him about that night but can find no sign of him. I can't sleep. Every time I close my eyes I hear him creeping up the stairs, coming for me. No one knows if he has run away or is hiding somewhere, waiting. Sita brings plates of food to my room; she sits by my bed and mixes it with her hand, feeds me. I can see that she too has not slept properly in weeks. The three of us have become gaunt female ghosts mourning our lost men.

My mother stares out of the window at the river. She puts her hand on the glass as if beseeching what is outside to come in. Her voice is ragged. "Why did he have to go out? I begged him not to."

I don't say anything. I stay very, very still. I know what she is thinking even if she never says the words. This is all my fault. She's lost him because of me.

Inside me, the dark waterweed stirs.

• • •

After the funeral, people come. Every tangled, twisted branch of the family, every far-flung relative, every department head and professor my father has taught with over the years comes.

They sit on our couches. Sita brings out sandwiches on a silver multitiered stand, cakes, a pot of freshly brewed tea with the smaller containers for milk and sugar, all the familiar paraphernalia. They sit and look at us with shrewd eyes and say, "He was so strong, no? Such a good swimmer. How is it possible?"

The men say, "Yes men, I was with him at university. He swam like a fish." Suspicion rises like clouds from them. My mother and I have crossed an invisible threshold. We are marked by worse than accidental drowning; we are marked by scandal.

After they leave, Amma cries, "What do they think? That I held his head under the water until he died? What the hell is the matter with people? It was an accident. He *fell* . . . in the rain. It was raining so hard. What the hell do they think happened?"

I sit next to her, rubbing her back, handing her my own hankie, hoping she does not turn to look into my eyes. We do not say the words we are thinking: *suicide, murder.* We lock these words in the boxes in our chests.

She turns to me wide-eyed and says, "Oh my god, your birthday."

I say, "It's okay, Amma."

She says, "Are you sure? Shall we have a cake?"

I shake my head fiercely. "No, really. It's okay. I don't want anything."

She looks at me even more closely, and maybe seeing that I am not lying, that I really don't want to be looked at or seen, she relents. She says, "Okay, but next year, I promise. A big, beautiful cake with roses on it. A party. Everyone will forget all this by then. Everything will be normal again. I'm sure." She looks anything but sure, but I nod my head. I know I am the mother now and she is the little girl. I fold her into my arms and let her cry against my small bony chest.

They come in their large rented car, the driver waiting outside. My mother's sister, my aunt Mallini, who left the island a decade ago with her husband, my uncle Sarath, and their daughter Dharshi, who is just six months older than me. Names I have associated with boxes sent from America, magazines and shorts, precious things.

Aunty Mallini is tall and dark, where my mother is small and fair. No one would ever think they are sisters. But now she is kissing my mother on both cheeks, holding her tight, and my mother is hugging her back. Uncle Sarath wraps his arms around both of them and they stand there for long moments, cocooning her while my mother's shoulders shake. I have never seen her accept affection like this. I realize that these are people she has missed desperately. People I don't even remember. I feel a stab of envy. These are people who have known my mother before I was born.

They turn to me, opening up their little circle, and Aunty Mallini says, "My god, what a long time it's been. Look at you.

You were only a little one last time I saw you. You and Dharshi. Both of you so small when we left." She turns to include the girl, says, "This is your cousin Dharshi." We look each other up and down. She is tiny, coming up to my shoulder. I had thought Americans were large, taking up more space than everyone else. But nothing is big on this girl except her coal eyes. Her hair swings loose to her denim shorts, which have frayed white edges just like the ones she sent me. Her toenails are painted a violent pink. I'm profoundly aware of my calf-length skirt, the baggy T-shirt I'm hiding in, my hair parted in the middle and tightly braided.

I say shyly, "Thank you for the magazines."

She nods.

We regard each other warily and my mother says, "Why don't you take her around the garden?"

She follows me as I show her the various landmarks of my childhood: the river, the hibiscus, the ponds and fish, the well in its overgrown corner. She looks at each politely. At the well she leans over the side says, "Oh my god! It's so deep. What if someone fell in?"

I say, "No one has fallen."

Our old dog comes up to lick her hand.

I say, "This is Punch. Judy died."

"Oh. Like the puppets?"

I had not expected her to know this. I nod.

She says, "Do you have MTV here? What do you do for fun?" And then looking at me from the corner of her eye: "My mother says you're coming to America with us."

I stare at her and ask, "What is MTV?"

• • •

Inside the house our parents are talking. We stand outside the dining room listening, some complicity binding us to silence.

Aunty Mallini's voice says, "You must be careful. People will talk. They'll say things."

"What things?" I can picture Amma plucking at the edges of her dress.

"Things . . . you know how people are."

"What things?"

"About how strange it is that he drowned. They'll ask what he was doing out at night by the river. It just doesn't make sense, you know. It's not me. I'm just saying what people are saying. And you have to be careful. You have a young girl. People have long memories here. They will remember when it's time for the girl to marry."

My mother says, "What does it matter?"

"It matters a hell of a lot. You want the girl to make a proper marriage, don't you? It'll be hard with this hanging over her head. And also how will you support yourself? You've never worked a day in your life."

Uncle Sarath breaks in, his voice practical. "Think about it. Very soon his relatives will come. They will want the house back. You don't think they will let you keep their ancestral house, do you?"

Amma makes a wounded sound. She knows this is true. Already the relatives are flapping around like vultures sniffing carrion. They want their house. They will get it back by legal or illegal means. Either way there will be a fight.

Aunty Mallini says, "What we are trying to say is that we think you should come with us. To America. We can sponsor you. The business is growing. It's only a small agency now, but everyone there has to fly home, and they all buy their tickets from us. You can stay with us, work with us. Until you get on your feet."

My mother says nothing. Aunty Mallini continues, "It's the best thing to do. You'll be able to give the girl a proper education. Nothing's happening here. Between the army and the Tigers, anyway, this country is ruined. Better pack up now and come with us."

Next to me Dharshi grins, whispers, "See, I told you we've come to take you away." As if they were rescuing us. Airlifting us from our devastated lives into some new and exhilarating reality.

Amma comes into my room as I'm falling asleep. She sits on the bed and talks about things that don't matter for a while. I wait and then she says, "Darling, listen. Aunty Mallini and Uncle Sarath, they think we should move to America. Live there for some time. Stay with them. What do you think? Shall we do this?"

In the last few hours I've thought about what to tell her when she asks me. I've thought about my father falling through air, about him getting off the train while we travel onward into the unknown future. I've thought about the small urn that held his ashes before Amma took me by the hand and we went down to the riverbank and let the water claim again what it had already taken. I can barely look at the river without imagining the waters closing over my father's head, without reeling with guilt. Everything that has happened is *my fault*. Everything in this place *knows it*. The monsoon, the river, the trees—all the nonspeaking witnesses, they know who my father's true murderer is.

And beyond all this, Samson. He may be anywhere, hiding, waiting. When I let my guard down, he will come, and then I know his punishment will be cruel.

I say, "Yes, Amma, I think we should go."

"Really?" She has not expected this.

"Yes. Otherwise if we stay, people will keep saying things. If we go, at least we'll be with family." It's the right thing to say. Her sister is the only family my mother has known. I saw it in the way they embraced.

She hugs me close, kisses me on the forehead. For a moment we clutch each other, panicked. Then she lets me go. I listen to her footsteps through the quiet house.

By the end of that week, it is decided. We will go to them as soon as we can get the proper papers. A new life. It's what we have to carve out now.

Months later, the house is returned to my father's people and our bags are packed. Puime and her mother come, both of them with worried eyes. I haven't seen them in a long time. I've stayed out of school, hidden in the house. Puime's mother sits awkwardly at the edge of the couch while Amma pours tea and tries to make small talk. When my mother releases us to my room, Puime says, "Really? You're going to go to America?"

I nod.

She comes close, tears suddenly welling in her eyes, "I'll miss you . . . a lot."

I feel a squeezing in my throat and say, "I'll miss you too. So much. I don't know anyone there. I don't know how they do things. Must be very different, I think . . ."

My voice trails off and suddenly I am shaking. How can I do this? How can I leave everything known? How can I leave language and belonging and familiar faces, faces that look like mine? How can I leave this patch of earth that has been mine? Samson taught me once that the hydrangea blooms in a range of shades depending on the soil it sinks its roots into. From faintest pink to darkest night blue, the flower reflects the acidity of its patch of earth. How am I different? This person I am, will I be killed in the transition across the planet? What new person will emerge in that other soil?

Puime wipes her face, takes a deep breath, and says, "At least you'll have the right clothes. Not like these old things." She gestures to the school uniform she's wearing and then her eyes get big, "Maybe you'll see Duran Duran! My god. That could happen there."

I nod. I hadn't thought of that. They are in America. I'm going there. I could actually see a concert. The thought makes my heart race. The idea of being somewhere new and bright and shiny. A place I have seen in my magazines for so long about to become real. Under the sadness, I feel a razor's edge of excitement.

I say, "Anyway, here, these are for you." I point to a stack of books, folded clothes. Her eyes sparkle. "My god. All this for me?"

"Yes. The jeans that you like, the strawberry-pink blouse. Lots of other things. I don't think I'll need them there.

"I'll keep them for you. For when you come back." Her fervent words: "You will come back. I know you will. I'll keep everything for you until then." She hugs me tightly and fiercely and then bends to examine her new cache.

The night before we leave, Punch raises his snout to the sickle moon and howls for hours exactly as Judy had before. The sound of it rocks the house, echoes through the garden. He has never done this before; he had not joined Judy in her funeral lament. Now it is as if he knows exactly what the suitcases in the living room mean. He cannot be stopped; he is determined to give voice to what we cannot.

I shut my door against him. I try to sleep one last night in my own known bed, but I toss and turn until dawn. At some point in that long night I dream that Sita comes into my room, sits on the edge of my bed, smooths my hair, and murmurs words of love and sadness. She will hand the house keys over to my father's relations in a few days, and then she will make her final journey back to the village of her birth. She had expected to die in this house. I had expected to live here all my life. But none of our expectations are to be fulfilled. We have all been tossed up in the air like pieces of confetti.

. . .

In the morning the driver comes. I say goodbye to the river and the garden, the house and the dog. I hug and kiss Sita one last time, hold on to her and feel like I will choke until finally she pushes me away, wiping her face with her sari pallu. We get into the car and behind us she waves goodbye, Punch at her side. I watch until they are tiny and then we drive away from Kandy and down into the hot, crowded press of Colombo. A week later we leave the island. Framed in an airplane window, it lies below us, its palm trees waving goodbye, its long white beaches like lit crystal, its bustle and boom forgotten. It turns smaller and smaller until from this distance it is a garden blooming in the sea. I put my forehead on the cold window to say goodbye to both my father's ghost and the threat of Samson. On a fulcrum in my chest, grief and relief are balanced in equal measure. Then we trace a path between the tempest-tossed ocean and the canopy of stars and are carried into a new world.

part two

eight

We land in Fremont, a suburb in Northern California full of wide-open freeways, a sky that turns plum at dusk. This is a place where life is lived inside houses on silent streets and in strip malls. There are some sari shops, a few "ethnic" restaurants, but the predominance of brown skin, of Afghanis and Pakistanis and Indians that will come to mark this place, is far off in the future. We are few and far between. These are lonely days full of misunderstandings.

In those first few weeks I saw unbelievable sights. A woman walking down the road with a small black dog on a leash, a plastic bag in her hand. At home a dog like this, a mutt, would be left to wander by itself. It might be beloved, but no one would leash it and walk it. It might perhaps follow at its owner's heels, but only a dog of some preciousness, a discernible breed, would be put on a leash and led. But much more than the dog, what catches my attention is that mysterious bag in her hand. Full of what? I watch astounded as she stoops down behind the dog's lowered flanks, the plastic bag spread wide in her hand, and scoops up shit, ties the bag, and walks away. As if the bag is precious, as if the dog has bestowed upon her a treasure that must be carried home and savored. How impossible to imagine, in this richest country of all, that people are saving dog turds? *For what possible purpose?* My imagination boggles at the question until Dharshi, my guide to everything in this new place, explains.

There are other, more serious differences. On the island we were fixed in place from birth. We knew where we fit. You were this person's older sister, that person's second cousin on the father's side, that one's oldest cousin. Names would tell you everything about a person's placement in the complex familial and community matrix. The naming described your destiny from birth to burning.

In Sri Lanka, when two strangers met, they asked a series of questions that revealed family, ancestral village, and blood ties until they arrived at a common friend or relative. Then they said, "Those are our people, so you are also our people." It's a small place. Everyone knew everyone.

But in America, there are no such namings; it is possible to slip and slide here. It is possible to get lost in the nameless multitudes. There are no ropes binding one, holding one to the earth. Unbound by place or name, one is aware that it is possible to drift out into the atmosphere, and beyond that, into the solitary darkness where there is no oxygen.

· · ·

But before all this, we stumble off the plane, jet-lagged and dazed, into America. In the arrival lounge are Aunty Mallini, Uncle Sarath, and Dharshi. And my story of America always starts with Dharshi.

We drive a maze of freeways through an alien world, and at the house she says, "You'll share with me," and leads me to her room. It is a cave, one wall covered floor to ceiling with posters of singers and bands in random jumbled order so that they overlap like a thick, scabbed skin. There are more huge posters on her closet door. It's amazing. None of my friends back home have anything like this. I go close to look, hear her say, "You like music?"

Nodding. Oh yes, I do. I like anything she likes.

She says, "Okay, this is Paula Abdul. This is George Michael. This is—"

"Duran Duran." There they are, hanging right over my new bed, in their huge-hair and eyelined glory. It feels like a prophecy. I hear Puime's words in my head. Maybe magic things are possible here.

Sweeping her hair from her eyes, she says, "Well, good. I didn't know if you'd know anything."

We have twin beds next to each other, mine bought when it was clear we were coming. I fall into it and sleep until the next evening, my dreams a tumble of time zones and clouds, and when my eyes open, she's sitting on her bed reading, like a tiny pixie. When she sees I am awake, she says, "Let me see your clothes."

So I stumble out of bed, pull open my suitcase, and take out various things bought at the Colombo shops, some sewn especially for me.

At each piece she wrinkles her nose and grimaces and finally says, "My god, are you really going to wear that stuff?"

I shrug. "I don't have anything else. I can't have new ones. Amma spent so much for these. What's wrong with them?"

She frowns and says, "They're not from here. No one wears things like that here."

My face falls.

She says, "Okay. Look, why don't you take some of mine. Let me see . . ." She bounces off her bed and pulls open the door to her closet. It is stuffed full, clothes jumbled in piles on the floor and askew on hangers, hung double and triple. She starts pulling out clothes, throwing them at my feet, a white minidress, a pair of denim overalls, a gray sweatshirt with the neck cut dangerously aslant. I look at the mess falling at my feet. It is the first act of generosity in this new and generous place, but I say, "Amma will never let me wear any of this!"

She turns to look at me and screws up her eyes. "You think *my* parents let me dress like this? Are you crazy? They have no idea. You just wear it under your clothes, then you take the top stuff off just before you get to school."

I stare at her. "What? You mean, at school? What about uniforms?"

She sits down hard on her bed, a pair of emerald-and-yellow-striped leggings in her hands, and says, "What uniforms? We don't have uniforms here!"

•   •   •

The first day of school. A blur of faces and places. English spoken in an unfamiliar disjointed way. Only weeks later do the syllables come into focus and lock into their proper place.

The English teacher pauses to take me in. The skirt that hangs in folds to my midcalf, the shirt buttoned to my wrists, a pair of white tennis shoes and socks on my feet. I hadn't taken Dharshi's advice on a covert outfit; instead I had let Amma choose my first day's outfit. It has not been a success; no one has talked to me all day. They have looked at me as if I am not just from a different country but from a different planet. He says, "Let's see. So you just arrived?"

"Yes, sir, we came two weeks ago."

"You don't have to call me sir, you know. And your English is very good."

"Yes, sir. We speak English in Sri Lanka. The British came and taught us." It is a cheeky thing to say, but I can't help it.

My mother and I have come armed with English; we have at least that much, unlike so many who have come without it. I can't imagine what it would be to come stripped of the carapace of language. In this one way, history has rendered us lucky.

I am fascinated by the girls. Girls with hair teased into stiff spiders crawling high off their foreheads, girls with eyes magnificently mascaraed and deeply shadowed. Walking into any girls' bathroom is to enter a hissing, stinging cloud of Aqua Net. There are girls standing with their heads between their legs shaking out their layered manes into a storm of spray. There are girls leaning into the mirror to paint their eyes, their lips. Their clothes, their hair—it is all dazzling. How do they go through this ritual of choice every single morning? If I had more than a few clothes, choice would paralyze me.

But I am learning that the rules are different here. These girls don't put their arms around each other as we did at home. Boys do not hold hands. Friendship is prescribed by the rules of separation and space between people's bodies. Instead, it is girls and boys who do these things together, who walk around in couples, their arms linked, or even kiss against the wall of lockers. The first time I see a kissing couple, I look away, sure that a teacher will burst out and slap the two, haul them by their napes to the principal's office, where their parents will be called, thereby bringing shame upon their families. When none of this happens, when nobody around me even notices, I see that I have indeed come into a brand-new place. Then I stare, mesmerized by the ease of it, the way bodies fit together so fluidly. I can't imagine that ease. It is hard enough to get used to the presence of boys. I have never before been around them in this casual, easy way. In class, it is hard to concentrate. There are so many of them everywhere. I sit lower in my seat, hoping no one will notice my accent, my clothes, my overwhelming difference.

The presence of boys also means other things. The hair on my legs is suddenly shameful, suddenly public, when before I had barely noticed it. Now there are the long fair hairless legs of the white girls gleaming below their cheerleader skirts to compare with my own limbs. I had been fair before; at home, the girls had called me sudhi, white girl. How ridiculous that name is now, in comparison with these actual white girls. Now I am clearly, irretrievably dark, and beyond that, hairy!

In our room Dharshi yells, "What about this for you? It's too big for me. You want it?" She throws a denim miniskirt at my head. I hold it up to myself in the mirror, see that it would come to the middle of my thighs.

"No way! I'd feel like a gorilla."

Her head pops out of the closet, eyebrows questioning. "Gorilla?"

I gesture at my legs, say, "Hair!"

She's out now, gesturing at my pant leg. "Okay, let me see."

I pull it up, displaying my legs.

She says, "Ah, I see," and then, "So we'll have to shave you." She pushes me into our shared bathroom, says, "Get in the tub, we have to use these." She is pulling out razors, shaving cream.

"What? No way! Amma will kill me."

"Okay, so you want to be a gorilla? You want people to look at you in PE and laugh and point?" She fills the tub and gestures at me. "Take it off." I pull her borrowed T-shirt over my head. Stand there in my bra and skirt. She flaps her hand at me. "All of it. I've seen everything already."

I sit in the tub, hugging my knees in the warm water. She squats next to me.

She says, "Okay, soap up to the knees." I do it, shyly.

"Is it going to hurt?"

"No, silly. Okay, like this. Drag it along the skin." She leans over the edge of the tub, puts the razor against the edges of my soaped-up leg, starts pulling it along the skin in a long, smooth stroke.

Later she runs her palm along the skin of my leg, says, "Yes, nice. Very nice."

And then, while she is scrutinizing my face, her brow wrinkles again.

"What?"

"Your eyebrows. We have to do something about them too."

"Oh no, no way, Amma will notice in a second."

"Really? Are you sure? We'll do it very lightly, just a clear-up so you look a little less . . . Brooke Shields. She'll never notice."

I make a choked noise.

She says, "Really? Do you think she looks at you, really looks?"

I'm quiet. She sees more than I think she does. I sit on the bed and her fingers pull and stretch the skin above my eye.

I squirm. "Oh god, oh god, is it going to hurt?"

"Well, yeah, if you jump around like that, I'll probably stab you in the eye."

"Oh god."

"Just settle down, okay?"

"Okay. Okay!"

I close my eyes and she goes to work. It is like being bitten by an insect several dozen times. I screech, "Argggghhhh!"

Afterward, I have to admit I look different, better, more

American. I start performing covert operations, hiding an entire outfit under my own, pulling clothes off in the girls' bathroom, displaying my new hairless calves. And it is true, Amma never notices. She hasn't looked at me closely since we lost Thatha. She has looked at everything else, but not at me.

When we first came to this country she slept on the couch all day and all night. She looked shell-shocked and barely talked to anyone. Aunty Mallini and Uncle Sarath left her alone for a few weeks, but now they take her with them to the office. They are teaching her how to book flights, how to use a computer and talk to clients on the phone. She works almost every day now. When I do see her, she is exhausted.

Instead it is Uncle Sarath who looks at me closely and says, "What have you done to your face?"

"Nothing, Sarath Uncle."

He stares at me, then says, "Ah, I see Dharshi has got at you with her tweezers. Trying to make you a proper American girl, ah?" He laughs. "Don't worry, I won't tell your mom." Then he says, "How are you? What do you think of the US of A?"

I shrug. I cannot tell him everything brilliant and terrifying that has happened in these few months. But it's the first time anyone has asked, and for this I am grateful.

On the weekends other families come to gather around the table and the food. At Christmas we throw a big party. I have never celebrated Christmas before. On the island only Christians marked the day, but in America, it seems even a household of

Sinhala Buddhists with a Buddha shrine in the alcove feel moved to celebrate.

Uncle Sarath brings a tree into the house. It sits in the living room shedding needles, releasing its scent into the air. There are presents under it wrapped in shiny paper. Amma and I have agonized about what to buy. We have spent hours walking the mall trying to understand what is appropriate. Our presents seem ridiculous. A perfume bottle for Aunty Mallini, a tie for Uncle Sarath. Clichés of the worst kind, but it's all we can think of to give. But when they open them on Christmas morning and exclaim in gratitude, we feel better, feel that we are in a kind of home, that we are indeed with family.

Various people come that night. There is a huge dinner, rice and curries made by my mother and her sister. Christmas cake, for which Dharshi and I had spent hours chopping fruits and nuts till our fingers ached. But now tasting the small rectangular pieces under their snowy coating of almond icing, we decide it was worth the trouble.

After the food is cleared away, they put on music. Aunties and uncles sing and hold hands like kids. A crashing of Christmas bells signals the arrival of Santa Claus, and the children's eyes grow huge. They had thought Santa was the exclusive property of their white classmates. But now here he is, wearing the proper red suit over the right belly, sporting the perfect snowy beard.

Old Sri Lankan Saint Nick sets himself up in a chair by the tree, picks up presents one by one to call out names. A six-year-old tugs at his mother's skirt to whisper, "Santa looks like Sarath Uncle." And Santa, hearing this, roars, "Ho ho ho! That's because

Santa Claus is Sri Lankan! Didn't you know that, little boy? Santa Claus flies through the air on his sled pulled by elephants. All that reindeer stuff they told you at school is nonsense! Elephants fly so much faster! It's a lonnnng journey from Colombo, but now I am here. Come and get your present, no?" The little one rushes up. His ideas about Christmas are now a little muddled, but he is much happier about this new version of the story. He will boast to his friends at school in the coming week that Santa Claus hails from the island, and they, finding flying elephants so much more evocative than reindeer, will have to agree.

On weekends Dharshi and I absolutely cannot go on trips to the grocery store or to the car wash with our parents because we have homework to do. We are at the kitchen table, our heads bent over our books, pencils working furiously as they get ready to leave. Aunty Mallini says, "Okay, ladies, both of you study hard. You have those math tests next week." Uncle Sarath ushers them out, winks at us behind their backs as they all leave. We wait breathless, heart-thumping minutes, our ears wide open for the sound of the car starting, the garage door closing behind them.

When we are sure they are really gone, we run into the living room. We turn on MTV and sing as loudly as we can into hairbrushes, jump from one end of the couch to the other. We cock hips and leer lips in the mirror. We are material girls; we just want to have fun. We are Billie Jean in faded denim with fluffy bits of lace in our hair and black plastic bands encircling our wrists. We are Billy Idol platinum blonds walking like Egyptians on Manic

Mondays. We tease our hair into giant sprayed edifices, draw long curling tails on the corners of our eyes. But when they come home, we are again safely parked at the kitchen table, studious, dedicated studiers of algebraic equations.

Some nights I wake to Dharshi shaking me hard, her fingers tight around my upper arms. I am startled awake, breathing furiously, the beast that sits on my chest slipping away reluctantly. She says, "Shh, shh." When I'm quiet, she says, "You were dreaming. You cried out. Your dad, I think."

I nod. She says, "You said a name . . . Someone else."

My voice is rusty. "What name?"

"You said Samson, like that guy in the Bible. You said it very clearly. You were saying no, over and over."

I say, "I don't know anyone like that."

"Okay." But she doesn't believe me. It is clear in her eyes as she turns away. It lies between us now, the first secret.

One day while both of us are lying on our beds reading, she says, "So what's it like?"

"What?"

"You know. Sri Lanka, the motherland, our ancestral place?" She says it with a roll of the eyes, but I realize that here is something I can give her. Here is something lacking for her. She had been there only once, in the nightmare after my father died, but she is asking me something else—not how it is to be there for two weeks as an outsider, a tourist, but what it is like to live and belong there.

"It was beautiful. We swam in the river and I had a best friend, Puime, she and I, we were so close. And I miss speaking Sinhala. And Sita's cooking. She could make the best moju." I stop, guilty for evoking all these lost and buried treasures.

"Whose cooking?"

A vision of Sita at the gate as we left, small and tired, waving as if her arm would fall off. Punch at her side. A sharp stab through my heart. But also the realization that I was not the only one who had lost home and gained America. Dharshi too had lost certain things, and for her, these are losses she doesn't even know she has sustained. I try to explain it all to her. But I know it is futile. She grew up in this soil; her shade of flower has taken on the colder tint of this air. Leaving is an act that cannot be undone.

We sit on the couch, watching *Gilligan's Island*, our feet resting on each other. She teaches me the joys of afternoon cartoons and how to eat Oreos. "Like this," twisting apart the cookies, her tongue languid in its swirl across the cream center. We walk to the drugstore for rainbow-flavored ice cream, delicious synthetic sweetness. We sit, heads close together over a single cassette tape recorded off the radio. We play and rewind and play and rewind, all the while our pencils scribbling like crazy to write down the lyrics, to penetrate the mystery exactly. We fill notebooks with lyrics. We transcribe parts of our favorite Wham! song so that we can reenact the video: "Young guns, having some fun/Crazy ladies keep 'em on the run." In those days she was the whole of the continent for me. "One, two, take a look at you/Death by matrimony." She is George and I am Andrew and we strut through the living room feeling dangerous and free. She twirls and glitters and I, star-struck, emulate her every move.

I hear Dharshi and my mother talking in the kitchen. Usually they just tolerate each other as if my mother can't deal with having another daughter and Dharshi can't abide the idea of a second mother. But now I listen and hear Dharshi say, "Aunty, who is Samson?"

My mother says, "Why, Dharshi?"

There's a pause that Dharshi doesn't fill, so my mother says, "That's the name of our servant back in the old house. Why do you want to know?"

Dharshi says, "No reason."

I wait for her to tell my mother that this is the name I cry out in my sleep. Sometimes in horror, sometimes in something far from horror. But she doesn't say it and I walk into the room and they both look at me. My mother with steely eyes asking whether I have revealed the secrets that will destroy us. In Dharshi's eyes is knowledge, as if now, without my saying anything, she knows everything.

nine

The white man opens the door with a flourish and my mother and I walk through the two-bedroom apartment, noting the worn magenta carpet, the windowless bathroom, the chilly rooms. He says, "It's not much, but the rent is good and your daughter's school is close enough."

And then we are alone, Amma and I. We have never been alone together in this way before. As if set adrift on an ice floe in this enormous new continent. We live together, both of us haunted by a place, absent people we must never speak of.

America: It is like being reborn as a blank, like being outside history. People look at me and then look past me because they cannot place me. They think I am Indian or Mexican. Innumerable conversations invariably follow this precise trajectory:

Person: Where are you from?

Me: Sri Lanka.

Person (*confused and incredulous, sure he/she has misheard*): Where?

Me (*in the monotone of a person delivering lines*): It's a small island twenty-two miles off the southern coast of India.

Person (*relief dawning in his/her eyes—a familiar word; visions of samosas, chai, and women in bindis*): Oh, so it's *part* of India.

Me: No, no, it's a separate island. It's its own country.

Person: Oh.

Me: It's a separate independent island nation. It has nothing to do with India.

Person: So is it Hindu or Muslim?

Me: Neither. It's primarily Buddhist. But there are Hindus, Muslims, and Christians.

Person (*eyes glazing over*): So it's not a part of India?

The social studies teacher says, "And as another marker of their primitive state, these people eat with their hands. They haven't discovered cutlery yet." She shows a slide of a family of Australian aborigines around a fire, the absence of forks and knives marking them as other, savage, frightening. I think of our dining room in Kandy, all of us gathered together. Sita bringing steaming dishes to the table, the luxury of my fingers moving through rice and curry. So this is what they think of us. Entire civilizations derided because of the way we choose to tackle our food. It feels unfair, but I'm careful after that. No outsider will ever see me use my hands. Always I will be proper and formal, employing my knife and fork.

After school, I let myself into the silent, empty apartment. Amma works at the travel agency from morning until well past nine. Uncle Sarath drops her home then, and exhausted, she falls into bed, sometimes forgetting to change her clothes. I've found her like that often, feet dangling off the side in her new sturdy flats. I kneel and ease her feet out of them, roll her over so I can cover her with the blanket.

Now I pull out the containers of food she has cooked on the weekend from the freezer, warm up the curries, and eat in front of my textbooks. The apartment has the quality of a place where no one had been for many hours. The sense of not being watched drops around me. It is lonely, but also safe. I can do anything I like, no one is watching me, there are no hidden eyes. A taste for solitude blooms.

In my bedroom, I am the queen ruling over her minute kingdom. This space is mine; no one can enter without my permission. When we left Dharshi's, she had pulled her old *Tiger Beat*s out of the closet and pushed them into my hands. Now I cut out one picture of Depeche Mode, put tape on the back, and place it carefully in the center of my wall. That night I hold my breath when Amma comes in, squints at these men in suits and manes of teased hair. "What is this?"

"Amma, it's what girls do here. All my friends have them. You saw Dharshi's room."

"Dharshi grew up here. She's not like you. These are men! In a young girl's room?"

"Amma, it's just what girls do here. Please."

I wait for the shouting, the ripping off of photos from walls, but maybe America has already worn down her ramrod sureness. She turns and looks at me for a long, searching moment, says, "Okay, but don't turn too much into one of these foreigners, okay? We also have things to be proud of."

I nod. I don't correct her. I don't tell her that *we* are the foreigners and that everything we had before is rendered useless here. I'm just ecstatic that she has allowed me to retain my poster. I have plans to turn the entire wall into a harem of wall-hugging androgens.

A postcard comes from Puime, a missive from a different world. I trace the florid plumage of birds, the spotted coat of the leopard with a finger. Such colorful, vibrant stamps, nothing like the red, white, and blue logic of my new home. Her rounded letters, now formal, as if we barely know each other.

She writes:

> Hello,
>
> How is it there? Have you met interesting people, new friends? Everything is the same here. We have exams in a month, so Ammi is shouting at me to stop writing and start studying. Anyway, I miss you.
>
> Love, Puime

I turn over the card and find the Sigiriya Queen. An image I have known from childhood. Here are her round breasts and face, her long, slitted eyes, her hand bent at an awkward angle as if warding off evil, holding a sprig of jasmine. I see something I have never seen before. This woman, centuries old, frescoed on the rock face of a single enormous bolder rising far above the forest canopy; this woman who was the beloved of a king who dared build his palace on this lofty, precarious height—this woman looks like me. Here are features from an ancient past, replicated on my face and figure. Here is an inheritance I've never even been aware of reaching down through the generations of islanders and touching my blood here now. Amma is right: perhaps we too have things to be proud of.

But that's not good enough. Looking like some ancient queen from a tiny island a world away will win me no friends here. Her sloped shoulders and gold skin are not beloved here. I would give up the resemblance in a heartbeat to look like the white girls with their long limbs and exposed cheekbones. I would sacrifice a kingdom to have their confidence, their utter and unquestioned belonging. I put away the postcard; it has nothing to do with me.

And yet a magic moment. Christina Green stops by my desk, looks straight at me, says, "Do you line your lips?" I shake my head in confused disbelief. Is it possible that this goddess is speaking to me? She tries again, this time pantomiming the movement over her own lips, tracing an outline. "I mean, do you use lip liner? Around your lips?" Again I shake my head. She says, "Because it looks nice. Like you have natural lip liner."

I stare at my lips in the mirror after this, study the dark pigment, their color and curl. She never looked my way again. But I had been seen. She had noticed something I had not ever noticed about myself, and this was powerful.

At breakfast one day Amma says, "The only *dates* in this house will be the type you can eat," and laughs at her own joke. I'm shocked. I didn't even think she knew the word *dates* in the context she is decrying. What she doesn't understand while she is yelling, "Cover up, cover up!" is that she is seeing me in a way no one else sees me, as desirable. At school, the boys are not looking at me. I am invisible. I simply don't exist in the way the white girls with their thick ponytails and their long, hairless legs do.

Instead I am "exotic," like a python or a large cat. One does not have crushes on these animals. One does not pet or caress or love these animals. One does not ask them to dances. One regards them with suspicion and perhaps admiration, but one does not approach them. I can wear a skirt shorter than any I have and no boy will come up to me because in so doing he would be marking himself also as strange, and no boy in this place and this time is willing to do that.

But more than this. Something that Amma doesn't see. I want to be like the white girls; I want to stalk the hallways like them and wear my hair in spiked shapes around my face like them. I want to feel some sort of belonging in this new place. But I don't really want to be seen by the boys. Not in that way.

Something deep in me shrinks every time a boy's eyes touch

me. Some memory raises its head from deep within and I have to walk fast past the boy before it rises fully and erupts out of the depths. Always the possibility that Samson's hands will reach out from these strangers' arms and grab for my soul. So though my skirts are short by Amma's standards, they are always far longer than anyone else's. The pivot point of fear inside my skin so much more a push toward chastity than Amma's lectures could ever be.

On the weekends, Dharshi and I comb the racks of the Salvation Army and Goodwill stores, looking for baby-blue jeans, fringed boots in soft white leather, sweatshirts that slide off the shoulder. I hide my loot in a garbage bag at the back of my closet. I wear it all secretly under my long skirts and shirts. So that when Amma sees me at breakfast, I am still her little girl.

I come home one day to Amma in my room, my garbage bag of clothes in her hand.

She shakes the bag and shouts, "What is this nonsense?"

"Leave it." I grab the trash bag, my precious hoard so carefully won, my ticket to an all-American girlhood. I tear it from her grip, and both of us realize that I am bigger than she is, that I tower over her, that she is small and cowering. I raise my hand and she shrinks, and in that moment everything is reversed: I am large and she is small. She steps back and stands by the door and watches me hang each piece up carefully in the closet. I no longer need the garbage bag. The tide has shifted; the power has slid my way. It's a heady victory.

• • •

We live alone together, but we never talk about what happened before. It is as if my father's death has rendered her mute. I catch her looking at me. For a quick second I read the distrust in her eyes. Always, I will be the daughter steeped in a secret and unfathomable shame.

We live alone together, Amma and I. Our living room window looks out onto the desolate landscape of a parking lot, but always beyond this, we hear the smash of falling water, see the curve of a moonlit tree over the rushing, tumbling river. The ghost of one drowned man rises from the water. The shadow of that other lost man waits on the bank. They look up at us in the window. They want entry. They want to be with us and live with us. But we never speak of them, never acknowledge their presence, never say their names or recount their deeds to ourselves or each other. This is the only way to survive.

ten

This happens when I am sixteen. She's in the shower. I'm in my room reading when I realize that the water has been running for a long time. I knock, ask, "Amma, are you all right? Is everything okay?" I am answered only by the hiss of water running. I stand with my ear against the door, the surface of my lobe melded to its cool surface. There are odd noises, small animal sounds. I sit on the ground, back against the door. It feels like those days when I was small, sitting outside her bedroom door, waiting and hearing nothing.

Time goes by. Maybe ten minutes, maybe twenty, then a quiet click. I jump up, grasp the knob, and turn. She is staring at her wrists held over the sink, blood dripping on the knife dropped there. The white porcelain is streaked as if with food coloring. I turn the water on, grasp her arms from behind, hold her wrists to the flow. Flesh opens; the water runs deep red, then rosy, then a delicate pink. She is muttering. "He left us. He left us. I didn't do anything. It's my fault. I didn't do anything."

I turn her to me, dab at her wound with a towel. Wrench the door of the cupboard behind her head open, grasp a tube and slide antiseptic gel along her wrist. A long thin cut revealing the layers of her flesh like strata: pink flesh, white fat, red muscle, the colors of her interior.

I pull the edges together, cleanly, neatly, wrap long strips of white bandage around her torn skin. I say, "Why did you do this?" She stares down at her wrists as if they belong to a stranger. She says, "Why did he go? Why did he leave us?"

"I don't know, Amma."

I put her in her bed. Take to my own bed. Lie there, my heart opening and closing in the rhythm of an anemone, something that passes salt water through its tender, delicate self in order to live.

I beg and beg for a pet. I miss Judy and Punch more than almost anything else. One day Amma comes home with a tabby kitten, all glinting amber eyes, rose-petal softness, and tiny thorned paws. He is supposed to be my kitten, but it is Amma whom he claims. Tucked under my mother's chin, the kitten falls asleep, and she whispers, "Isn't this the sweetest thing?" Her hand covers the tiny body. She says, "So small and all alone. No one to take care of him. He must think I'm his mother." Tenderness in her voice.

Catney Houston, she calls it, ignoring gender and after the pop star who is singing her heart out on the radio, newly discovered, young, and luminescent. The kitten reminds her of the singer, my mother says, something about his meow—loud, soulful, and diva-ish.

I hate Catney Houston as much as I hate Whitney Houston. It is impossible to turn on the radio without the singer crying out about an adulterous love affair or issuing passionate invitations to dance. At home my mother strokes the kitten, follows it with her eyes, talks to it in that baby voice. I hate the way it winds around her feet and insists on sleeping curled next to her. When it comes meowing to me, I push it away with my foot. Not so very hard, but enough to make it jump in surprise.

At home alone, I slip scissors around its whiskers, snip on one side, and then quickly before he leaps away, on the other side. The cat looks lopsided now. When she comes home, Amma says, "Why did you do this?" with a bewildered look and holds it even tighter. I shrug. I don't know why I did it. I was just bored. There was nothing else to do.

Another day, Amma is late from work. I lie on the couch waiting, watching TV and trying not to pay attention to the ticking clock. On the ledge the cat is also waiting, and from its suddenly pricked ears and the steam-engine rumble in its throat, I know that my mother is approaching. The door opens and she stoops to sweep up the animal in a hail of kisses, a soft glut of love noises. "I'm going to bed," I say. I get up and stretch, and still they do not look at me.

Now always this animal is on her lap or next to her head on the sofa. The cat, sensing my rancor in the way that animals do, hisses when I come near, shrinks away as if I have hit it. Amma says, "I don't know why he doesn't like you. He's so loving with everyone else."

One evening she looks at the dishes I washed in the morning, says, "What is this?" Her nail scratches at a bit of dried-on egg. I say, "I'm sorry, Amma, I didn't have time. I had to do homework." I had rushed out that morning, the horrors of chemistry homework left unfinished the night before snapping at my heels. I see the tensing of her shoulders, her jaw moving, and I back away toward the door.

"What the hell is wrong with you? Look at this! Can't you see this? Can't you do anything right?" The plate flying past my head smashes like fireworks against the wall. The cat zips out of the way. I run to my room, throw the door closed, slump down against it. I wish there was something heavy I could drag against it. Instead I have only my body to keep her out. I hear the usual cacophony in the kitchen: exploding plates and glasses, the smashing of glass. Then her crying, and after that, silence.

Hours later I hear her just outside the door. She says, "I'm sorry, I'm sorry. I didn't mean it. I'm so sorry." I stay quiet. Through the wood she whispers, "There's only us. Only you and me. We have to stay together. I love you. My little girl." She continues, "I was so young when I had you. Only eighteen. Just a few years older than you. Can you imagine? I didn't know how to do anything. And when I was small . . ." She pauses, takes a breath before she goes on. "Mallini and I . . . we were like luggage. Moved from place to place. We never had anyone." I stay stiff and silent, wishing I could be like the cat, sinuous and bending to all her moods, loved.

I've learned just recently in biology class that a female human carries all of her eggs in her from birth. So whatever Amma has survived, as a child, as a girl, I had been there inside her, waiting to spill into the me I've become. The ache of her brokenness, wherever it came from, is also mine. It must have entered me then, when I was just a curl of a creature. I must have absorbed it along with every other nutrient she fed me through that thick and rootlike cord. She stays outside my room for hours. I do not answer her. Eventually she goes to bed and I too turn my face to the wall and try to sleep.

There was the before-mother and here now is the after-mother. Another way of saying it: the Sri Lankan mother and the American mother. Whereas the earlier had been delicate and controlled (except when she was not), kept like a hothouse flower amid the beautiful carved furniture, the American mother is broader, a part of the world, out there among people in a way that would have been unthinkable in the world she grew up in.

Between my aunt and uncle and Amma, the travel agency is growing. There are always islanders willing to pay for passage home. There are always relatives dying, getting married, being born—so many reasons for return. My mother is there when they call. She says, "Yes. You can take a flight out on Sunday, early in the morning. I can book it now itself, if you like."

Behind her head at the office is a lurid Technicolor poster of a Lankan beach, a lone palm tree stretching long over the tranquil water. This is what paradise looks like, all white sand and light playing on waves.

But Amma has never thought of home as a tropical paradise. She has never lain down on such a beach, and even if she had been forced to, she would have cowered under the shadow of a giant black umbrella, fearful for her complexion. And yet she longs to return, speaks often of going back, of reclaiming our house. Her true life is not here. The food is still strange; the people are cold. The only thing still holding her here: me. She can't go while I am still here. She won't leave me here alone. For this I'm grateful.

We are seventeen, Dharshi and I, giggling at her father's birthday party. We slide away to her room, where with a flourish she pulls out a secret stash of cigarettes. We light them up in the bathroom with the fan turned on and end up coughing and choking. She frowns and says, "What the hell? I thought it'd be more fun." She waves the stubbed-out cigarette around and puts her other hand on her jutted hip. She says, "This looks cool, right? Super sexy?" I nod. She is beautiful, with or without the cigarette.

We go downstairs and find a table loaded with curries, a crowd of people singing old, forgotten songs, a cake Aunty Mallini has made in the shape of an airplane with a goggled teddy bear pilot whose billowing scarf proclaims "Fifty and Still Fabulous!" Uncle Sarath dissects a piece of teddy bear ear, holds it up to feed his wife and then his daughter. He wipes tears from his eyes and says, "So happy to have all of you. What a lucky man I am." I kiss him on the cheek.

In the later stages of the party, baila music blaring, dancing aunties and uncles all around, Dharshi and I sway our hips. We hook arms and swing around each other. This is as much at home as I have ever felt.

A few months later I open a fat envelope with trembling fingers and buckle in joy. An acceptance letter to UC Berkeley. Amma holds me and cries, openly joyous; everything has been worth it, all her long hours, her weariness, America itself. She holds my face in her hands and says, "I am so-so proud of you." My heart leaps. This is all I've ever wanted. To be told I am worthy of her love.

In September, she drives me to the leafy campus, my many new college-student necessities piled high in the car. In my room, she packs my tiny fridge with containers of rice and curry. Then I bundle her out and watch as she drives tearfully away. I feel guilty to be leaving her. But more than that, I am finally, gloriously free.

I have done it. I have won the immigrant prize, a scholarship to an American university. In just four years I have achieved this holiest of miracles. Below me, the campus spreads out like an ancient city waiting to be unearthed. This is the place in which my life will change, the place where my life is finally my own. I lie on my small bed in my dorm room. My roommate is coming tomorrow. The hours are my own. Sunlight pours onto me from the window like a rainstorm. It flames into the room, sets everything aglow, a thousand shades of burnished gold. The doors of the world swing wide open. I see my future self beckoning me with both hands. She is beautiful. She wears my face. It has lost the soft padding of youth. She is lined around the eyes and the mouth, silver glittering in her tumbling hair. Her body is heavier, rounded. It is exactly the body of the Sigiriya Queen. Her eyes, they shine with so much that is coming. "Hurry! Hurry!" she says. "Come now and grasp our life! I have been waiting for you, and I am *everything*."

eleven

Dharshi calls from her dorm at the University of Texas in Austin. She too has made good, made her parents' college dreams come true. She says, "You won't believe what my mother is on about now." I can picture her eye roll, the phone balanced against her ear as she walks around her room, excited to feed me some tidbit of gossip.

And I, equally eager for her news, say, "What, what?"

"Okay, are you ready?"

"Yes, for god's sake. Just tell me."

"Okay. So get this. She says I'm running wild at college, so she thinks it's high time I settled down and got married."

"No!" I suck my teeth to express my horror. "Is she mad? It's still only our first year."

"I know. You won't believe this. She's already written my

matrimonial ad. She wants to put it in those awful Lankan papers that run in Toronto and London and Australia."

"Oh my god. Do you have it?"

"Yah, listen to this. 'Parents of Sinhala Buddhist girl. Govigama caste. Wheatish complexion, well educated, looking for similar boy. Must be well educated with potential for financial growth and strong family background. Dowry and astrological details to follow.' And then there's pictures of me."

"Wheatish . . . ha-ha!"

"I know, right? I'm much darker than that. He's going to have a fright when he sees me."

"Why is your mom doing this?"

Dharshi sighs. "She says dating like Americans is stupid. Leaving everything to love that can end at any time. She says marriage needs to be based on something much stronger, you know, wise parents who can pick properly for you without being confused by hormones and whatnot. She says she'll find me an amazing guy. And also she says architecture school is expensive. If I get a nice guy with loads of money, then he can pay for it."

"What'd you say?"

"I said if that's the case, she should marry him and go to architecture school herself."

I can picture my aunt's face when Dharshi said this. We break into peals of laughter.

She sighs. "I think she thinks she's just being practical. We aren't rich, and architecture school *is* expensive. Amma and

Thatha had an arranged marriage, you know, and your mom married your dad, who was older and richer, so she thinks it's normal."

I stumble at the mention of my parents' marriage. She and I have never talked about the things that had happened before we arrived on the set of our parents' lives.

"So what'd you tell her?"

"I said if she ever talked about it again, I'd go out and find the whitest boy on campus and marry him."

"Even better, you should have said you'd find the blackest boy."

We giggle, imagining my aunt's face if Dharshi ever said this. We are both well informed about our parents' hierarchy of desirable husbands, a perfect portrait of the recent immigrant's inherent racism. At the very mucky bottom layer of this pyramid and completely undesirable is a boy of the "duskier races." To bring home a black or Latin man would be to risk forced smiles in the living room and a great deal of screaming after said male had departed. Directly above this layer is another, smaller layer made up of respectable, educated white boys with old families and lots of money. Not really acceptable, but less horror inducing than the darker Americans. Above the white guys, an even thinner stratum of other kinds of South Asians: Indians, Pakistanis, Bangladeshis. Higher still would be other kinds of Lankans: Christian Sinhalese, Burghers, or god forbid, Muslims or Tamils. They weren't "our people," but they were as close as possible to the zenith. And there, poised teetering on a glorious throne at the very top of this pyramid, is the prize, that almost mythic being: a Buddhist Sinhala boy of a "good old family" with "excellent earning potential."

She says, "What I really told her was that if she made me do it, I'd kill myself."

I'm silent for a moment, some sharp knife point of panic breaking my skin, and then she starts laughing. "Don't be an idiot. This is all stupid. She'll forget about it soon. She'll have to."

I hang up ten minutes later, go back to my studies, and forget all about this. There is so much on campus to catch my love. The old, venerable buildings so different from the suburbs I grew up in, the miniature redwood forest in the middle of campus, the fat gray squirrels that come up and chatter like old friends, the color and hustle of Telegraph Street, with its marijuana haze and dreadlocked denizens. There are lectures in gorgeous brick and ivy buildings. There are new friends and beers in the evenings, plays and films and books. All of it alive, all of it exciting.

In our junior year, this happens. In the middle of the monsoon season on the island, Uncle Sarath goes back for the wedding of his cousin's daughter. Aunty Mallini refuses to go, claiming she is too tired for the two-day crossing of the planet, the checkpoints, and the curfews. So she sends Uncle Sarath with a suitcase full of presents and he goes alone to Colombo.

It is a year of a merciless monsoon. Rain smashes down until the roads are flooded, cars stuck tire deep in the mire of Galle

Road. The power is cut daily. When the rain stops momentarily, people wade through knee-deep water to get their necessities before the deluge returns. The family of the bride whom Uncle Sarath is staying with are disheartened. How to have a wedding in the midst of this monsoon madness? The hall has been booked for months, the flower girls and poruwa makers are all sorted, but what if it floods on the day? What if the guests can't make it to the hotel? What will happen to the fancy saris and expensive hairdos in the onslaught? The father of the bride seeing his investments—the costs of the hall, the caterer, the dowry—swept away in the flood walks about with a stormy face. The bride breaks into tears at every opportunity. The mother of the bride has even wetter, more thunderous breakdowns.

Uncle Sarath remains in his room and tries not to get in their way. They have exclaimed over his presents, Mallini's cast-off clothes and handbags and his own old shirts and trousers, but now they seem to have forgotten him in the fervor of their wedding-day anxieties. He stays in the house for a week, and then perhaps deciding that he has had enough, he decides to go out into the street, face the rush of water head on. I imagine him excited at the prospect. Looking forward to being showered in the monsoon, as surely he must have been while growing up in this city. He must have decided to walk somewhere, perhaps to the Vijitha Yapa bookshop or to the Saraswathi Lodge for one of their legendary thosai. His destination will remain one of those little unanswered mysteries in our lives.

But Uncle Sarath has been in America for so long that he has forgotten the rules. He steps out onto Galle Road, sinks into water up to his calves, and raises his face to the sun, which is breaking through the clouds. Then he does a sudden dance. People hurrying by with their umbrellas finally folded think he is making a joke, welcoming the brightness back. But when his face goes black, they realize that his slippers have been swept away and he has stepped on a live wire under the water.

There are frantic, panicked calls to America. Aunty Mallini cannot comprehend what is being said. Someone she barely remembers from her own wedding decades ago, her husband's cousin he says he is, is sobbing and saying, "Sarath has died, Sarath is gone." My mother calls me and tells me to come now, immediately. I call Dharshi's phone but get no response. I take the train and my mother picks me up at the station, her face ravaged. We drive to the house that was our first home in America. There are people sitting in the living room. I push past them into Dharshi's room. She is sitting cross-legged on the bed, her face perfectly wiped as if she is made of plastic. I go to her and she crumples. I had read this phrase before, but I had never seen it, the way a person's body literally deflates under the rush of grief. I hold her in my arms for hours while she shakes, her face against my chest, her hands clawing the bedclothes.

From the next room we can hear Aunty Mallini raging, "Why did he go there? Back to that cursed place? Why? He should have stayed here. We were safe *here*." My mother tries to comfort her, but there's so little that can be said. We are again in a house bereft of men. We are again surrounded by haunted shadows and disbelief. How can two sisters lose their husbands to the rage of water? I am plunged back into those days after Thatha died. The same static hum has descended on this house. It sits eerie and everywhere in these rooms as I cook and clean and make sure these women are taken care of.

But whereas Dharshi's family had swept in during our time of tragedy to offer us succor and taken us with them to the far, golden edge of the new world, now there is nowhere farther we can take them. The four of us, we are two widowed sisters and their fatherless girls. A coven of women left by their men.

I stay for a week. But then I can't swallow it anymore. The house, the heaviness of female grief, the hum of loss that hangs so heavy in the air that it vibrates at its own frequency. This is the kind of grief I do not want to remember, do not want to enter, because I know that if I do, I will never leave this room of sorrow.

Every night I dream of my father climbing that curving tree in the rain, pausing at the top as if waiting to hear me call him back, and then dropping into the water. I had not seen his face after they pulled him out of the river. Amma had acquiesced on a closed casket, but I see his face now, bruised and torn and blue tinged over the brown, the destroyed unseeing eyes. I wake up shuddering in the dark. I remember what it is to lose a father, to feel unmoored in a great rushing stream one had never realized before rushed just under one's feet. I remember what it is to be uprooted, in deep water, so that your feet are over your head, the

feeling that they will never again settle peacefully on solid earth.
I know there is nothing more I can say to Dharshi that will bring
her quiet.

I tell her I'm leaving, going back to college. She lies on her bed
next to mine and stares at the ceiling and says nothing. I pack
slowly, waiting for her to ask me to stay just a few more days. I
roll my few clothes into balls so I can stuff them in my bag. I heft
the bag onto my shoulder. For a long moment I stand by the door.
I memorize her face, her small body, her pale palms flopped away
on the comforter like doves, the tears rolling slowly down the
planes of her face. I know that I love her and that things will be
forever different, and then I leave.

I go back to college, get wrapped up in the rhythm of it—classes,
lectures, papers, all-nighters. But it all feels different now, more
serious. I start studying harder. The difficult subjects, science and
math, these are my solace. For the first time I consider medical
school. It would make my mother happier than anything. Like every other South Asian of a certain generation, she worships those
in the doctoring profession. I've never been able to figure out
whether this cultural worship of doctors is due to the saving of
lives or to the fat paychecks or to a combination of the two. Pos-
sibly it's just a holdover from some other decade when medicine
was a noble calling. In the end, I am practical. Med school will
take too long, cost too much. Instead I decide on nursing. It's
practical and lucrative. I know that the sight of blood does not
make me queasy, the secrets of the body do not frighten me. On

the contrary, I am thrilled at the idea that the interior labyrinths will be revealed to me. This is all my desire now. I throw myself into schoolwork with a vengeance, nursing school in the cross hairs of my ambition.

I have new friends now. Boys and girls to sit on the lawns with, to study into the night with, to eat all the greasy requisites of student life with, to stand outside clubs with, and to smoke cigarettes with, which feels naughty and subversive because all around us is the message that smoking will kill us. The act feels at once calming, dangerous, and sexy, so I light up and feel part of a quiet community, those of us pulling smoke into our bodies.

Yet there are moments when I feel a continent apart, when their belonging seems easy and unforced and my own is only pantomime. How casually they bring up parental divorces, molestations, and assaults as if these are badges of honor, horrors they went through and survived. When these conversations start, I want to escape to the library, the quiet stacks of books, anywhere but here. I don't want to hear these secrets told, witness these family closets flung wide open. I pull my hair over my face because invariably I know their curiosity will turn like a searchlight my way and then there will be prodding and poking as if they are fishermen trying to hook and reel in some deep-sea fish from my memory, up through my throat out of my body. So when I feel the tide of the conversation turning toward me, I slip away to the library, to my room, anywhere that the fortress of my solitude cannot be breached.

This too is happening: sex. In huge quantities and at all times of the day and night. Undergraduates slip in and out of each other's rooms, wander home disheveled in the early hours, dressed in last night's short skirts and stockings, shoes in hand. My roommate comes giggling to the door with whatever specimen of beefcake she has currently won, and I gather my books and leave them to it.

I kiss a few boys and let one do some other things to me. But it's never worth it. There is always an accompanying panic, that seething of the waterweed all along my veins, a rancor rising in my throat, and I must push the boy away, leave before he realizes I am gone, shut the door as he says, "Hey! What's wrong?" I walk home pulling my sweatshirt hood over my face. I turn my body into a castle, inviolate. If no one gets into my body, nothing dangerous can burst out of it, either. In this way safety is won.

In my room, under the covers I push the knife tip against my pulse until I am recast in time and space, and only then can I breathe again.

When Dharshi calls, months later, I don't recognize her voice until she says my name the second time. We chat of different things, but I hear a flatness in her words that wasn't there before. I'm castigating myself for not calling earlier, for forgetting her so completely in the midst of my own life and plans. My mother had said she wasn't doing well, had asked me to call, and I had forgotten or let myself forget. Then her voice gets steely and she says, "I need to tell you something. I've decided to do something."

"Dharshi? What?"

"I'm getting married."

I start laughing. Surely she's joking.

"No, really. I've decided. It's the best thing."

"What? To who?"

"A guy. His name is Roshan. Amma found him. He's nice. He'll take care of me."

I can feel my eyebrows rise, my mouth make that *oh* of absolute shock. "What? Why?"

"I didn't get scholarship money. This is the only way. Amma says this is the only way. Thatha lost a lot of our money, you know? We're poor now." An accusation. My mother has told me that Aunty Mallini is floundering. The grief is too heavy; she does little but sleep and cry, and she leaves the agency entirely to Amma.

"I'm going to marry him. He'll take care of me."

I'm silent. Ridiculous, but what comes to my head are those Wham! lyrics we used to spend all day bending over the old tape recorder to write down: "One, two, take a look at you/Death by matrimony."

I say, "Do you love him?"

And knowing that this is the trump card, the one thing that will shut me up, she says with a twist in her voice, "Yes. I love him."

I call my mother. "Why? Why is Aunty Mallini doing this? Why would she push Dharshi like this?" Amma listens, and then she says, "A mother shouldn't eat off her daughter's body." There's silence. But there's more she wants to say. I can feel it, heavy in the air, so I wait. She clears her throat like something painful is caught there and says, "After our parents were gone, there were only the two of us. She had to take care of me. There were relatives, but we were nobody's children. So when Sarath came, she didn't love him, but he fell hard for her. She was so pretty. He wanted to marry her without a dowry, and his people were well off, so she did it. To save herself and me, do you see?"

I don't see. What does any of that have to do with Dharshi? Amma continues, "She thinks it's Dharshi's responsibility like it was hers. To save them both. She thinks it's the only way."

I say, "But that was a different time."

Amma sighs. "It's what she knows. It makes sense to her."

"I don't understand. They've been here forever. Why would Dharshi agree?"

"Sometimes the old ways are easier. Don't you see? Love is difficult. There are no guarantees. But this way is easier, safer. Dharshi's chosen safety for herself, for her mother." She laughs. "Don't worry, I won't try to make you do this. I know better."

I am grateful for this. Amma might throw plates, lock herself in the bathroom for hours, and cut her wrists. She might scream and yell, but this is something she could not do, this selling of a child to the highest bidder. For once we are united.

I throw myself back into school, try to forget the whole thing. Mostly I do, but in my dreams I see Dharshi's beautiful face and some other unknown one next to it. A frog, not transforming into a prince but shape-shifting into something frightening. The metallic taste of these dreams tinges my mornings like a flavor stirred into my coffee.

Aunty Mallini calls. She makes small talk and I force myself not to let the venom rushing through my body erupt through my mouth. Finally she says, "So you must have heard . . . Dharshi is getting married." I mumble an affirmative and she says, "You two have always been so close. Like two little birds in the corner twittering away. Right when we brought you from Sri Lanka, you were joined at the hip, isn't it?" I say nothing; I wait and then she asks the question I know she has called to ask. "Darling, will you be her bridesmaid?" I want to say no. I want to scream at her that I want nothing to do with this marriage. But more than all this, I want to see Dharshi one last time before it happens.

I say, "Okay, yes."

There's relief in her voice. "Oh, good. Dharshi will be so happy."

I wonder if this is true. It has been months since we last talked.

The night before the wedding I take the train again. Retracing the journey I took on that other awful night. I've come late, so I've missed the dinner, and at the station it's Aunty Mallini who picks me up and takes me to the house, talking nervously all the way, filling the silences.

Dharshi opens her bedroom door. Hanging on her closet door where all her posters used to be is a white sari encrusted with gold filigree dripping to the floor. Her sari blouse hangs next to it, stiff as a piece of armor with the weight of beads. My own terrible pale-pink bridesmaid sari hangs next to it. Her wedding jewelry—earrings, bangles, the headpiece that will hang along her hair parting—is lined up in velvet boxes on the dresser. High-heeled jeweled shoes balance on their box in the corner. She looks at me and then away. I start pulling clothes out of my backpack, taking off my jeans to pull on my sweats. She says, "How are you?"

"Good, I'm good. What about you? How's it been?"

She shrugs her shoulders, drops them, turns to the jewelry on the dresser, says, "Look at what Amma gave me to wear tomorrow." She pulls out a large ring gleaming with brilliants in a paisley pattern, slips it on her finger; it catches the light with its gleaming surfaces.

She says, "Amma wore it at her wedding too. It was the first thing Thatha gave her."

"Is that right?" I can't keep the serrated edge out of my voice. I finish changing, say, "I'm going to sleep," and slip into my old bed. She has kept it here for whatever reason. Perhaps some reminder of how it used to be. I hear her sigh, hear her clothes thrown off. I hear her get into her bed just feet away from mine. I pull the blanket even higher around my shoulders, stare at the wall. She switches off the light, and I am falling asleep when she whispers, "Are you awake?"

I hiss, "No."

She says, "Do you think I'm doing the right thing?"

"No! Of course not. This is stupid. I don't understand."

The silence falls thick around us. An impenetrable wall of bricks rises from the floor to the ceiling. I hold my hands between my knees, my heart thudding. This is it. This is the moment she slips away forever. I keep my eyes open, stare blind at the wall I know is just in front of me.

She stretches her hand over the miles that separate our beds and catches my shoulder in her fingers, the grip of a drowning woman. She pulls me toward her and I reach out my hand and she takes it and I tumble out of my bed onto the floor and then am dredged up into hers. Then we are against each other, body to body, and she sighs against my cheek, and when we kiss it is rougher than I have imagined but also delicious and her body with all its gentle fallings and swoopings and depressions is melting against mine. She pulls off the heavy sweats that cover my skin. I feel like a snail slipped from its shell, vulnerable but also released. The white sari hangs like a threat in the corner. It glows, the only point of light in this room. I grab fistfuls of her hair and pull it around us like a tent of silk. It blots out the sari, the room, everything. It is squid's ink, a darkness where no one will ever find us. I realize I'm not scared. That my pulse is not thrumming through my body as it has every other time. I feel only love and desire. Her chest rises against mine, our legs dovetail. There are mutterings and moanings and softness. I lick the salt at the corners of her eyes. There is the slide of skin, a tumbling together, her sobbing softly against my chest. Her opening for me, my bare feet against hers. Later we fall asleep tumbled together, entwined in the tiny cocoon of her single bed.

. . .

In the morning we hear a voice just outside the door, and we jolt apart as if electrocuted. I have barely jumped into my bed and pulled the covers over my bare shoulders when Aunty Mallini comes into the room singing, "Good morning, darling. It's your big day!" She leans down to kiss her daughter. Both of us holding our breath, hoping she doesn't note the scent of sex that hangs heavy in the room. But it must have been too long since she had known this particular perfume, so she doesn't seem to notice. We don't look at each other, both of us startled by this thing that has happened.

Aunty Mallini sits on Dharshi's bed, my thrown-off clothes right at her feet. She ticks the day off on her fingers. "First we have to go to the hairdresser's. And then after that, the makeup artist's, and then we have to dress you. That will take time because we have to make sure the sari is draped perfectly. It won't be easy with that much work on it. And then the boys will bring the bouquets. Red roses. Such a good choice, no?" She turns to look at me then, and I, the covers still pulled to my shoulders, nod frantically. She rotates back to her daughter, says, "And then there are photographs to take and then the poruwa ceremony in the hall and then of course dinner and dancing. So hurry up, girls! Get up!" We are both terrified that she will pull the covers off Dharshi, reveal her small, naked body, when instead she jumps up and flounces out of the room, no doubt remembering some urgent wedding business.

Dharshi's face has gone black and uninviting. I don't dare talk to her. I wrap the sheet around myself, rise to grab my sweats, and pull them on with my back to her to hide from her eyes the body she has kissed and loved for hours. When I come out of the bathroom, she's already gone to the many hands that will transform her into a bride.

When I see her next, it is in the wedding hall. She is draped in the white sari, a row of deep red rosebuds like bloody spearpoints in her elaborate folded hairdo. Her face is painted several shades lighter than her jawline so that it floats disembodied above her darker limbs, a beautiful mask. Her long eyes are shadowed and outlined, the lashes coaxed to sweeping stiffness, her lips coated in scarlet. The shape of them reminds me of Samson's orchids.

Her husband is handsome. He's tall and well built and towers over her. His jaw is sharp, and a tumble of hair falls over his eyes. He might be kind or he might not be. It is impossible to read the quality of his tenderness from where I sit. I remember Dharshi jumping from couch to couch with the hairbrush clutched in her fist yelling about how much fun girls want to have, about being a material girl, about feeling like a virgin. I have to turn away so that no one sees the lone bridesmaid in the terrible pink sari tearing up.

When we hug goodbye, she says in a shaking voice, "He's handsome, right? You should be happy for me." I nod against her neck, kiss her under the ear where her own dark shade is spared. A surge in my heart almost spills through my lips. The thing I want most to tell her: "I love you. Come away with me." But the words stay stuck, and then the crowd carries her away from me, a hail of confetti obscuring the bloody rosebuds in her hair. She climbs into a car bedecked with trailing jasmine; Roshan follows her. The car starts and she is gone. In my hands, her bridal bouquet, crimson roses so dark their edges crisp outward toward midnight.

part three

twelve

So much happens *before* we are born. We come into being in the middle of the narrative, midway through stories that have been unfolding long before us. We totter in on our fat infant feet and attempt to take our places on the stage, but we know only a fragment of the bewildering plotline, only a sliver of the odd characters we encounter. The big people have been practicing their lines and playing their parts for decades.

I pitied my child from the moment she dropped away from me. Even then, tiny as she was, she tried so hard to understand events that had started decades before her birth. She moved her head, looking from one face to the other, back and forth, trying to read the emotions, the moods, the secret signals that would reveal what had occurred before she came. She was wise. I looked into her eyes and saw that she had come armed with ancient knowledge. But at the same time, so much of what came before was beyond her knowing. This is the worst kind of disability, the primary disadvantage of childhood.

But that was much later. At this moment I have outrun all my nightmares. I am a young nurse working at the old brick hospital in the city. There is a saying: "Someone who saves one life is called a hero; someone who saves thousands is a nurse." It is my guiding principle in these days.

I live in a brightly lit apartment over a Mexican grocery store in the Mission District of San Francisco. This is a mountainous city of dramatic views, great steel bridges rising in either direction, their heads lost in clouds. This is a place where one is shaken awake by earthquakes in the middle of the night. The planet beneath you moves in long liquid waves or quick gasp-inducing shrugs. It jolts you awake and reminds you that this is a precarious spot on the earth's skin. You wait to see if the bookshelves stop moving. When they do, you go back to sleep.

We are casual about it, but we know that one day the Big One will come, the colossal, catastrophic earthquake that will destroy us. It will snap the bridges like long beans. It will smash the buildings, as if under the invisible foot of a Japanese movie monster. The sea will rise and swallow this place; it is an apocalypse in waiting.

We know all this and are willing to ignore it because we are seduced by these forty-eight square miles. Here are streetcars rushing up and down the sinuous slopes, ferryboats skirting the island of criminals, with dolphins rollicking in their wake, sunshine falling like a blessing of the gods through the whispering fog, raucous crowds in Dolores Park, ice cream worth waiting in block-long lines for, a park that stretches even farther and more luxurious than Central Park, with bison and boats on lakes, street-corner flower shops spilling blossoms onto the streets, and it is all completely magic.

On a corner, tucked on a slight hill, is the old brick hospital. I spend my days and nights here, and I'll tell you this: when you are dying, small and alone in your hospital bed, it will be a nurse who will make your existence horrific or bearable. It will be a nurse who holds the bedpan, catches your quivering hand, gives you the begged-for extra shot of morphine. It will be one of us who shifts the bed those few inches that make the difference between agony and, yes, even pleasure. It will be one of us watching over you as you face the toothed abyss.

I work in the ICU, which can be either a place to heal or an antechamber to death. Not much is beautiful here, and yet there can be a grace, a certain painful dignity that happens to those lucky ones when the time has come. I walk from my apartment for the night shift. On the quiet streets the curtains are drawn. I see a few TV watchers awash in the blue glow; the sight of a shambling hobo with hands sunk deep in his pockets makes me sink my own cold hands deeper. Then I enter the hospital and the night is banished. It is always such a relief to arrive and be encased in these ringing halls, to be enfolded into the multitudes working, living, healing, and dying here.

Here then are the evening's cases: rival teenage gunshot victims from the Mission in cubicles down the hall from each other; a girl in a room waiting for the rape kit, realizing she is still wearing her rapist's sweatshirt and screaming anew; an ancient-faced meth-head scratching deep rivets into his legs. I have heard each story a hundred times. I know how to tend their wounds and their souls.

This is a place with its own specific codes: blue for heart failure, some serious malfunction of that most important muscle; pink in the case of a child abduction. When we don't want patients and visitors to panic, there are the secret codes. When the system pages Dr. Stork, it means that a woman in labor is in crisis. A call for Dr. Strong means that there has been a security breach.

But there is no code to signal our most important visitor, no announcement when he comes. I see him often, the night-winged angel of death perched on the highest gabled roof of the hospital, his inky eyes searching for the souls that fly out of our windows. His, the reign of this entire kingdom.

In the wards, the doctors come and go like gods, consecrated by their white coats and stethoscopes. They pronounce and diagnose and stand in judgment. Then they leave and we are still here. In the ICU you are reduced to your barest essence. No possessions, no homes or wallets, all you bring here is your body in whatever state it has fallen into.

There is always a rhythm to it. The family comes in in shock.

What happened to the son, the lover, the brother who said good-bye this morning and went to jog along the Presidio? How has he been transformed into this shattered thing? Why are these tubes piercing every part of his tender and beloved body? They will cry, they will rage, they will be exhausted by the decisions that have to be made, the arrangements, and the paperwork. Yet in a few days they will accept this new reality and do the best they can. Tears will become an unnecessary extravagance.

Then another relative will arrive from somewhere farther away and he or she will be shocked by everything all over again. There will again be tears and denial. There will be anger. Then in a few days he or she will also be exhausted, accepting. The cycle will resume. These are the rhythms of our days.

I have seen miracles too. Once a girl came in, gaunt and wasted. Twenty-six years old and dying of a disease that made her prone to stomach cancer. They had cut out two-thirds of her intestines, so she was a tiny wasted thing in the bed. Her mother gave her things to throw and she exorcised her anger by screaming across the room and throwing teddy bears, paper plates, cutlery.

I didn't try to stop her because her screams were weak, more like long, exhausted sighs. The objects she threw fell a few feet away, rolled under the bed. I didn't try to stop her as I might have with a louder screamer, a more adept thrower, because I didn't think she'd make it through the weekend. We made her as comfortable as we could; we checked her vitals hourly, gave her a heady concoction of sedatives. The chaplain came and she wept through instructions for her own funeral. Various family members trooped through the room saying their farewells. And then they left and we waited.

And then miraculously she didn't die. Her vitals went up and she survived the weekend. Then she survived the week and did not stop surviving. There was no explanation for either her having this rare disease so young or for her remaining among the living.

She comes to visit us sometimes. She brings flowers, cookies, balloons. She fills the ward with her laughter. She hugs me tight and says, "I couldn't have made it without you." She looks deep into my eyes as if she sees me. She makes my heart pound. She is beautiful, thin as a supermodel from the lack of so many coils of intestine, and the men love her for it. They do not realize she is a miracle.

She brings flowers for the nurses, large, waxy white orchids. They are supposed to be for everyone, but I know they're mine. I was her principal care nurse; I watched over her in those crucial days. Once when no one was watching, I folded a sprig of her orchids into my jacket as I left the hospital. I took it home and put it in an old painted vase I had found at a thrift shop and sat it in the middle of my kitchen table.

Then I poured a cup of tea and stared at those incandescent flowers. They lit up my kitchen. Three blossoms climbed the curved stalk, which ended in two perfectly rounded buds. I looked at the flowers with their large creamy wings lifted in flight, the mysterious interiors with all their carvings and curvings, the yellow passages into their hearts. I brought my face to the sprig. There was no scent, only the purity and smoothness of skin against my lips. I couldn't resist. I dipped the tip of my tongue into the innermost crevice of a blossom and the inner lips pulled at me as if to hold on forever.

Here is the secret of that girl, the one who was cured and who brought us flowers. When we were alone, when even her mother had left, I held her clawed hand and I prayed to whatever power was poised above us, enormous and invisible, weighing her life on its scale, fingering the cobweb of her breath, scissors opened around it and ready to snip. I begged this unseen creature for her life, and somehow it was pacified. The scissors were withdrawn; her life was spared. He looked at me once before he left, the mighty winged angel of death. He promised me he would return, but then I didn't care. We aren't supposed to do such things, of course. We aren't supposed to pray or have favorites, but I did. For her, I prayed. These flowers are my just reward.

thirteen

In these years I stay away from men; I stay away from women. I avoid love; I shun desire. I am creating the purest monogamy. My body belongs only to myself. My heart is as contained as a creature hidden deep in its shell. I know that the hungers of the body, its needs and impulses, are dangerous. They can maim unnamed but important parts of you. It's easier and safer to break the body into its working parts, to learn the names of bones and the functions of organs, the uses of chemicals to stunt or stall the advent of disease. These are the only acceptable ways I can delve into the physical.

There are men who like my slim tallness. They like the tumble of hair that releases when I refashion my ponytail. There are men at the hospital who look at me—doctors, sometimes recovering patients, a fellow nurse. They ask if they can come over and cook me dinner, maybe a spicy curry. I would like that, wouldn't I?

They make it easy to reject them. I am a hunger artist in the realm of love.

Amma, who has guarded my virtue like a dragon at the door, is now obsessed with its end. She calls to say, "Yes, it's good for a girl to have a job, to be able to take care of herself. Good-good." I can hear Catney Houston purring next to her; the cat is ancient now, half blind and mangy, but still alive, still passionately in love with Amma. My mother goes on. "You've done really well . . . But . . ." I wait for her to pick up the thread she has left dangling from our last conversation and of course she does, "You need to start thinking about settling down before you get . . . you know . . ."

"Get what, Amma?"

"You know, dried up."

"Amma! I'm not a sponge."

"Yes, darling. But good to have someone, no? Look at me. All alone. You mustn't end up like me. You can't be happy all alone. With no one to take care of you."

"I'm fine, Amma. I *am* happy. I have my work, my place. I like my life." I say this emphatically. Later after I hang up, I think about what it must mean to her that I live alone. In the place she came from, the only reason for this solitary state would be widowhood.

If we had stayed in Sri Lanka, there would be a hundred voices a day reminding me to find someone, to get married and settle down. Everyone from the aunties to the fishmonger would be asking where my husband was. If I revealed that he didn't exist, they would pantomime shock and proceed to tell me about their father's uncle's grandson who had just returned from abroad and was looking for a wife. Here, thank god, only my mother calls to harangue me and warn me against getting "dried up." I know that she doesn't mean I'm getting wrinkles. She is referring to a more intimate sort of desiccation. I look out of the window at the city street and laugh.

If love is absent, belonging is not. This apartment poised above the Mexican grocery is where I have felt the most at home in years. It is my small kingdom, my patch of earth. A tumble of green vines spills over the bookcase; an anatomy map in lurid detail rests on the dining table; a globe sits on the side table so that I may spin it and come to rest a finger on that single spot of green island in the wide blue sea that was my home a long time ago.

On a dresser by my bed is the aquarium, a two-by-three universe lush with plant life, a stream of silver bubbles constantly rising. It was once populated by a kaleidoscopic array of flitting fish, tiny red shrimp, snails who slid across the glass and participated in huge snail orgies, their shells turning this way and that as they fucked in whatever way snails can be said to do that. But over the years a few careless overfeedings on my part, a few ammonia blooms, have made the fish arc themselves out of the water. I would find them later, tiny and dried as wood chips on the floor. I mourned over each minuscule life and couldn't bear to replace them.

But one has survived. One shrimp has outgrown his kin by inches and outlived all his kind. In his red carapace like a king's mantle, his antennae bristling, he moves about the aquarium, climbs rocks to survey his kingdom, brings pincers to his face to feed himself. I call him Godzilla for his ability to survive devastation. He reminds me of those days when the river was my life. The days before water became dangerous, but here water is small and contained. Here I can watch Godzilla in his busy life and wonder if he too watches me as I come and go. He is my closest companion in these solitary days.

Days off I spend among flowers. When I first saw the dahlia grove at Golden Gate Park there was a moment of breathless recognition. How I had missed the flowers I grew up amongst! Those luscious crab claws and jacaranda of childhood. But here too are monster blossoms with wild faces. Not the same, because this soil, this air, yields different beauties, but likewise seductive. I gaped at them, worshiped their tumbled madness or precisely placed geometry. From the lightest champagne pink to the bloodiest midnight dark they turned their bold faces to the sun, and I wanted to kiss each one. So I cajoled and worked my way through the ranks of volunteers until I am here once a week. My fingers in the dirt, stripping away dead leaves, loving these flowers.

This is my life. A private undertaking. A place of refuge and solitary pleasures. And then, as always, everything changes.

Most evenings I am home curled up with a textbook. The human body doles out its secrets bit by bit, so there is always more to learn. But this night I am restless. A warm spell has fallen over the city. It is a rare enough thing to make people spill out into the open, everyone giddy at the thought of walking the streets without jackets, sweaters, scarves. There is the feel of a holiday. I feel a pounding restlessness in my blood, and soon the textbook is abandoned and I am pacing the apartment, not sure what to do with myself. My phone pings. It is Nadine, a nurse on my floor who has been after me to come out for ages. She has said, "You need to get out more. You're alone too much." Now she texts, *My new dude is spinning. At the Elbow Room. Come?*

I thumb back, *Yes* ☺

What? Really?!? ☺ ☺ ☺ ☺

I am already pulling on my shoes.

I walk down the long stretch of Twenty-fourth Street to the bar, where shimmering curls of silver ribbon hang from the ceiling and throw swirls of light around the dim interior. It's packed and loud; it feels like we are all swimming underwater, moving through some green, lightning-streaked liquid. Nadine grabs my hand as I walk by, pulls me into a booth, pushes an icy bottle of beer into my hand. A man she knows crowds in next to me and suddenly I am at sea.

He doesn't look at me. I don't look at him. We don't talk to each other. But I can feel his long thigh resting against mine, the heat of it almost too much to bear. He talks to the others squashed into the booth with us. I can't tell who they are. Everything is loud and overwhelming. I sit mute. Nadine is already drunk. She points at me with her beer bottle and says, "This is . . ." But my name is swallowed up by the music and the voices.

I feel my face flare up. He turns to look at me, says, "What *is* your name?" And I lean into him and whisper it like a secret, and he looks at me and nods; some recognition sparks in both of us.

He says, "Let's dance." And I am shaking my head. "No, no, no. I don't dance." But he is laughing and saying, "I bet you do," and he reaches out and our fingers interlock and we stand up and then he is pushing through the crowd, pulling me along.

On the floor, a crush of bodies, sweat spilling from skin to skin. I am shy, but then the music enters my bloodstream. It takes over my pulse and my feet. My fingers are undulating and I am unwinding and uncurling and expanding and laughing riotously with this man who has appeared like something mythical, something magnificent. We dance for hours, his body connected to mine by the music. We stomp and twirl and make faces. We are camp to Frankie Goes to Hollywood, melancholy to "True Colors," singing at the tops of our voices along with the crowd, sweeping our arms in poetic gesture, then frenzied when the DJ reverts to drum and bass and the whole place is only bodies moving to rhythm.

Then the lights turn on and we are all blinking in the glare like beached fish and he turns to me. His eyes are startlingly blue in the sudden light, blue as deep water. He says, "Do you want to come and see my view from the roof?"

I've never done anything like this before. Later I will feel surprise and even shock that I agreed so quickly. I, who am so used to dodging love. But at this moment I know, with a sureness I've never felt about anything else in my life, that this man is magic.

. . .

We walk up the hill to Noe Valley, suddenly awkward. He lives
in a house perched on a side street off Twenty-fourth. He has
three roommates, he says, but they are all probably out on this
beautiful night. We enter the house. His room in the back is large,
cavelike, and high-ceilinged, and on every wall are paintings that
looked like they have been ripped out of art books, bought at
thrift stores, some framed, some taped from the back. Along these
walls turned away from sight are stacks and stacks of canvases.

He goes to get us wine, and in the dim light I study the painting on the wall closest to me. A Japanese print showing a few figures hurrying across a bridge, bare pale legs, the shards of a
storm coming down, a riot of waves rising underneath. I move to
another and see a woman writhing on the ocean's edge. She is
caught in the coils of a giant octopus, tentacles snaking all over
her body. I look more closely, feel my face flare up. She's rearing
back in pleasure, her fingers at her crotch, her snorkel mask forgotten at her throat, and the water gathered at her back. The octopus, enormous and frightening but also erotic, holds her captive.
Its tentacles stretch around her ankles, drape around her arms;
one encircles an aroused nipple as she pleasures herself. I imagine
these tentacles moving around me. How heavy they would be,
how easy it would be to succumb to that embrace. Daniel next to
me, hands me a glass of red, says, "Teraoka. Do you know him?" I
shake my head, embarrassed that he has seen me looking.

He must sense this because he says, "Come on." He grabs
a throw from its place on an old chair and disappears through a

window. I push through behind him and am borne into the night. He spreads the throw on the roof and we sit. It is astoundingly warm. There is a downward slant on the slate under us, making our toes curl in vertigo. Below us, late-night stragglers, arms around each other's waists, stumble home to bed. We perch above them, unseen, but seeing everything in the dim light of the sharp sickle moon. We talk shyly and carefully through the wine. I don't remember what was said, just that it was said breathlessly. When he reaches over to kiss me I surprise myself by not pulling away as I have done so often. Then there is a dizzy roll, a loss of gravity, a sort of slipping and sliding. His mouth and his scent and a thousand giddy kisses, a hungry taking of tongue and breath and taste, and somehow we have rolled to the very edge of the roof; just below us is a drop into the now-silent street. We look down and laugh because we are invincible, and nothing, not even that empty space just below our heads, is frightening.

And then he says, "Bed?" and stands up and I follow him as he scrambles up the roof and stumbles through the window and toward the bed. He pulls my hand, kisses me more softly, seeing that the atmosphere has changed, but I shake my head and pull away. I cannot do this. There are terrible memories in my skin. I walk out of his door as he calls out, "Can I call you?" I shake my head hard, say, "No, absolutely not. I'm *not* available." It is a warning and a threat. I close the door quietly behind me and pray never to see him again.

His name is Daniel. He is an artist, a painter in oils and gauche. In the daytime he handles art for museums and collections; at night he paints. He's twenty-nine, a year older than me. Nadine tells me all this. She tells me he's been asking about me, asking for my number. She asks if she can give it to him and I say, "No!" and then I go home and look up meanings of the name Daniel. It means "judgment of God." I shudder. That's the last thing I need. I read this about men of this name: "Daniels tend to be passionate, compassionate, intuitive, romantic, and to have magnetic personalities. They are usually humanitarian, broad-minded and generous, and tend to follow professions where they can serve humanity. Because they are so affectionate and giving, they may be imposed on. They are romantic and easily fall in love, but may be easily hurt and are sometimes quick-tempered."

I look up that artist—Teraoka, he had said. I find a cross-eyed geisha, her long tongue intent on her ice-cream cone, characters caught in a shipwreck, and many, many women writhing in the giant octopus's embrace.

I slam my laptop shut and shower as I always do under burning hot water. I eat my solitary dinner, my eyes on the textbook in front of me. And later I look down to see that I have drawn his name in looping octopus curlicues in the margins of my perfect and ordered notes.

I wait for Nadine to ask again. I have to wait days, but then she asks and I say yes, give him my number, and I ignore the Cheshire cat grin that stretches across her face.

He calls. We talk. I tell him I prefer texts because I am busy. So then he texts and asks me out. I say yes. He will pick me up on a Saturday morning. I am beside myself that morning. What will I wear? I throw clothes on the bed, huge discarded piles of everything I own. I strew shoes across my perfect apartment. Godzilla watches me from his tank; he has never seen me so nervous. I settle on the most innocuous clothes—a sweatshirt, jeans. I cannot bear the thought that this man might see he has unsettled me.

He picks me up. The sun is shining. We drive toward the water. I had thought we would have lunch, see a movie. Instead he says he wants to walk the Golden Gate Bridge with me. I've never done this. It's always seemed the dominion of tourists. We park and walk along the bridge. Water crashes blue-green under our feet. We hang our heads over the edge and watch the ocean dashing itself against the rocks, breaking itself into a million silver bits. We turn to look up into the sparkling sky, the arches of the bridge stretching high into the air above our heads. I point to the other side and say, "That way is Asia!" Excited as a school kid, he laughs and grabs my hand. We walk along in the most perfect silence, our heartbeats in synch, our bodies reaching out to each other, our nostrils flared to catch each other's scent.

Later he kisses me slowly and carefully. I feel the tightly wound cocoon of myself loosen and begin to unravel, but it is months before I am convinced into his bed. When he enters me, I hold on to his shoulders and weep. Here are memories under the skin that are being released. But for him I can bear them. He asks with his eyes if he should stop and I shake my head and hold on harder and his tongue shoots out and licks away my tears and I sob until he comes. Just before we fall asleep, I whisper, "If you leave, I will die." He's mostly asleep, but he kisses my eyelids, whispers, "Never." Sated, still and calm, I fall asleep with him still softening inside me.

It is astounding, the way we fit together. And there must be some alchemy that happens in sleep on that first night, because this is how we sleep from that day on. My back cleaved to his front, his lips against my shoulder, his long body curved around mine. He holds my wrist between his fingers, his thumb on my pulse. Our moving and shifting in darkness is always choreographed—an elbow accommodated, a neck nuzzled, knees folded into each other. There is never an expanse of sheet between us. Always just the sacred resting of these two bodies entwined.

We learn each other's lives. He grew up in West Virginia, a place that feels as exotic to me as Sri Lanka must feel to him. I say, "Coal? Isn't that what you have there?"

He laughs. "Yes, but my dad is a doctor. We lived in Charleston. It was as big as a city gets out there, but I wanted out as soon as possible. So I did what all the kids do. I packed up and went to art school in New York." He says he went to a place called Cooper Union. I don't know what this means until I look it up later and realize it's the best art school in the country, that they accept only a handful of the most talented young applicants every year.

"Why didn't you tell me?" I ask. He makes a wry face, says, "New York . . . all of that. It didn't end well for me." He won't tell me more. I let it be. We all have our secrets.

For money he works as an art handler. There are five of them in the company. All young artists, driven and talented but forced to handle other people's work to survive. They drive to rich people's houses in Marin, in Pacific Heights, to install the private collections. The most expensive collections are in the houses where Broadway meets the Presidio, he says. He tells me about a house perched over the city that feels exactly like stepping into an eighteenth-century Italian villa. Another house is so modern that walking in, one is greeted by a cement wall and a huge photograph of a woman pissing into a man's upturned mouth. He has put up displays at MOMA, at the De Young, at the Asian Art Museum. "What's the most incredible thing you've touched?" I ask.

"The Monets," he says. "To be that close. To see the brush-strokes . . ." He shakes his head and has no words for what it felt like to be that close to genius.

All around his bedroom are large and small canvases of his; others are stacked under his bed. He pulls them out to show me and I see the progression of his thoughts and talent. The early paintings are crowded and full of color. Later his style is simpler and cleaner, more graphic and beautiful, intensely emotional. One painting I love shows a young girl standing in an open doorway holding out a letter, a stork taking it from her hand. Overhead a whole gaggle of birds is flying past. It's called *Special Delivery*, he says. It's a metaphor for a young girl's losing her virginity, becoming pregnant. I hadn't seen it. They are messages, I realize. Each canvas a short story. He shows me piece after piece after piece. He asks, "What do you think? Do you like them?" Yes, of course, I like everything about him. Already I am a mirror. He is the image.

We talk for hours into the night; we show up to work bedraggled but shiny-eyed, like religious converts or victims of starvation. Friends are forgotten, work is a hindrance. I cannot remember the last time I went into the dahlia garden, but then what is blossoming in my life is so much more imperative.

In bed, he answers my questions, sharing a long snaking ribbon of women starting with junior high crushes, high school sweethearts, art school fuck buddies, long-term girlfriends. He first kissed a girl when he was twelve. He lost his virginity at fifteen in the basement room of a girlfriend, her mother watching TV in the room above, loud enough for them to hear the muted sounds of the show. Sex has been easy for him, a natural part of his life. I picture these women. Each one brings a quick stab of acid to my mouth. I want to know their names, their ages, which ones he still keeps in contact with. I keep smiling as he reveals everything. It's clear that he has never been taught shame.

Then he turns those blue eyes my way, nestles his head against my bare shoulder, sucks the skin in a kiss, and asks, "What about you?" I throw an arm over my face, say, "There isn't a lot to tell. I lost it at twenty-two. In college. A guy."

"What guy?"

I sigh. "I don't know. I don't remember his name. He was the brother of a friend. He was spending the night in the house we were in. It isn't important."

He rolls over me, pulls the arm away from my face. "It *is* important. It's important to me." I look everywhere but into his eyes. But he holds my head carefully in his hands and won't let me look away even when the tears well up in the corners of my eyes. His gaze feels like knives carving away layers of my skin.

I push away from him, sit up with my arms around my knees, and say the easiest thing. "It's fine for you. You grew up in America, where virginity is no big deal. But where I'm from, it's the biggest deal. It's a matter of life and death. It's what mothers look for when they choose a bride for their sons. When the couple comes back from their honeymoon they have to bring the sheet with them to prove she was a virgin. Otherwise the family can decide she's spoiled goods and discard her and then no one will marry her. And an unmarried woman . . . she's nothing back there. That's what I was brought up with. That's why I didn't lose my virginity until I was twenty-two. Are you happy now?"

He pulls me gently back into his arms, kisses my face, whispers, "I'm sorry, baby. I'm so sorry." I sigh into his shoulder. I have misled him. But this is what he expects to hear; this is the narrative people expect from me. Is it so bad to give it to them?

Later in the fogged bathroom, the heated water pulsing against my flesh, I wonder, when *did* I lose my virginity? Was it at twenty-two when that boy entered me? Or was it much, much earlier? Was it when I was a little girl with a spot of blood upon the curve of my foot? Was it in the months and years after that, when every footfall felt like a threat? And *what* was it that entered me? Who? I try to think about it clearly, but a white fog rises, makes me sleepy until the question itself loses meaning.

At first I say I can't spend the night. I say I can't sleep in a bed that isn't my own. But a few months into our relationship, I get up to leave and he tugs me back and I fall asleep cradled by his body.

The nightmares come. Sharp objects. Skin tearing slowly. A child crying in a hidden place. Water crashing over my head. I gasp awake, gulp air. Daniel's hands are trying to soothe me. He whispers, "Shh, shh. It's all right."

I regain myself quickly, my thudding heart reclaiming its pace. He says, "Jesus, what were you dreaming about? What happened? You were fighting me off. I've never seen anything like that. What was it?"

"Nothing, just bad dreams." I grab my thrown-off shirt, wipe off my torso. He says, "Maybe you should see someone, see what they have to say. Seems serious."

"Everyone has bad dreams."

He says, "Not like yours. What was it?"

A corner of the room flares alit. Samson's eyes. He is here, water falling from the surfaces of his face. He is alive, watching. I am filled with the certainty that, as was true in my childhood, there is nowhere to hide.

I say, "There's nothing. I don't remember. They're just bad dreams." I lie back.

He picks up a long curl of my hair, kisses it, says, "You can tell me, you know. It's okay. You can tell me anything."

I nod, but I know that there are some things you *cannot* tell. If I tell, he will know what I am, he will see through to the corrupt core of me. He nestles against my back and falls asleep, and I lie wide awake, jaw clenched through another half spin of the planet.

I expand into love. This man named Daniel is mine. I own him; I love him. From his tumbled brown-blond hair to his long, stretching limbs to the arching span of his belly to the uplift of his cock that grows against my fingers or my lips. The smooth, flat expanses of his skin are like cream to my kitten tongue. I can't stop touching him. Suddenly I understand all the pop songs with their terrible love lyrics. I don't want to slow down this slide and tumble. I am high on brain chemicals, oxytocin flooding my system.

He is slow and careful with me. He lets me want him. I have never wanted a man before. Now with him my body is at ease enough to hunger. A bud closed tight since childhood explodes into full blossom. All through me surges a rush of chemicals attuned to his scent, his lean long frame, his skin. My whole self glowing, growling, ready—it wants such things. It accepts the adulation of his mouth and fingers and skin and desires more.

He pulls me astride him so that he is below, perfectly still, and I start to move. The bounce of my body, a specific friction, a mounting of heat and flush. As if our two bodies are kindling, this friction causes a fire to catch and spread all through me. He watches my face rapturously, waiting for that telltale shudder. A bursting open as if he has reached in and clasped my soul and thrown it outside my boundaries so that I am flying free, rising outward into the boundless dark. I gasp and fall upon him. As I fall asleep he runs his fingers along my skin, and it is as if his fingers and not his mouth have said, "Beautiful."

Later I'm sitting sedate on the bus on my way to work and am overcome with the memory of his breath on the pulse of my throat. My blood jumps and I am wet and throbbing and tumescent from the thought. I have to squeeze my thighs together, shift in my seat, try to look respectable, responsible. I hunch over my hospital notes, scribble tiny lines covered by my other hand. I don't think I'll have the courage to give him this scrap, but it reads: "You make me cream my undies; your tongue makes me insane; the memory of your body on mine bucking like a wild horse drives me to distraction; I want to ride you for hours; I want my nipple between your teeth; I want to bite you and scratch you; I want your blood in my mouth; I want you."

Who am I? Someone I barely recognize. Someone driven by lust, bold and brazen. A stranger to the way I used to be. He has split me apart and released the fibers of my being so thoroughly that they reach into him and pull us skin to skin. At my apartment that night, I cover my face with a napkin and hand him the torn scrap of paper. I watch from behind the cloth as he squints to take in the tiny writing, his lips moving. When he is done he looks at me with a shine in his eyes, an admission of the hugeness of this thing between us. He reaches for me, pulls me onto his lap, and covers my mouth with his.

All through the days I carry the smell of him. On the weekend, I shower, am ready to head out to a shift, scrubbed clean and dressed, but he pulls me back into bed, groans, "Don't go, stay here with me. Fuck me all day long." And I do, and afterward there is no time to shower again; soon I realize how glorious this is. At work I catch just the tease of a scent, a cobweb wisp floating in the air to my grasping nostrils. If I open my legs a little wider, sniff the air, the scent of us mixed together—a potion, a seduction, an obsession—carries up to me.

I wonder if he carries me around in the same way. On his skin. Perhaps for a while. But it's not the same, is it? It's not this tiny scent parceled out bit by bit all day. I have a secret, a heady pleasure that makes my head spin when I go to piss and drop my head between my knees, inhale the soft silk of my panties.

Can other people—my fellow nurses, my patients, the doctors—smell it? The subtlest hint of our mingled sex? I don't care. I had always felt cold in this foggy city, my circulation slow. But now the very temperature of my body seems to be raised, my skin alight like a match has been struck from the inside.

He moves in after three months. It makes more sense, since I own this apartment while he has always rented. I make more money than he does. We both know this and I don't mind it. He's supremely talented. It's only a matter of time before other people see this. I am convinced of it. I have never accumulated much, so it's easy to nestle his books among my own, to hang his clothes in half the closet, install his canvases and paints and turpentine in the back room, put up his paintings everywhere. I introduce him to Godzilla, who stands on a rock and waves his antennae in a friendly seeming way, making us laugh and hug. This is what it means to be happy, like letting the river take me effortlessly into its broad, warm embrace.

He says, "I want to tell you something." He looks intent, serious. I know that he has seen through the disguise to what I truly am. He is going to leave me. Why would he stay? Why would anyone stay? I am shattering inside when he says, "I love you."

I burrow against his skin. He needs me; I am special; I am chosen. I feel him move into my body, our blood mingled. The paths of our lives uprooted from their previously separate soils and replanted entwined.

Yet here is another and important part of our story. Daniel is white. Creamy skin that tans in botchy spots if he has too much sun, blue eyes, blond hair, a little more than six feet of white man. Here in America, for someone like me, to love someone like him, what ignoring of history do I have to do?

But in love, history can be ignored. Indeed, perhaps, in a love like ours, history *must* be ignored. What do plantations and shadows hanging from beautiful trees have to do with my lover and me? What does a history of colonialization and enslavement have to do with us? What does a queen's pounding of her children's heads in a mortar have to do with us? After all, my past is hidden behind the thick curtains of a different country. I will choose not to part these particular draperies.

Even more truthfully, perhaps, I am secretly thrilled at being noticed and chosen by *one of them*. As if he makes up for all those white boys in high school who had looked past me. To be desired like this feels like being lifted into the very bosom of America.

We put our arms, one dark, one pale, next to each other and exclaim at the difference. Next to him, I am irrefutably, undeniably dark brown. Such a malleable concept, one's body. It exists only in contrast to the bodies around it.

Then too, we live in a time and place where it isn't particularly remarkable to be interracial. There are couples like us everywhere in the city, mixed in every variation possible.

But there are also the battle stories. A black nurse who does shifts with me tells me of driving at night with her white husband, their car pulled over at a DUI stop. They had not worried because the husband had been the designated driver and had not drunk at the party. But the officer had shone the light in her eyes and wanted to know what her relationship to the driver was. He had asked questions until they realized he thought she was a prostitute out with her white john. It was only the proof of their shared name, their matched rings, that convinced him and freed them to go. Always between this couple, the way the officer's eyes had misread love for commerce.

Once Daniel and I drive across wide stretches of land, and in Utah we stop at a motel. I stay in the car looking at a map and he goes inside. After a while, bored, I wander into the lobby and go up to the counter, where the woman behind the desk is talking to him. I enter their conversation and it takes me a while to realize that she is talking to him, but not to me. She is looking at him, but not at me, and nothing I say, no ferocity with which I stare at her face, will make her turn and look at me and admit that I am here with some claim on this man who in her opinion should not belong to me. I am invisible, kicked in the chest by her refusal to see me. When she slides the room key across the counter, it is toward him. It is a gesture marked by an unmistakable ignoring of my outstretched palm. I storm out, and later in the room he says, "Shh, who cares? She's just a stupid, racist woman. Don't worry about it." And I nod and let him comfort me.

In the summer he takes me to visit his parents, who are good people living in a good place, a small town an hour out of Charleston. On the drive to their house, I open the window, and it is humid in a way that reminds me of the island. My skin opens up as if I am coming home, the biology in me tricked by the weight and temperature of the air, by the myriad shades of green rushing past.

I say, half joking, "It feels like home. We should move here."

He grips my knee and smiles, says, "Give it a minute." We pass a small church with a sign outside that reads, "Jesus, stripped, abused, assaulted, violated for you." I raise my eyebrows at him. He says, "Yah see? Not exactly home."

His mother is silver haired and soft shouldered, his father taller but stooped now. They hug me and are sweet. But they are not prepared for their son's choice of someone like me. Someone from such a faraway place, a place they have never heard of before. They have not been abroad. They were born into this place, this life, and have never left or even felt the need to. Their ancestors had come here fleeing terrors, and once they had been planted in this soft and welcoming earth, there had been no need to ever leave again.

They had expected that same life for this one child of theirs. Instead he had moved across the country, found me. They never know quite what to say to me. There are awkward silences and strange questions. They ask if I like the food, if I need more spice. I do—the things on my plate are bland and everything seems to be submerged under a white blanket of cheese—but I shake my head. I want desperately for them to like me. They are not bad people; they are simply people who have lived in one place, even one house, for all their lives.

He's strange around them. Different than I have ever seen him. When they ask how his painting is going, he almost snaps at them. But it is clear they are supportive. All around the house are his paintings, from the juvenilia of high school to more polished pieces, landscapes, portraits, still lifes. A jumble of styles as he was heading toward his own. That night in his narrow childhood bed I ask, "What happened at dinner?"

"What?"

"Your mom asked about what you're painting now and you snapped at her. What *was* that?"

He's lying on his back, hands behind his neck as if we are outside and he is gazing into the sky. His eyes are closed, but I can see them flit under the lids. Then he must have decided to tell me because it comes out in a rush.

"Okay, here it is. In New York a few years after graduation, I was in a group show at a very serious gallery. The kind of gallery that kicks off major careers. The owner was this really great guy. He had sunk all his own money into the gallery because he believed in it. Somehow, through some miracle, it was doing extremely well. He called and offered me a solo show and I was over the moon. It meant I was done struggling, that I was about to get discovered. Be a real artist. I could quit the day job and just paint. It was all I wanted to do. As we got closer I got more and more elated. This was going to be it. My life would change."

He pauses and I wait, my palm on his chest, feeling his heart thudding under the skin. He takes a deep breath, says, "And then a few weeks before the show, someone called me. The owner had been hit by a car. He died on arrival in the hospital. His wife was devastated. She sold the gallery immediately, and there went all my grand dreams in a puff of smoke." He opens his eyes to look at me. "I was crushed. I felt like someone had wadded up all my freedom, all my possible talent, thrown it in the toilet and flushed. I saw that . . . all my life being flushed away. I was gutted."

I nod in the dim light, our faces near each other. He says, "I stopped painting. I drank a lot. I smoked nonstop. I didn't eat or shower. I lost my handling job. I just closed up like a book. Withdrew into my apartment, into myself. I didn't want anyone around me. It was the worst time of my life. My folks finally came and found me and dragged me back here. That felt like death, but they probably saved my life. It was the worst humiliation. Having to move back to my parents like a kid. I lived with them here for about six months. In this room. I felt so guilty, I had gone to this great art school, done well, almost made it big. And then back here. And for those six months everything went dead. I didn't care. But then slowly it came back. My fingers would ache and I realized they missed the feel of a brush. My mother left out my old art books, things I thought I had outgrown. A book of paintings by Leonardo da Vinci. I used to look at his weird backward writing and those tremendous faces he loved, those craggy profiles, those massive rumps of horses, until I couldn't help getting paper and pencil and trying for myself. Then it all came back in a fever. I moved straight out to San Francisco. Got a crap job. And painted. God, did I paint. But this time just the sensation of the pencil on paper, the drag of the brush and the turpentine in the air, the working out of the ideas in my head, that was everything. This time I didn't give a fuck about the galleries or sales or numbers. This time it belonged just to me. This time it felt pure." He leans forward and kisses me. He says, "So that's why I get annoyed when they ask about painting. It's stupid of me. But it reminds me of that time when I felt like an absolute loser. I almost died. Then I came back to life."

Later when he falls asleep I lie there thinking about everything he has revealed. What must it mean to love something the way he loves painting? What must it be like to have your soul claimed by something in this way? I don't have this. It is the difference between him and me. The only thing I love in this way is him.

We drive away, his parents waving at the door. We go back to our beautiful city and resume our life together. The trip and all that bland food has made me long for simmering curries in creamy coconut milk. I start to cook, remembering how Amma had learned in those early years in America, when for the first time she was without Sita. I cook eggplant moju, chicken curry, pol sambol, and he loves it all. At first when we sit down together, I eat with a fork and knife in deference to a long-ago social studies teacher.

But one day, annoyed by the inability to form perfect mouthfuls, I put my fork down, put my fingers in the food, mix, and eat. I say, "Oh god, that's so much better." He stares and I feel like I have dropped my clothes in the middle of the street. But then he lays his fork aside too, tents his own fingers, and mimics my movements. He tries to make neat balls of rice and curry like mine, tries to keep his fingers clean past the first knuckle, makes a mess until we are both laughing.

He says, "Is this how you're supposed to do it?"

"Yes."

"Why didn't you tell me?"

I shrug. "I don't know. You're American. You might not like it."

He smiles, says, "It does taste better." Then, "How do you do it so easily?"

"Like this, like making a ball." I push the food against my tented fingers with my thumb, make a ball, and hold it up to show him.

He says, "Mine doesn't looks like that."

I shake my head, sassy. "Then use a fork, white boy."

"But this is the right way, right? I want to do it the right way."

A hardness in my chest, held since I was a child, new in this country and told how to be, crumbles away.

My mother calls and makes small talk for a long time. I'm saying goodbye when she finally can't stand it anymore and says, "You're still seeing that foreigner?"

I want to say, "I'm doing a lot more than seeing." Instead I say, "He's not a foreigner, Amma. *We* are the foreigners."

She says, "You know what I mean—foreigner, white person, same thing."

"Yes, Amma. I'm still seeing him."

"Is it . . . you know . . . serious?"

"What?"

"Because you know . . . these people. They have different ideas. They're not serious like we are. He might use you and then leave you high and dry. It happened to my friend Vishanthi's daughter. She 'dated' one for years and then he just up and left her. Poor girl. She was such a mess. And then the mother. My god, what a long time it took for her to get over it. Now, of course, the girl is happily settled with a boy from home. So all I'm saying is be careful, okay?"

"Okay, Amma, I'll be careful." As if falling in love is a disease I can protect myself from. I picture a giant condom, stretched all the way around my body and tied off neatly at the top with a bow. I fight the giggles.

She senses this and changes the subject. She has just gotten back from Los Angeles. She and Aunty Mallini had gone because there had been a memorial service for a young girl a few years older than me who had gone back to the island to teach art to war orphans. She had gotten on a bus and there had been a suicide bomber on it. The girl had died in the explosion along with scores of others. Amma tells me about the chaos of the house, the weeping parents. She says there had been a picture of the dead girl—pretty, laughing, her arm around a grouping of kids with big smiles and amputated limbs. The girl had had an older sister who had been there with her. They had made the sister identify the body. My mother uses the word *shattered* to describe her, this returned, shell-shocked sister.

I don't care. None of this has anything to do with me. I feel a stab of sorrow when she describes the sister's face, but these events, these people, feel far away. Their lives have nothing to do with my own. I wish she wouldn't tell me these stories about other Lankans. I wish she'd pay attention to my life and what I'm telling her about it instead.

. . .

Later when Daniel and I have been together for years and it is clear the "foreigner" is going nowhere, Amma asks, "How is your friend?"

I know what she means, but I always ask, "Friend?"

She's awkward, embarrassed. She says, "You know, that boy you see. That 'artist.'" The word *artist* pronounced with as much disdain as if she were saying *prostitute*. It makes her crazy that I've chosen this man whom she sees as a boy for daring to imagine his preoccupation with color and line is anything more than a hobby. "Why can't he get a real job and do this painting thing on the weekends?" she has grumbled to me more times than I can remember.

I pick a different battle today. "Amma, he's my *boyfriend*. Not my friend. You know that."

But *boyfriend* is an impossible word for her. Her mouth cannot form its syllables in relation to me. There are boys, fiancés, and husbands. Not *boyfriends*. Yet she says it often enough in the context of other people's wayward, rebellious, slut-whore Americanized daughters. Those girls have "boyfriends." I have a "friend" who is also a "foreigner."

These are the pleasures of love. They pour into every crevice of my life until they flood and overflow. I am on a train, thundering through the tunnel toward Oakland. I look around at this momentary gathering of strangers: the father with his baby daughter strapped to his chest. He shows her the pages of a soft book and she reaches out with her chubby infant hand to pat at the animals. There are tourists shivering in sweatshirts they have bought on Fisherman's Wharf because "who the hell thought California in July would be cold!" In the corner seat, a homeless man covered up to his eyes in newspaper. They are all luminous; they are all beautiful. I could grab any one of them and love them. I could sweep the homeless man into my arms, I could dance with the new father and his babe; even the tourists I could kiss. I have to contain myself, hide my aching, flooded heart behind my smile. I am vibrating with the fact of love.

I take Daniel to the park and stand with him in front of the dahlias. I have not told him about this obsession. He considers them silently, taking in the riotous, tumbling profusion of colors and shapes, the mini explosions of petals like the wheeling birthing of galaxies. He says, "Jesus, they're incredible. I've never seen flowers like this. They're like aliens." He points out the mighty scarlet ones, which look like spiky insects, the ones I have always held as my secret favorites, and I grip his hand harder. It feels like a secret sign. One more way our souls are made of the same substance.

We walk into the Conservatory of Flowers and our skins instantly drip sweat. I exclaim, "This is what home feels like! This is how hot and wet it is." He says, "I'd love to see it." I think about him there, in that place that was my home. It's a dream I almost cannot let myself have. These two parts of my life, can they be seamed together? It would be miraculous.

We sit on the lush and spreading greens. He reaches for me and the picnic is forgotten; we are kissing and rolling about and lost entirely in each other. We hear shouting, pop up, and see a group of cyclists riding by, wildly cheering us on. I hide my face in his neck. Embarrassed but also elated.

He wants to hike and camp. Things that brown people decidedly do *not* do. "Sleep outside? In a tent? Why?" I ask when he first suggests it.

He's astounded by the question. "I don't know . . . I can't believe you've never been camping."

I narrow my eyes and say, "But why would anyone do that? We can sleep in a hotel and go out for food, no? We can hike and that kind of thing in the day."

"It's not the same."

"Really? There are bugs, right? And weird people in the woods. I've watched all the movies, I know what happens out there."

"You'll love it. I promise." A kiss by the corner of my eye.

I'm skeptical. The idea of being outside for no reason, of "communing with nature"—these are new ideas. We used to go on trips all over the island in rented minibuses full of cousins and aunties and uncles. But we always stayed in hotels or guesthouses. In those places there was no question of sleeping outside where a wild elephant or a boar could find you. I remember singing loudly as the bus careened along graphite mountainsides or followed the curve of the southern coast. We sang baila, but often everyone's choice was "Hotel California." As if there was a yearning for a view completely at odds with what was around us then. This is a song about an arid landscape, a place that sucks you in and doesn't let go (and drugs, of course, but we didn't know that then). We sang "Hotel California," but never once did I think that one day I would be in the landscape of the song. Now he wants to show me what it really means to be in California.

I protest, but he is persistent, and weeks later we are out in the woods, walking deep into redwood groves. At a certain point he pulls a sketchbook and pencils out of his backpack. He wants to study how the moss clings to the bark, he says. He wants to capture the various permutations and textures of green. He says he'll be quick, but I know he'll be lost for hours. I kiss him and walk off on my own. The ground is rough beneath the new sneakers he has insisted I buy. I walk along, sweaty and slightly annoyed. There are noises I cannot identify. What creatures live in this place? Are they dangerous? I don't even know. Then the wind rises and ruffles my hair. A short way from my feet there is a great drop and the valley spread out beneath. In the distance a silver river snakes through the lush growth. I drop on the ground cross-legged and study the valley, the smooth velvet slopes, the craggy mountain edges. It feels like I am drinking beauty. An intoxicating beauty that rises in waves stills my breath. I lie back on the bed of the earth. It cradles me, soft as down. Far above, birds wheel, small in the distance, carried on the current. I lift my arms and am carried high into the sparkling air.

Later that night, when we are lying side by side in sleeping bags, staring into the exuberance of redwoods far above, I say to him, "It's like being a child at a party. The grown-ups are so much bigger than us. They've been here so much longer. We can see only their calves." I point my chin up at the trees. He laughs. I say, "No, really. Think about how old they are. We're like infants to them." He falls asleep and I lie there in the magic grove, being hummed at by trees with ancient memories, lulled by their stately breath, held in the embrace of their roots. I feel the sway and pull of the planet, the curve of it under my flesh, that gorgeous, voluptuous roundness. The stars spin circles overhead until I too, lost in this darkness, fall asleep.

He takes me to Lake Tahoe on a certain specific weekend in October. He wants to show me something, he says, and is as gleeful as a child. We stay in a small hotel because now it is too cold to sleep under the stars. We head out in the morning, walk through a parking lot into the woods. It's pretty, with meadows and, just off the path, squelchy wetlands, signs set up here and there to illustrate the life cycles of frogs and water birds. He stops to read each one, and I am bored but humoring him. I don't see why we have made this trip in a month when the sunshine is watery, but then he takes my hand and we round a corner and I gasp at the sight.

Almost at our feet: a creek, narrow and tumbling over rocks, and in the water, hundreds, thousands of flame-colored fish. So many they push into one another, each of them pointed upstream, swimming against the water's flow. I go closer so the fish are directly beneath me, oblivious of my presence, fighting the water to get up, up, up. The stream is narrow but deep, and there are layers and layers of fish. The living flash bright red, and under them, the dead, silver fleshed, flaking, blind eyed. Konakee salmon, he says. They spawn only here in this creek. They come from Tahoe and then swim upstream.

I wonder about this, the obsession with home, with finding their way back to the place they were born. "They aren't native," he says. "They escaped here from the fisheries." So this is their adopted home, I think. This place they are fighting to recover, it is not their native place, but still beloved, still worth fighting for, dying for.

We walk around the rim of Lake Tahoe, its cold, perfect blue bowl of water reflecting the sky. A silver line at the horizon. The depth of this lake is unfathomable, leagues and leagues of water, down to the unknowable depths. We hold hands and walk in step, our motion rhythmic and in synch. We walk out onto a pier that stretches long and narrow over the frigid water. At the end of it I lie longways on my stomach, my head dropped over the side so that my entire vision is taken up by blue. He sits cross-legged next to me, talking to my dropped-over head so that his voice comes to me as if it belongs to the lake itself.

He says, "Do you know the story about Jacques Cousteau coming here?" I shake my head, just feet over liquid, the tips of my hair almost piercing the surface. He says, "I don't know if it's true or not, but they say that Cousteau came here in the seventies and dove down in one of his submersibles. When he came out hours later, he was terribly shaken. He said, 'The world is not ready to see what I have seen.' He left the country and never said what he had saw."

I say at the water, "What was it?"

"He didn't talk about it till years later. Then he said that it was the scariest thing he had ever seen. The cold, it preserves everything, and so he saw bodies, lots of them. Native Indians, Mafia hits, drowned swimmers. All of them jumbled together, as perfectly preserved as on the day they died."

I scramble on my knees, leap to my feet, and start walking fast down the pier. He runs behind me, says, "What's wrong? You're shaking. It's just a story. Something people say. I'm not even sure it's true." But I can't shake the image. Those layers of bodies, just like the salmon, all held unmoving in water, the sins of this land held in perpetual silence like the layers of a grotesque cake. All water is connected, and my father's body was pulled from a river. I remember his closed coffin. Samson, who might be captured in water or not. Nothing is forgotten or finished. All of history is lodged in the earth, in the water, in the strata of our flesh.

We drive to other places. Gorgeous high vistas opening onto unreal views, pine ridges, the lake like an emerald cut askew, shimmering far below. We see silent-footed deer deep in the woods, wild turkeys so large and regal I vow never to eat their domesticated brethren trussed and carved on the Thanksgiving table again. But I'm quiet through it all. A certain cold came up from the lake and dipped a finger into my jugular, and all his talking, all these beautiful sights cannot melt the icy shards in my veins.

I tell him about my father's death that night. He holds me close in our hotel bed as I shake and cry and tell him what water means to me, what the image of bodies in water does to me. There are other memories I cannot speak of, but now I fall asleep in his arms and feel that I have reached safe harbor.

fourteen

In these early days I wonder if it is possible to be heartbroken with happiness. Yes, a cliché, but in the cavity of my chest, in the embrace of my ribs, my heart unfurls. There had been a whorled shell around it, like a ripple-edged, tightly closed clam. My heart had been a pearl in the center of it. He had slid a knifepoint into a crevice and prized with all his strength, and this covering had cracked open. The heart muscle, freed now, expands and fills as if with tide-pulled liquid. The sound of his voice, the silk of his skin—these are the sum of my treasure. I calibrate my days around his presence; I weave my life around him. This is what he does for me: he breaks my heart with happiness.

In some far part of myself, I know that it is dangerous to love like this. I know that this love has meant letting him occupy the space of my spirit. But my spirit was a room I had left long ago. Letting him reside there, letting him be the whole of my interior, is to feel my ghosts rise and leave. Pain retires to the far shores; it is a glorious and complete inhabitation.

We have six months in our kingdom of two. It is everything I've ever wanted and I could have lived like this the rest of my life, but one weekend morning he says, "We should go out and meet everyone!" I don't want to. I haven't returned calls for months, and now my phone barely rings. I have him. Who else do I need? "We need friends," he says. "You should call yours. I'll call mine." I don't, but he does, and quickly I learn that there are many people who adore him. We go out with them. They hug him tight and ask, "Where the hell have you been?" and he introduces me and they say "Oh!" with surprise in their eyes.

Now I see the ease with which he fits with these people. I witness their delight in shared memories, the way the conversation rolls off their tongues, the loud laughter. These are folks he has collected throughout his life. There are a few from high school, who escaped the same dreary little hometown and came west; a whole contingent from his art school years; and some other friends he's made in adulthood. They are mostly American, mostly white. They have a kind of perfect belonging, a knowing of where their earth is, where their roots sink. Next to them I feel like a hydroponic plant, roots exposed and adrift.

We go to parties, dinners, bars—a whole series of events to make up for the six months they refer to as his "kidnapping." A term that makes me feel like the kidnapper. As if those first glorious months had not been mutual, as if I were the aggressor and he the taken. I don't like sharing him; I dread these nights. It never feels easy; there is always some discordant note.

My English is perfect, but maybe too perfect, because when I say certain words they ask me to repeat myself. I say *boot* when I'm referring to where to put things in the car, and there are generally puzzled faces until, laughing, he explains, and then I realize he is my interpreter to these people. In their presence, the word *dance* comes out of my mouth in a way I can't control, clipped and British, and quickly becomes a running joke. "Say it," they urge, and I shake my head and find a hundred other ways to refer to what happens in a club. "But we love the way you say it." They say, "It's so proper." They'd mimic it back to me, making me feel tight and self-conscious. It isn't aggressive, it is perhaps even a sign of affection, but I can't stand to stick out in this way.

At a dinner a woman turns to me and asks, "Have you read that book about Sri Lanka?"

"Which book?"

"Island something." She snaps her fingers. "It'll come to me. It's about the war there. A Sri Lankan American woman wrote it."

I shake my head. As if a Sri Lankan in America could write truthfully about that war, or even understand it from this huge distance. As if this woman talking to me about it could understand anything about where I come from by reading a book. I want to laugh, but instead I smile politely.

And yet these women are mesmerizing. Like grown-up versions of the girls spraying mists of Aqua Net in the high school bathroom. But instead of those stiff constructions of hair, these women have smooth, flawless ponytails or bobs that skim their perfect cheekbones. I watch them like an anthropologist. The way they sip their drinks, the way they speak to each other, to the men, the way their clothes hang—all of it crucial knowledge because they have known him before me, because they have access to a him I never knew. And this lack of knowledge feels to me like a crippling disadvantage.

But I am becoming a master of imitation. I have started to pull my hair high into a ponytail just like that girl Marnie. He says they were best friends in art school. Did they "date"? Has he made love to her the way he does to me now? Has he seen her naked? Has she touched his cock? Have they kissed? He says no, no, they were just friends, close friends, but I don't know. When I see them laughing together, the thought comes splintering into my brain that there was more, that there is more now, that he loves her and feels nothing for me. I smile at her, but on the inside, I am ripping up her face.

If he knew, he would be disgusted. At a party he bends to talk to her and I walk into the bathroom and lock the door, sit on the toilet shuddering for long moments. I get up and stare at the face revealed in the mirror. It slips and slides. I can't make the parts reassemble into familiarity. I have to clutch my hands at my sides to keep from smashing the soap dish into the silver surface. If I could just do that, see the blood snake down my wrists, I would slip back into myself, I would calm down, my breath would return. Someone knocks and I dash away the tears, blow my nose, and slip out past the waiting person.

I smile, I laugh. *I do not let them see me.* The conversation washes around me, and I know I am the cuckoo in the nest. The mother cuckoo lays her egg in the nest of a different species. When the chick hatches, always earlier than its nest mates, it pushes the other eggs out of the nest. The parent birds feed the one hungry baby they have left. They can't imagine that it has killed their young. But the cuckoo chick always gives itself away by growing too large, even bigger than its unsuspecting adoptive parents, and one day it will be seen for what it is and thrown out of the sheltering huddle.

I live with the thudding fear that I will be exposed, that one day one of them will see me watching them, will realize that I am an impostor, will turn to whisper this knowledge into Daniel's ear. Who will it be? One of the men? Or Marnie with her French-manicured nails. She will whisper in his ear that I am not like them, that I am the overgrown, feathered parasite. What will his eyes look like then? What color will they be when the scales fall from them? I am waiting to be thrown out of the nest. I can feel the long fall to the ground, the impact, the agony of lying on the ground in a twist of bones.

I can't lose him. He says, "I love you. I can't believe you're mine." Joy floods through my body. I kiss his skin in a frenzy. He laughs and holds me away, but I squirm until I am right next to him again.

We cross the bridge for a party in Oakland. I had wanted to stay home with him, alone after long, frantic days at the hospital, but he has insisted. He goes to get us drinks and I walk around and lose sight of him and talk to someone else and then look for him and he's in a corner talking to a woman with striking skin, long, tumbling red hair, and tight black pants. I try to come upon them as if by accident. I try to make it graceful, but still, I see the quick twist of annoyance around his mouth before he says, "Hello, my love, meet Moira. She's an actress."

I say, "Wow really? That's great."

"And she's invited us to her new play. On Saturday. Can we make it?"

I shrug. A vague gesture that means maybe yes, maybe no.

He turns to the woman and says, "Tell her the details."

The women opens her mouth, which is painted scarlet to match her hair, and says, "Well, we're doing a version of *Love's Labour's Lost*, but here's the thing: we're doing it at a bar, so there will be drinks and specials and things. I'm playing a nun."

I try to keep the acid out of my voice. "Really?"

She laughs. "But you know, a sort of sexy nun. A bawdy nun."

I say, "But what will you wear? A sexy habit?"

"No. But it's long, so you never know what could be under it."

I say, "Oh, you should wear black lace panties and nothing else under it."

He says, "That's hot." They laugh.

Knives peel my skin, a red mist of rage. I dash my glass at the ground; it shatters, glass and ice everywhere, alcohol pooling on the wood. I spin on my heel, tears coming fast, push past shocked faces to the door, out onto the cold street, fumbling with my car keys. I'm starting the engine when he comes up, bangs his fist against the hood. "What the hell happened? What's happening?

Why did you do that?" And then when he realizes I mean to drive away, "Wait! I'm coming with you."

"No!" I shout against the closed window.

"But what happened? How will I get home?"

"Maybe your sexy nun can take you."

I peel away as his palm slaps against the hood. At the door of the house, a small crowd of shocked mouths, raised eyebrows. I see someone come out to put an arm around him and lead him inside. I don't care. I leave them all behind, drive over the quiet bridge shaking, silent tears running down, soaking my blouse. At home I lie in bed, curled into a comma, the heart ripped out of me. It lies next to me in a nest of bloody veins like the site of a detonated bomb. I watch it as it bleeds itself out on the sheets, thuds a final time, and starts to turn gray at the edges, and then I fall asleep.

We make up, of course. I cried. He was shaken, but he forgave me. I promised I wouldn't do that again. We started making jokes about sexy nuns until it entered the language of our relationship and neither of us could remember the details of that party. I was happy again. There is nothing I want more than him. He is the whole of it.

Months later, we are at a Chinese restaurant in Berkeley. We are sharing brown rice and broccoli with veggie chicken. I eat the forested tops of the broccoli and he spears the trunks, which I

cannot stand, off my plate. This silly synchronicity in our broccoli desires is something that has always felt auspicious to me,
another sign that cosmic forces had taken an interest and said
"These two will do nicely" and nudged us toward each other that
night three years ago. I am talking about my last shift, a particularly daunting patient, the frustrations of conflicting medications
and a family that doesn't trust us.

He says "Uh-huh" and "Hmmm" as he folds a sheet of paper
over and over, making it take the shape of a tiny white crane. I say,
"Are you even listening to me?" He says, "Yup, uh-huh, yes," and
slowly, carefully writes something in minuscule letters on the bird.
He looks at me with that deep-water gaze and holds the origami
out on his palm. I take it and stare at the tiny writing until I
understand that it is asking me a question.

I raise my eyebrows. "What?"

"Why not? I love you."

"My god. Are you serious?"

"Yes."

I can't think of a single reason why not, and so we do.

We are married under the golden dome of City Hall at the top of
the curving marble staircase on a silver day in May. I wear a long
slinky white dress and carry a jumble of dahlias in every shade of
red I can find. His parents are here, wearing formal but sensible
clothes, looking surprised but happy.

My mother comes in a worked sari. I know this is not what
she had envisioned for me, the bridegroom being a tall white man

instead of a dutiful Lankan boy, an artist instead of a doctor, engineer, lawyer, even for god's sake, a professor. And the wedding too must be a disappointment. What she would have wished for is a hall full of people, a spread of food, a flowered poruwa, young girls in white ruffled half saris singing the proper verses. Without these things, is it even a wedding? She would have wanted everything Dharshi had at her wedding for me. She must feel bad that Aunty Mallini gave her daughter these things, married her the proper way, but that she cannot do the same for me. But if she thinks these things, thankfully, blissfully, she doesn't say them. A wonderful thing has happened. After we have lived together for years, instead of leaving me as she thinks all white people are prone to do, Daniel is making me a legitimate and lawfully married wife, and for this she is thankful enough to stay quiet.

Then too she has told me this. Soon, a few months after our wedding, she is moving home. When she told me this, I said, "Where?" before I realized she meant she's moving back to Sri Lanka. I was incredulous. "Why now?" and she said, "You're settled now. There isn't anything to keep me here anymore. Even the cat is dead." I feel guilty for not asking after Catney Houston, who after hanging on for this ridiculous length of time has finally died. Now there is truly nothing holding her here. She says, "I'll get a place in Colombo. Or a house in Kandy. In any case you're settled, so I can go now." I can hear the determination in her voice. She wants to reclaim what was lost. My wedding will be the last time I will see her for years. I am sad; I am relieved; I am joyous.

A month before the wedding I open the mail and find a package from her. A sari froths out. A white sari studded with paisley in golden sequins and shining crystals. It's beautiful. I throw it over my shoulder and am transformed. An instant bride. But then the memory of that other sari glowing in the dark, hanging over the door, and below it two bodies tumbling together in love and desire comes to me. I haven't seen Dharshi for years. She has been taken into a different life, become a person I don't know. Our connection has been diluted to seeing pictures of each other on our computer screens. I have seen pictures of her and Roshan, rounder now, and claimed by two children, hanging on to her from all angles. A sort of yearning shoots through me. She had been my first love. I know that now. I put the sari back in its box. I tell my mother it's hard to wear a sari, I don't want to stumble on the steps, I don't want to trip under six yards of floating fabric. The truth is, I want nothing that reminds me of who I was before this man came.

On my wedding day I wear a clean white dress, a satin dress that spills to the floor. A dress that is not ivory or champagne or any other corruption of white, but is instead stark and startlingly white. A dress that he had bought for me a few weeks before, wrapped and packaged, a huge crimson rose held by a ribbon to the top of the large white box. "Here," he said, "this will fit you perfectly." I opened the box and exclaimed, "Oh my god. It's beautiful." I pulled the dress, slithery and heavy as an animal skin, out of the box. I could feel how expensive it was, how exquisitely, elaborately one of a kind. I couldn't imagine how he had paid for it. He must have saved for a long time. I'm touched by his generosity when this money could be going to other, more practical concerns. He said, "Put it on."

"But you shouldn't see me. It's bad luck."

He laughed and said, "What? You've turned traditional? Go, put it on." I went into the bathroom, stepped out of my clothes, and pulled the dress over my head. It sighed against my skin, settled. I came out, shy, the cloth slinky against me, my arms bare, the entirety of my silhouette exposed. He looked rapturous and said, "Yes. Amazing. It's perfect." I loved that he said the word *perfect*. Not a stain or a blemish anywhere on me. He pulled me close, searched my face, touched his thumb to the mark beneath my right eye, high on the cheek. "This is my spot. This I claim," and put his lips against my skin exactly there, a slight suction. He thought it was a beauty spot, but it was a scar from a childhood cruelty that had faded now into this slightest demarcation.

The dress *is* beautiful, a long sleek column of white with silver straps that slide against my shoulders and make them shine. But under this, a thought like a splinter under the skin. On the island, white like this, unembellished and not lit up with gold embroidery or jeweled sequins, is a symbol of death. This is something my American fiancé cannot know. White was the color I should have worn to my father's burning. Instead I had worn the slightest shade of pink. Now when I should be as adorned as a goddess, I am wearing the perfect white of mourning.

After City Hall, after the judge has said the solemn words and the rings have been slid onto fingers, after Daniel has been told to kiss the bride and I have acquiesced and after the few assembled friends have whooped and cheered, we go on a pilgrimage to the water. His parents, my mother, the chosen friends. We stand on the cliffs over the Sutro Baths, the churning sea stretched far below us. This is the distant edge of the world. There are apocalyptic clouds above; the red bridge is framed in the distance, the entire world painted in shades of gray, silver, and emerald.

Someone pops open champagne and it froths over all of us, making us giddy. He pours it into gushing flutes and hands them out. We are toasted in words of love and blessing. The wind flings itself in our faces and we fall silent then, because it is beautiful, and just like that I know I will belong to this man for always. I, who have sailed these seas in storm and peril, who had felt ever wind-tossed, ocean-flung, have come home to dock in these safe and sunny harbors. I throw my bouquet over the cliff down into the rushing waters and the sea takes my offering, unties the silver ribbon that holds the flowers together, tosses them until they are scattered on the waves, tiny as single petals borne away on that salt tide.

part four

fifteen

Three years pass faster than I can imagine. We learn the rules of marriage. It is a closed system with its own weather, politics, and machinations. It is a loyalty constructed out of inside jokes, the sharing of fears, and predawn recounting of dreams. It is a shifting of personality toward each other like two plants in a small pot striving for the same patch of sun and in the process becoming entwined above and below ground. His roots take hold in the earth of my body.

Soon enough comes the inevitable question. Hamlet grappled about whether to be or not to be. Our burning existential question becomes to baby or not to baby. His parents drop subtle American hints, "It would be so nice if you did. And it would be so beautiful. A lovely shade of caramel. Like Halle Berry." My mother on the phone doesn't hint. "So when are you going to do it? Better now than when you're even older. What are you waiting for?"

I say, "Amma, we just got married."

"Three years ago. Don't you know what comes after marriage? The baby."

"And after that?"

"The second baby, of course."

"God, Amma, you'll have me with a herd if you had your way."

She says, "I always wanted a lot of kids, but then I couldn't. You should. It'll be good for you two, make you settle down and grow up. Maybe it'll make that hubby of yours get a real job."

She's set up in Colombo now. She rents a house, has a servant. She says the country has changed so much, I wouldn't recognize it. The war is over, of course, but more than that, money is flowing in, roads are being built—freeways, just like in America—there are shopping centers, and everyone has a cell phone. She says that the only thing that would bring her back to America is to see her first grandchild. I don't tell her the truth. That neither of us really wants children, neither of us is pulled in that particular direction.

She goes on. "You know Dharshi is pregnant again."

I say, "She's having another baby?"

"Yes, her third. A girl, they say, this time. Two boys before, you know."

"Yes, I remember."

"You know, I think it worked out. I think she's happy. They look good together now. Mallini got her married so young. But now she's settled. And the babies, Mallini has her arms full of them, lucky lady."

I sigh. She says, "What darling? I just want you to be happy. How can a woman really be happy without children? All that other stuff, career, love, what have you, it'll all go away, but a child is yours forever."

I don't tell her that I've never felt those urges other women talk about. I've never looked at babies with longing, never envied women with newborns in their arms or toddlers hanging off them. My uterus has never throbbed at the sight of a newborn. The biological imperative, those essential hormones that make women stare at babies as if they are delectable, they must be missing in my particular chemical makeup.

And yet the baby-hunger is all around us. I know women with a baby-desire so deep their breasts automatically weep milk when they hear other people's infants crying. I have friends who after years of focusing on careers are issuing baby ultimatums to stunned husbands or boyfriends.

Daniel's male friends sit at the table and talk about being surrounded by women who are newly rapacious for newborns. One of them says, "I feel like they just want my sperm. A woman actually said to me the other night, 'I want to have your blond baby.'" He looks terrified. The rules of dating have changed under his feet. It's no longer lighthearted or spontaneous; the objectives are different.

The opposite too is happening: men we have known for years are saying to their wives and girlfriends, "Give me a baby or I'll leave." Formerly happy couples are breaking up, and the one left behind sheepishly, heartbrokenly mutters, "She/he wanted a baby. I'm not sure I do."

Daniel and I listen to all this and turn to each other, delighted that neither of us are pulled in this way. Instead we clink glasses long after our friends with children have gone to relieve their babysitters. We loll in bed, take hiking trips into the desert, go to Mexico, and congratulate ourselves for not falling into the trap that has enmeshed so many of our friends.

Child free is the term we use to describe ourselves. In this choice, we are wholly and luxuriously selfish.

But it's not only our friends who are heeding the call to procreate. The grocery store racks are full of magazines that follow the progress of pregnant celebrities with the concentration and enthusiasm usually reserved for sporting events. It's a nationwide obsession that follows a predictable path in the headlines. First, the all-important photos of the woman showing off the sparkling chip of compressed carbon gracing her finger. "He proposed! She said yes!" Then the exclusive shots of nuptials: "The Fairy-Tale Wedding. Flowers. Cake. Dress." Immediately after follows a giddy anticipation of that lauded physical manifestation of fertility, the baby bump. Who has it? Who is showing? Almost immediately after the baby is born, the most important part of this equation comes into play: How fast does the woman regain her "bikini body"? How quickly can she shed the grotesque signs that her body has harbored another being for the last nine months? If this shrinking takes longer than a few months, there must be something wrong with the mother. She must be lazy or depressed. After all, this is her job as a celebrity, isn't it? To model for us how our own bodies should act?

The message is loud and clear: women's bodies are supposed to swell up, drop babies, and then shrink back down to a manageable size. The baby? Another perfectly designed accessory to match her heels and bag. All around us, this ambient roar of fecundity, and I for one am happy to be outside it.

Yet just a few weeks after the conversation with my mother I think back to it and wonder if it was a trigger. If all those nights Dharshi and I spent in twin beds next to each other had synchronized us so that even though I haven't seen her in years, perhaps her body has somehow reached out and whispered to mine, because now I am late.

My period has never been regular, the ebbs and flows of it impossible to regulate. Also maybe having to pay so much attention to other people's bodies makes it hard for me to pay attention to my own. I realize that it's been some time since I bled, at least a month, if not two. I wait another week hoping and praying, the question gnawing at the back of my mind. What could have happened? I'm on the pill. But is it possible I have missed one here and there? Could his sperm have breached the gates in a moment of hormonal confusion, a morning where I rushed out without popping a tiny pink tablet? It's possible. I've been working mad hours; I haven't always paid perfect attention. I don't tell him because a part of me is convinced I am being stupid. I am not pregnant. Soon my period will come and then I can tell him how scared I was and we will laugh at my silly anxiety and toast to our child-free-ness.

At the end of the week I buy a pregnancy test. Hands shaking, I squat and piss. I lay the test on the counter, wash my hands. I stare into the mirror at my terrified face. Then there are those long, long minutes. I go into the kitchen and eat a cold chicken leg I find in the fridge.

Minutes later, there it is, an unambiguous plus sign.

I sit on the old gold couch we bought together at a garage sale when he was moving in, and my entire life shimmers and vibrates and changes in front of me. How can it be? Even now, in some secret passage of my body, some tiny, unwanted *person* stirs and dreams. When did this presence come? Where did it come from? Can I get it out? It's shockingly like being possessed by some outside force. I think about my skin moving outward and stretching taut, about pushing out a living creature through an orifice that seems far, far too small. I press my hands across my belly, imagining a tiny speck of life floating there. What will I do? What will he think? How will our lives be? Should I abort? Should I carry a child? Give birth to it?

I pace the room and the lost men come to me. My drowned father, Samson. Between them, they had crafted me. How can I pass on such an inheritance to a child? How can I conjure up some miniature soul from the mysterious unknown, feed it upon my blood, and then push it kicking and screaming out of my body into this world? Existence has been heavy enough for me. Would it be a blessing or a curse to bestow it upon some small, unknown stranger?

But then this tiny thought unfolds. It whispers hope. It says that perhaps *here*—far away from the island, far from those malevolent spirits, far from those cruel hands, in the arms of this strong and loving man—it could happen. Perhaps I could be a mother in a different way. Perhaps a child would be born who is a new thing, not an entity ruled by ghosts. A child made by him and me would be born of love, even if accidentally. And this accidental child, born in this safe place, it would love me unconditionally, and for this I yearn.

When I tell him, his eyes widen and his brow rises. He spreads his hands on the table, pushes himself up, and goes to stand in front of our window, his back to me. He looks down onto the street where the late October sun is falling like weak drizzle. I say, "Say something."

He says, "I don't know . . . A baby?" His voice trails off and he stands there for minutes. I stay quiet, waiting. He comes back, squats next to me, holds my hands. "I just . . . I don't think we can. Do you want this?"

I shake my head and then I'm not sure. "I don't know. I never thought I wanted to be a mom, but maybe with you . . ."

He says, "We've talked about this so much. You've always said you didn't want to."

I shrug my shoulders, my hands on my stomach pointing out

that the decision has been taken from us, has been made by un-known, unseen forces.

He says, "But we're so good. Look how much freedom we have. How easy our lives are. It'll change everything. I don't want it to change. I love our lives. I love how we are together."

I counter, "I love our lives too. But maybe it'll be like us mul-tiplied. It'll be us times ten. You, me, and a little one. A tiny one just like you or me. It could be good."

He says, "Have you even thought this through? Do you know how much time and effort and money it'll be? I'm just trying to get off the ground. I mean, if I sold some paintings it could be dif-ferent."

"Yes, of course. I'm not proposing we adopt a puppy." He lets go of my hands, gets up, and paces the room again. He says, "I don't know."

I say, "I have to go to work," and stand up. Something in me is far away from him, but he must feel it, because he comes and holds me close to him, strokes my hair with his palms. I rest my face against his chest. He says, "We'll figure it out together. I promise." His voice sounds like it has traveled miles to me, but I nod against his skin.

I go to my doctor and find out that I am about seven weeks preg-nant. At home despite my trepidation I open my old nursing man-uals, and there are the lists of attributes:

The embryo is around 13 mm (1/2 inch) in length. The heart is beating with one chamber. A dividing wall is formed in the heart. Arm and leg buds are beginning to grow. The lower jaw and the vocal cords are beginning to form. The mouth opening is forming. The inner ear is being created. The digestive tract is developing. The navel string is being created. The following organs are being formed: the lungs, the liver, the pancreas, and the thyroid gland.

It sounds like a poem, like the lines of the most beautiful poem in the world.

Inside me, these things are happening. The delicate whorl of an inner ear, its complicated mechanisms beyond the grasp of all science to create, is being created. Inside me, organs that pump blood, breathe air, secrete hormones are coming into being, forming the tiny swirl of life that will be this miracle, a new human being. A childhood memory rises, of listening to the Buddhist verses that extoll the sanctity of life, verses that claim that a child is a child from conception and that the months we spend in utero too are marked as a year of life.

I can't eat, I can't sleep. I am as devastated as a bombed-out city. He tries to hold me, but I don't want him. I walk my shifts like a zombie, go through my paces at bedside on automatic. Nadine tries to talk to me, but I push past her. I wonder when one of the others will report me for being careless, for more than once pushing the needle into flesh rather than vein so that patients gasp and swell and complain. There is a time bomb ticking inside me. This is one problem with a deadline set in stone as much as in flesh.

At the grocery store and at the park, I stop to watch women with their children, the way they look at their little ones and the way that longing gaze is returned. No matter how far the child might stray, there is always that look over the shoulder to make sure mommy is there, mommy has not left. The mothers always know where their children are, even as they hold coffee and talk to the others. Always, this invisible umbilicus stretching between a mother and her young.

To be adored like that. To be loved unconditionally, to extend the way we are together, Daniel and me, to this other unknown person, who is also both of us. Could we be like that? Happy? All three of us in love with each other? It seems the last thing missing in the life I have built.

He comes home one night, sits on the edge of the bed with his face in his hands. He looks ragged, like he too has been crying. I feel a rush of love for him and then he says, "I'm sorry, I just can't do it. I've thought and thought and thought about it, but I just can't. I'm sorry, but I'm not cut out for being a parent. I can't do it. I think you'd be a good mother. But I can't do it."

"What are you saying?"

"I just mean maybe it's important for you to be a mother. Maybe more important than being with me."

"What?"

"I'm just saying that if you want the baby . . . you know. More than you want me, I understand. I love you and I want you to be happy."

I understand then that nothing is more important than him. I will give up this baby for him. I am not strong enough to carry it without him.

I make the appointment. It's on a weekday, so he won't be with me. The doctor says it's not a big deal. I'll be sedated and afterward he'll pick me up. I'll sleep a lot, she says, and then I'll heal. It'll be like it never happened. We can go on with our lives and forget about it. I'm so glad I live in a time and place where this is easy, where I don't have to risk my life to do this. But I also know I will be haunted by this day. Haunted by this scraping out of the material that could have been our child. Right now just a curl of life, but also within it the possibility of a whole human existence with its entire weight of experience, memory, connection.

I'm sitting in the waiting room, trying to get myself ready for what happens next. I stare at a magazine, but I can't make out the features of the happy women in bikinis on sun-bleached beaches. Instead I see a jumble of limbs, flashes of what will happen inside me in a few minutes. My heart is thudding, the pages of the magazine fluttering with my hands. The breath is stuck in my rib cage like a trapped bird.

Daniel walks in. He sits down next to me. He takes my hand and I clutch his fingers as if I am drowning.

I stare at him. "What are you doing here?"

He says, "Do you think we can do this?"

I say, "Yes, if we do it together. If you stay with me."

The nurse comes to the door, calls my name. I stand, but he pulls me back into the seat. He says, "No, it's okay. We've changed our minds." She looks at me to be sure. I nod at her. He kisses my cheek in his special spot and whispers, "We're going to have a baby."

We walk out together. I leave that room as if I am walking out of a bad dream. I'm too happy to say anything.

After that, he's kind; he's solicitous. He cooks the foods of his childhood for me, bland white-colored foods that ease my rising nausea. He brings me large-faced flowers, filling the apartment with gardenias, camellias, huge waxy magnolias that glow like full moons. Our space is a swirl of scent. We fall asleep lulled by the perfume of these blossoms. We never talk about what almost happened. We pack our fears into a Pandora's box and lock it securely away. We have decided that the story was always that we both wanted this accidental child. We have no more use for doubt.

He says, "You'll be such a great mother. I just know it." He says, "What shall we call him or her?" and compiles a long scroll of names with beautiful doodles of animals in the margins. He gives me a red pen and asks me to circle the ones I like. He has taken the names that have run in his family, and here are the names of our brethren dead and alive. Generations of names. A way to connect this child to the ones who came before.

He moves the art supplies out of the spare room. He starts painting a mural but says I can't see it until it is done. He goes around with paint on his face and splattered all over the old gray sweatshirt he loves. Then he leads me to the door of the new nursery, his hands over my eyes. "Look," he says, and the room is transformed, a secondhand crib, a stack of diapers and baby wipes, and a changing table, and on the wall he's painted two beavers in perfect detail. One of them is stretching up to draw a perfect, anatomically correct rendition of a majestically large-antlered deer. The other has drawn a child's stick figure of a deer with red crayon, has trailed off the red crayon into a corner after having gotten some of it on his face, and is grinning at us from the wall. "This is you," he says, pointing to the artistic beaver. "You've got it figured out. This mother thing. You're going to be great. This is me," he says about the crayon-besmirched beaver. "I'm a mess, but with you, I can figure it out."

I think: here are the two souls who will love me without condition, without artifice. I know I will never again wander pathless and unsure of who or what I am. Instead I am this one's wife and this one's mother; I will be called by these sacred names: *wife*, *mother*. I will be fixed, stable, and held in place securely between them.

sixteen

It's an easy pregnancy. I have some morning sickness, the skin stretches and hurts, I can't sleep much, but at five months there's a softness emanating from deep inside me. From the ultrasound, the doctor has confirmed what I already knew: we are having a girl. I feel her move in the seas of my body and it makes me breathless. I pull Daniel's hands onto my skin and we stare into each other's eyes in wonder. How is this possible? How have we made a new creature, a person who will have her own life? A new person who is both him and me. The immensity of it makes us grin in delight.

His parents come to visit and we take them out to dinner. When he tells them, I watch their wide, ecstatic faces. His mother says, "Oh, I thought you weren't going to. I mean, I didn't know you were trying!" Then there are the cries of "How lovely. Congratulations. How wonderful." The clink of champagne flutes for everyone but me. The father looking at the mother, saying, "We are going to be grandparents," with so much joy.

My body stretches, craves strange things. I had always thought they were old wives' tales, but now I realize that pregnancy cravings are real and insistent. I want foods I have always hated: brussels sprouts, raw carrots, and broccoli. I eat oranges by the ton as if unable to get enough of their sweet, sun-blessed flesh inside me. I eat apples fresh and unwashed from the farmers' market. I like that bit of grit on them. This too satisfies some strange pregnancy desire.

The sight of meat nauseates me. The veined slabs of it make me feel as if my own flesh has been filleted and displayed behind the grocer's glass. I have to avoid that entire section of the store now. How had I eaten these things before? They are so clearly organs, the workings of bodies so similar to my own, merely the skin stripped away to reveal the working muscles underneath the surface, living beings reduced to meat.

So many things I cannot have anymore! Wine, hot dogs, sushi, mushrooms, cigarettes. Such strict rules governing my body. At lunch if I even glance at a salmon roll, there are disapproving looks, which might lead to lectures about contaminated seafood and my child's development. The other nurses eat crap and smoke like mad, but now that I am pregnant, they all have strict opinions about what I can and cannot do.

I realize that my body, which had always been my secret realm, is now public property. Women stop me at the grocery store to ask if it's my first child. When I say yes, they nod knowingly as if they are the guardians of ancient and secret knowledge. "It hurts," they say. "It'll be the worst pain of your life," as if I don't know this, as if I am not already dreading what is to come. Perfect strangers come straight up to me and, if I don't fend them off, put their hands directly on my stomach. People ask if I am eating enough folic acid, if I'm taking pregnancy yoga.

There are too many eyes upon me. It makes me long to hide away. This body that is expanding into something I barely recognize, it proclaims itself so loudly. I remember that other life, even before I met Daniel, when I belonged only to myself. Sometimes, traitorously, oh so insidiously, I crave that privacy, that perfect self-containment.

There are ways to rebel. There were those first illicit cigarettes with Dharshi in high school; then the habit picked up in college, compounded through the tough nights of nursing school. There had been sacred moments when we all gathered outside buildings to stand silently and puff together, the communion of drawing the smoke into our lungs. A hushed and long drawing in, an instant serenity, the ecstasy of the exhale. I had never drunk much, I did not have lovers, but this ritual, in the form of a small box in my purse—*this* I had loved. In those years before him, it had been my only vice. After we were married, it had dwindled down to whenever I was stressed and could hide it from him.

Now a sharp hunger grows. Once a week or so when I can't

stand it, I hide and smoke. The first few puffs calm me down. But then a hail of images of what havoc it might be causing within me rises. I imagine her, tiny inside me, gasping for air, twisting and hurting. Guilt paralyzes my throat. How weak I am. How selfish, not to be able to fight off this craving now when it is so important, when it can change everything. I throw away the butt, promise myself it is the last. I go a week without, and then like a person glimpsing an oasis after crossing the desert, I must have a cigarette.

One day I heft my bulk through the front door, and hitting my elbow on the jamb, I drop my purse. A hundred things roll out, the most secret of them landing at his feet. My heart in my throat, I watch him unwrap the toilet paper to reveal two cigarettes. He looks at me with narrowed eyes, sudden disgust. "What the fuck is this?"

A sort of chaos inside me. He has never raised his voice before. My mouth spits words: "Nothing. They're not mine."

"What? Whose then?"

"They're Alice's. She likes to smoke after work."

"Who the fuck is Alice? Stop lying. *I knew it*. I smelled it on your clothes. I didn't say anything. But what the fuck is wrong with you? How could you?"

I'm trying to figure out what to say. Can I conjure up an Alice, who could be a friend, who could smoke, and who stores her cigarettes in my purse? Would he believe that? What lie can save me? My pulse is racing. I am a child again, exposed, in danger. A flash of Samson's face. I have to claw my fingers against my palms to stay present.

He throws the two cigarettes on the floor, squashes them beneath his heel so that flecks of tobacco worm out of the paper.

"You're a goddamn nurse. You know what could happen to the baby if you smoke."

"I'm sorry, I'm sorry, I'm sorry. I didn't mean to."

I just want him to hold me and love me again. It feels like the world is ending inside my skin.

"No more cigarettes, okay? It's too dangerous." Then, his voice changing, "We don't want a messed-up baby, do we?" He screws his face into a mask, grasps his hands into hooks like a mini Godzilla. "Look at me. My mom smoked when I was inside her and now look at what happened to me. I wish she hadn't done that." The voice becomes plaintive. "I wish I coulda been a nice normal bay-bee."

The terror abates. I walk into his arms, his kiss. The earth slips back under my feet. But now I also know this: he loves this creature growing inside me more than me. Now I am only a body holding another body whose needs are more important than mine. Now an interloper lives between us, separating us with her inescapable presence.

seventeen

I have put off telling my mother, but now it's time. I have to catch her in those slivers of time appropriate to both of us, the hours of waking or just before going to bed. I tell her and I hear the joy bloom in her voice. She asks me to come and let her take care of me. Or, she says, she could come to me. This is the way it should be. Always among mothers and daughters on the island, this tradition: a woman is taken to her mother's house far away from her husband. She is hidden away from men and tended to by the women of her family until the baby comes. For months after the birth she is not allowed to work. The women will surround her, will ensure that she and the baby are properly loved and tended until she is healed, until they are bonded, and only then do they return to the man's house.

I say, "No, it's fine. Come later when the baby is born. Then I'll need help." I can tell she doesn't want to listen, but she has no power now. The baby inside me is already changing me from subject to queen. Now I am the mother and she has no choice but to listen.

Being pregnant is like falling into an alternate universe. In the places that are overrun with the fertile population of the city, young women in yoga pants pushing strollers, fathers with babies strapped to their fronts—a café in Noe Valley, for example—I feel a sort of beaming acceptance. I am being welcomed into an elite club. It is a cool club, a hip club. We are not parenting in the old-fashioned way our parents did. No, sir. This is all new. We are a new breed of parent, knowledgeable about water births, orgasmic births, prolonged breastfeeding, the fathers as conversant as the mothers in all this complicated jargon of the reproductive body. We won't do anything our parents did, is the mantra. We are so much better than they were at this, is the unspoken mandate.

There are smiles and questions about my due date, my diet. The women with toddlers running around their feet relate their battle stories: twenty hours, thirty-six hours, forty-two hours in labor. The woman who says, "Pssshh . . . try sixty-five hours" is looked upon with the awe due a goddess.

One says, "I did it all naturally. Because you know, it's better for the baby."

Another says, "I had a home birth. Just Joel and the midwife and the doula. It was transformative." They flash perfect, glossy smiles, kiss their cherubic children, and hand them to the Guatemalan or Salvadoran nanny waiting patiently by.

In another part of town, in the Mission, young hipsters look at my rounded bulk with the distaste of people who have just seen the movie *Alien*. They are skittish around me, as if at any moment my belly will rip open and a fanged and phallic monster will burst out to chomp at their own delicate flesh. Young women give me a wide berth as if sitting next to me on the bus will cause their own taut bellies to pop into eminent, bursting heft. Men with beards glance past my body as if unable to see it. My female body, no longer in any way desirable, but instead reminding them of the ugly end result of sex.

Environmentalist friends wrinkle their noses. "But it's such a huge decision, isn't it?" they say. "Such a drain on the resources of the planet. My god. Seven billion people." They shake their heads. One friend of Daniel's sniffs, "I wouldn't ever do that. If the polar bears are dying. And they *are*." She fixes me with a hard stare. "Dying because of us, you know. I don't know why I have the right to reproduce if the polar bears don't. It's their planet too, isn't it?"

I shake my head at her, not sure how to respond. Daniel says, "Yvette, how about we leave the polar bears outta this, okay? It's just our baby. Hers and mine. We don't have to bring the fate of the whole planet into the situation." I press his hand in gratitude. With him next to me, I can do anything.

We learn that there are many things to buy. Strollers and car seats and nursing bibs and breast pumps and rocking chairs and clothes and pacifiers and on and on. I understand now why young parents look buried alive under mountains of things, why they buy larger cars and bigger houses. There is so much paraphernalia! His parents send us fat checks that he is loath to accept. But I tell him it's not a time to be picky. We need the money, and if they can be generous, why not? It's their first grandkid, after all. These days I'm paying most of the bills. We don't talk about it, but I know it cuts him.

We go shopping at a place that proclaims, "We deliver everything but the baby." I wander the aisles, thinking this is how a fifties housewife might have felt when she was asked to choose the perfect bathroom cleaner. If she could just master the uses of all these new scientific products, she would be *perfect*. Now an avalanche of things is targeted at me. I need to pick carefully so I can be the perfect mommy. It is a very, very important job. The most important one in the world, as the ads keep reminding me.

And lost under all this noise, the looks and the stares, the baby bump mania, the obsessive accumulation of things, is the absolute miracle of what is happening inside my body. Every week I read to him the newest accomplishment of our very small person, the acquisition of earlobes, the lengthening of the spine like a taproot, the spreading web of capillaries and arteries, the minuscule but rapid beat of that forming heart, the way this tiny human in me is replicating step by step the journey of our entire species, from tiny fish to curled-up mammal. We watch the sonogram screen and hold our breaths to see our baby girl. The technician knocks at my belly as if on her front door to make her move so that he can check her neck. It will reveal a wealth of information, he says. We watch spellbound as, legs tucked, hands in prayer, she turns to us with her huge, closed alien eyes. She is sacred; we are in awe.

These days she moves constantly. I can touch a hard place on my belly and say, "This is her head." In another place, "These are her feet." We watch the way my belly moves like a wave as she stretches an arm, moves a leg. Not gently, as one would expect, but assertively, just under my skin, as if she is saying, "I am here; I am alive; I am coming."

Then as if one miracle engenders another, I walk into the apartment and he hands me a glass of sparkling apple cider, clinks it with his own rare tumbler of whiskey. His eyes are sparkling, some deep emotion barely contained in his body. I rest my hands on my aching hips and ask, "What's happened?"

"You won't believe it. It's crazy. I've just sold *The Coming*," he says.

"What? But that one's not even in a gallery."

The Coming of Civilization to California is an oil he completed in the Oakland warehouse studio he shares with three other artists. It shows a covered wagon cresting the horizon, pulled by a steer, a woman in lingerie splayed on its back. Small panels show parts of the steer, cuts for sale, the woman too dissected into bits for consumption. A Mexican man in a sombrero looks agog at this insertion of commerce and commercialism.

"I know. I've never even shown it. We were installing a private collection in that house in Woodside. A bunch of modern pieces. Stuff that's super delicate, so it's been days of unpacking the boxes and carefully placing them where this rich woman tells us. Then last week she mentioned that she was looking for a big painting. Something specifically Californian. And Marcus pointed at me and said, 'You should look at this guy's work. It's damn good.' She said, 'Oh yeah?' and I said I have pictures on my phone. I was joking, but she looked and then she wanted to see them and then today she came in. I didn't want to tell you. I didn't think anything would happen. But she loved it and she wants *Cry of the Rain Crow* and *The Unmaking* too."

We stare at each other, eyes huge. This would mean more money than Daniel has made in all the years we have been together. Can it be? Is it happening as we have wished and hoped and prayed? The baby gives a kick from inside me. I put Daniel's hand on my belly and we grin in hope and joy.

I am eight months along. She lies inside me, head up, nestled below my heart, and now I am afraid that she may not turn in the appropriate direction, facedown like a diver waiting to arc out of my body, but might instead attempt to exit in this dangerous fashion, feetfirst. The doctor tells me to try speaking to her. She explains that there are invisible bonds between mother and unborn baby that no one understands, a certain chemical language, perhaps, or an emotional one. It's said to happen. She says, "You might be able to get your baby to move yourself."

I sit in the quiet of our apartment, on our old faded couch. I reach for my girl with my mind. I explain to her what will happen soon, the right way to turn so that this will be easy for both of us, so that soon I will be holding her. After an hour of sitting in the quiet and speaking to her, I feel her turn, a push and roll inside me, and my good little baby girl has listened, has turned herself upside down. I sit in wonder, my hand on the skin of my belly, which is still moving with the force of her turning. She reminds me of how little we know. How much about ourselves, the animal bodies we inhabit, is unseen and mysterious to us.

Later, reading, with my feet in Daniel's lap, I say, "Oh my god, listen to this. Her cells come into me through the placenta. A few of them. And if my organs are ever damaged in any way, the baby's stem cells can come in and help damage the repair. Can you imagine? Her cells will be in me all my life. They could be in any of my organs, my liver, my heart."

He kisses my hair, nods. This makes it all worth it, the pain in my joints, the way my stretched hips make me feel like a jointed doll coming apart. All worth it because we together, he and I, are making something new, something safe, a family.

The question of naming rises again. Such a difficult thing to decide, the sounds she will carry with her, the name we will call her, that her lovers will call her, the one that will be spoken at her deathbed when we are long gone. What an awesome responsibility. I can't believe someone is letting us name a child. Then I remember that someone is actually letting us bring a child into existence. She will be our creation and our responsibility. Who let us do this? It's madness. I try to focus on the smaller question of her name. I look over the beautiful illustrated list he's made me, but nothing stands out. I turn to him. "What are we going to call her? She needs a name! We can't have a baby without a name."

He looks at me over *The New Yorker* and makes a face. "Constance. It's a good old family name."

"Constance? That's ridiculous. That's like something from the Civil War."

"You wanted old family names. That's a good old family name from way back in the day. Great-Aunt Constance would be proud."

"Oh, in that case, if we're doing old family names, I can go all the way back to the village. How about a nice old Sri Lankan name like Iranganihami?"

"No. I like . . . Petunia-May."

"Isurusahani."

"No one can even say whatever you just said. Prudence."

"Chathurangani."

"Ezekiel!"

"She's not a boy!"

It goes on like this, us laughing, us terrified. And then one morning as the last shreds of a dream are leaving me, I hear her name whispered into my ear as if someone is standing by my bed.

I stretch and smile. "I know what to call her," I tell Daniel. He gathers me closer in his sleep. I lie there, knowing who is coming to us. Her name will be Bodhi for the ancient sacred tree under which the Buddha was said to have found enlightenment. On the island the tapering leaves of these trees rustle and spin even when there is no wind; they are said to be the abode of deities and gentle spirits. It's a masculine name, and I like this—our girl will have a taproot of steel in her.

He adds to it, Anne. A quiet, settled family name. His mother sends us pictures of various Annes, a line of grandmothers, great-aunts, and cousins. Bodhi Anne then, this is who we are awaiting.

My date is close, March 15. She will be a water baby, born under the sign of twin fishes swimming tail to head. I am ready. I want my body returned to me, and I want my baby. It's been an easy pregnancy. I'm scared, of course. What woman close to labor thinks about what is coming and is not frightened? But I am ready. More than anything I want to avoid an emergency cesarean. I know what they look like. I don't want to be that woman who is wheeled off after hours of pushing and propped up behind the blue screen. I don't want layers of me cut into, organs removed, placed into a bucket by the bed, my uterus lifted up, my baby popped out like a man poking his head through the neck of a sweater. Women are not supposed to feel it, but a part of them always remembers that muscular tugging and wrenching of their deepest beings.

. . .

I've thought about getting a home birth with a midwife. I mentioned it to my doctor, and she shrugged and said, "You can do it, but if something happens to your baby you'll never forgive yourself." And this specter of something happening to the baby is too frightening to overcome. Daniel says, "No way. I want you in a hospital with a doctor and a medical team."

I know what the word *midwife* is conjuring up for him. A greasy-haired witch with dirty fingers and bad teeth, boiling water while I scream. We burned women in the early days of this country. Women who had too much knowledge of herbs and plants and who knew how to deliver babies. Those early witches, they were midwives, setting up competition for the new science of medicine. So they were burned and their knowledge was lost, and since then there has been this drive into the hospitals. A gleaming, sterile place to have a baby. A place where any risk can be managed and altered with the knife, with the drugs.

The most experienced midwives know how to deliver babies without knives, without drugs, but I am too scared to challenge the wisdom of modernity and science. I'll have my baby in the hospital.

March 15 comes and goes. My bag is packed. At every twinge, Daniel looks at me with alarmed eyes. My body is huge, the baby moving all the time. I feel like a whale holding an ocean in its abdomen.

I am awakened by a movement, like a menstrual cramp but much sharper. I lie in the dark; he's asleep next to me. Another hard twisting inside me, and I gasp aloud.

He's instantly awake. "What's happened? Are you starting?"

I say, "I think so."

There are hours of walking and waiting. Holding his arm, I pace; the pain arrives and recedes. We walk around the block. I stop, have to lean on him, gasp and shudder. We go home and I bounce on the exercise ball. I won't go to the hospital too early just to be turned away. The magic 3-1-1. It's on our fridge door. Pains three minutes apart lasting one minute each for an hour, this is what we are waiting for. The pain mounts. I want to walk away from my body, leave it like a shroud fallen on the floor behind me. I realize this is not possible and am terrified.

It takes twelve hours. Then the worst car ride I have ever taken in my life. It's a ten-minute ride, but it feels like hours. At the hospital we are checked in. Contractions are coming like a knife stabbing from the inside. I lean on him. He grips my hand. When the pains come, he looks into my eyes and counts while I breathe. It calms me down a little bit.

The nurse checks me. She puts her hand inside of me and sees how many centimeters my cervix is dilated. She says, "You're a seven. That's great. Keep working, mama." I have become my cervix, this number more important than any other now. She pulls her gloved hand out; it's covered in my blood and mucus. I turn my head and sob.

I can't do this. I don't want to do this. I'm so scared. I've been ripped away from my life, my normal life. Everything is pain, a kind of pain I cannot describe. Our cozy apartment feels a million miles away. Instead I have been dropped into some nightmare. The curtain has been pulled back and I see what we really are, glorified beasts that deal in blood and sweat. I try to remember that I'm a nurse. Bodily secretions are not frightening to me, but it's different when you are the body on the table. It's different when you are not the one in control. I refuse the epidural, of course. I know the right way to have a baby. No matter what, it is important to say no to the epidural. And through the raging pain I think, this is the way the species is perpetuated, what the fuck?

I want to die. It won't matter. If I died, they could cut me up and take out the baby. She would live.

They call in the anesthesiologists for the epidural. I sit on the bed, curve my back into a C-shape, and hold a pillow to my stomach. I stare into Daniel's eyes and try not to think of what they are doing or of the needle so big that they did not show it to us in the birthing classes. I try not to think of the fact that they are going to jam it into my spine. *My spine.* I try not to think about the fact that what they're doing could paralyze me. But I'll do anything to leave my body at this moment. The shot slams through me, an electric bolt so strong my legs jerk out.

I lie back, ignoring the tube entering my spine. How wonderful to be pain free. How miraculous to have that horror lifted. The monitors show that I am contracting wildly. But I have cheated pain. I'm shuddering all over. The nurse says it's my body reacting to the trauma of pain. I fall asleep.

. . .

The nurse checks me. I'm finally a ten. It feels like I have to take
the most giant shit of my life. The epidural is wearing off. They
won't give me another because they say I have to feel the pain to
push. I'm terrified of the pain coming back full force. My vagina,
my ass, it's all already on fire. I'm on my back with my knees pulled
up, Daniel and a nurse holding my numbed legs, another nurse
with her hands in me as I'm grunting and crying and pushing as
hard as I can.

The epidural makes me disconnected from my body, yet also
and at the very same time, I am slammed into it in a way I have
never been before. It feels like a war. I don't want to be here. I
want to be anywhere else but here. Any battlefield, any war zone
would be better. I fall asleep for minutes and then am jolted back
to this place. The nurse looks up at me from between my legs.
She locks eyes with me, says, "You're not trying hard enough. I
want you to *really* try." What the hell does she think I am doing?
She says it louder, almost shouting, "Come on, *harder*, you can do
this. Push your baby out."

Delirious, I remember a friend in high school saying, "Do you
want to see me feed my snake?" I remember her dropping in the
mouse, the snake unhinging its jaw, the way it swung open un-
naturally wide and open and then sucked up the mouse's hind-
quarters, then its belly, until only its mouse face poked out of the
serpent's mouth, a moment before the rodent disappeared into
that black abyss. And now my hips are dis-attaching like the
snake's jaw, carving an opposite trajectory, from darkness into

light. I picture that curve inside me, the long slide that she must travel, and I push specifically into this place. I feel a wave, some specific energy flowing through me. I feel myself opening up; I feel myself tearing open. Everything is getting big. Pressure and expansion. The nurse says, "She's crowning. Reach down and touch your baby's head!" And I do and I'm crying because there she is, her head lodged between my lips. I push and grunt inhuman noises and the nurse tugs and then I open and she slips free from me. I'm crying, high as a kite. Daniel is leaning over me. They put the baby in his hands. He stares at her, his eyes huge, streaming. They put her on me, between my breasts. We watch astounded as she snuggles, moves her head looking for my nipple, smelling for it. When her mouth latches onto it, an electric current runs through my whole body.

She is born with her eyes open. Her gaze is regal and composed, like a queen surveying this strange new land she has come upon. Her head is elongated from the pressure of my pelvic bones, evidence of the journey we have completed together. I stare into those eyes, the strange shimmery surface of them.

I can do anything, go anywhere. I have completed this journey that lay unknown within my body all of my life, the ability to open and bring forth life. This secret knowledge held in my cells until the right moment; it makes me feel suddenly aware of the unseen rhythms of the world. I can sense the curved migrations of whales traveling the oceans, the opening of tiny flowers to minute winged pollinators, the pinecones that open in raging flame—all these unknown events and us too a part of it all.

We sleep and eat. She nurses. Daniel holds me while I hold her and it feels like hibernation or burrowing, like we are a nest of small furry animals—squirrels, perhaps, with our tails wrapped around us for softness and warmth. She lies on my belly. Her small face opens in my hands like a flower. She is fair, almost milky white. Nothing of me in her. She is all his from birth.

Later they will say that I didn't love her, that I had no feelings for her. They are wrong. The first time I saw my daughter, I fell in love with her. I could feel the chemicals running through me. It all worked exactly as it should. I fell in love with her; oxytocin was released in the right amounts. I felt warm and fuzzy. I felt deeply connected. Here was a creature that would love me, despite everything I am. His arms around me, my arms around her. We are perfect; we are beautiful.

eighteen

Motherhood. With her birth a new person is released in me. A person who has nothing to do with the person I was before. I had not known until I crossed into this new land what would be asked from me. What is asked is everything.

In that first devastatingly exhausting week, I fall asleep with the baby in my arms and my mother walks into the room. I think this cannot be. She lives far away. She cannot be here; it is impossible. I try to tell her this. She waves away my words, says, "That is my baby. Give her to me." I'm crying, but I know she is right. This is not my baby, this is *her* baby. She reaches down to grasp Bodhi. I don't want to give her up. Both of us are tugging on her, so she wakes squalling.

We go to the throne of King Solomon. And he, magnificent, purple-robed, seated on his golden throne, pulls out of its sheath a curved sword. It catches the light. It is sharp enough to cleave the child in two. He will give us each a part to carry away, he says. I am happy. I hold the child out for the sword's swing, and the king stands, comes forth. But my mother cries, "No, let her have the child!"

Then everyone knows that the baby belongs to my mother. Everyone knows she loves her properly while I am only an impostor. The king takes the child from me, hands her to my mother. She walks away with the baby and I am left alone, milk soaking through the fabric of my shirt, turning it a deeper crimson.

A year passes. What do I remember of that first year? There was sleeplessness and joy. A sleeplessness that felt like jet lag, the same suspension of night and day, the same grit-eyed, vertigo-tinged jolting between wakefulness and dream as comes from crossing the planet.

I kissed her face while she slept. We marveled over her feet, her hands, the small face like a flower. Her cooing laugh became my favorite sound in the world. She smiled at me and my entire body lit up as if we were still connected, as if the umbilical cord was still trailing out of my body and attached to hers. I could feel that tug at all times. I would steal minutes to shower, the hot water like baptism, and there would be a clenching of my abdomen and I would know she was crying, grab the towel, run out.

Because she needed me. This need was huge and everywhere. It was the definition of my life.

What happened in that year? Everything changed. We were different people from who we were before. It wasn't just her arrival, though of course that was the most important thing. In that year I was born as a mother, and Daniel too was born into a new life, not just as a daddy, but also as an artist. That's the year he became a star. Those first paintings went to the woman in Woodside. They say she discovered him, as if he hadn't existed before, as if he hadn't painted before she saw his work. But then after the "discovery," paintings flew off the wall. Galleries called. Everyone wanted him. Money flooded in.

We bought a house, of course. My beloved Mission apartment in those first months was already too small for the three of us. So we joined the flight out of the city and bought a house in Oakland, near the lake. This is where we live now. There are two bedrooms, one for her and one for us. Her toys are strewn around, the breast pump and bottles on the kitchen table, my rocking chair in the living room, her stroller folded up by the door. This is where I spend all my days. In these six rooms where the sunlight filters through the air, painting everything a pale gold in the late afternoon, where she sleeps in her crib in a room he has painted like a jungle. All around her, chubby cartoon lions and tiger cubs stalk one another through the grass, reach up to swat at flitting butterflies. Two long-eyelashed giraffes, necks entwined, reach up to puffy blue skies. What a lucky girl she is. How much love her daddy has spent making this jungle kingdom for her.

. . .

The making of Daniel had started like this. He had called, breathless. "A gallery show. In New York." Relief flooding his voice. He had named the gallery. It had meant nothing to me. I had stopped listening, all my attention focused on the baby, who was starting to wake up, who would scream in a minute if I didn't get my blouse undone in time.

A little later. His paintings sold. More than this, they wanted him for a solo show. He flies to New York when she is three months old. He comes back and says, "It's happening. It's finally happening. Everything I've always wanted." I smile and say, "How wonderful."

The art-handling job is long forgotten. Now they say he is the real deal. A painter the likes of which they haven't seen in years. He gets a studio space across town. When she is seven months old, I strap the baby in, go to visit. It is cavernous, a row of giant oils along the walls. He comes to us, grabs the baby and kisses her, snuggles her against his chest, where she coos, gloriously happy.

He lives in a different world now. Peopled by art dealers, museum curators, rich benefactors. I leave her with the sweet old couple next door and go with him to an opening in the city. We walk in hand in hand, but then he is swirled away from me. Everywhere people in angular clothes, women in sharp lines and black that drapes away from exposed shoulders, large-framed glasses and red-lipsticked mouths. I feel my body under me still ungainly, still bloated, an oddity among all these slim and svelte physicalities. On the wall, his new paintings. They are huge, bursting off the wall in riotous colors, none of that disciplined illustrative style he had had before. These are bold figures, almost abstracts. I go from one to the next. Each of them is a stranger to me. I do not recognize our life together anywhere.

A woman slips next to me, says, "You're his wife, right?" a glint in her sideways glance.

I nod, startled to be recognized.

She says, "What's it like?"

I raise my eyebrows at her and she says, "You know, to be married to so much genius?" She waves at the vivid canvas in front of us.

I turn my eyes away from her. "Amazing. So inspiring. To see that his talent is finally being rewarded."

"Oh yes, you were with him through the lean years, weren't you?"

"Yes. We were together."

"You supported him? Financially?"

"We supported each other. It's what couples do."

I walk away. She's right. I had supported him. I had been the pillar and he the creeping vine. I had worked. And because of that, he can do this. I had been such a good nurse. It comes to me in a flood. I had been good. I had made a difference. It had been important. The difference between life and death, even. While what he does, this glorified playing with color, it cannot even compare in importance. But there he is, in a knot of people who will praise him, who will buy his work, who will pay him so much more than I could ever even have dreamed of.

But I am mommy now. Every single other thing is secondary. Even if I did go back to work, back to that other life, that umbilical cord stretched thin would nag and pull and then perhaps snap, and this I cannot risk.

We have agreed I will stay home for the first two years. These are the most important times of her life. These are the years that will dictate the whole of her life, that will set how she feels about love and need and desire. I will give her all that. The whole of my world revolving around her. She is the sun and I am every planet. I love my baby.

He's gone a lot, but I don't complain. I walk around with her. We sit in the rocking chair, her lips latch on my nipple, those eyes look up at me, her head rests in my palm. We follow the sun and the shadows across the rooms of the house. It is silent except for my voice, her small sounds, her crying. A sort of peace. Just her and me, like a big animal and a small animal curled together for safety. Like all the pictures of mother animals and baby animals in her picture books. Here is the mama duck with her soft yellow baby under her wing; here is the mother horse with her foal between her legs; here is the sow with a row of pink piglets suckling at her. We are just like them, I tell myself over and over. This is the most natural thing in the world. This is normal. This is only a mother and her child alone together.

But then why is there this noise like nails on a chalkboard somewhere behind my eyes? Why is there a thudding panic in my blood? Why do I feel as if some childhood door is inching open? Sometimes when he's gone, something secret happens to me. Sometimes I put her in the crib, go into our bedroom, close the door, and fall into bed.

Her screams come loud and piercing, but the heaviness is stronger. I can lift no inch of myself. It is as if I inhabit a different planet where the rules of gravity are stricter, each of my limbs pinned mercilessly to the bed. I lie there listening to her scream and rage and sob, and then, maybe hours later, silence. Finally, finally, she has released me, and sleep drops over my head like a shroud.

I wake up in a panic, shoot out of tangled, humid sheets. She is tearless, her eyes huge as I lift her out of her crib. She is learning the unnatural lesson that crying is in vain. Already I have trained her well. Her diaper sags heavy. I clutch her to me, kiss the sweet slope of her forehead. I coo and rock her. I change the filthy diaper; I pull out my tit and attach her to it. I think I'll never do that again, never. I won't leave her despairing, unsure if I will ever return.

By the time he comes home, the baby and I are starved for his love.

nineteen

A year after her birth, and my body has shifted into shapes previously unimagined. In labor my hips had unhinged, and they have not swung back to where they were before. I remember in nursing school learning the signs by which a female cadaver could be identified as having borne children or not, that irrevocable spreading apart of the hipbones. My child has crossed my threshold and in so doing has marked me forever.

The outer signs also: my abdomen now slack, stretch marks puckering the lower skin. On the street, people's eyes slip by me. They might bend to coo and talk to the baby, but I am no longer *seen*, am only the adult attached to the adorable baby. When they *do* look, I flinch from their gaze. I know what they are thinking. I want to say, "No, I haven't lost the weight yet. Don't you know what my body has undergone? Months of reshaping from the inside, a complete structural transformation, bones sliding around, skin stretched to tautness. I'm not going to spring back to my pre-baby 'bikini body' any time soon." But this is exactly what every look on the street is projecting, what every celebrity magazine and TV show is shouting.

More than that, there has been another, more intimate kind of stretching. "It will go back to normal," the doctor assures me. But the truth is that no one knows if this will actually happen. I think of taking a mirror and looking at myself down there. But it's too frightening. It feels like the site of a battle. I want to ask other women, "Is it the same for you? Has this happened to you too?" But I can't make myself approach the other young mothers with their designer baby bags and expensive strollers.

Between baby bottles and diapers and my baby's screaming, the last thing I can think about is sex, and when he tries, I push him away. My ungainly, unlovely body doesn't feel like it belongs to me. It belongs to her now. These breasts are hers; my belly and skin and lips are hers. When he touches my breasts, I can't stop myself from swatting his hand away. He rolls away, but not before I see something flash in his eyes.

He tries again months later, putting a tentative hand on my breast, kissing the corner of my face, and again I can't stand being touched. I don't want more hands on me, another piece of me taken away. Her need is already deep enough to engulf me whole. I can't withstand his.

I wriggle away. The space on the sheets opens like an abyss. I hear an edge of frustration in his voice when he says, "Baby, why not? It's been long enough, hasn't it?"

"Long enough? For what?"

"For you to be healed. For you to be ready. I love you."

Some terrified tumble in my blood, my body stiffening from head to foot. I say, "I'm a mom now. That's all I can do. I can't take care of you too. Don't ask me to do that too."

"I'm not asking you to *take care* of me. I love you. I just want us to be together."

"No, not like that."

He shifts closer; he says, "You're a mom, but you're still my lover." Instant tears spring to my eyes. I can't imagine myself this way anymore. I'm not his lover. This body belongs to her more than to him or even to me.

He pulls me close. I let him kiss me on the mark on my face he has claimed as his own. He sighs. "It's fine. I love you. We'll be fine. We'll be like an old married couple. We'll just love each other and it'll be fine."

I know he's trying to convince himself. Deep in my body I know that sex is too powerful a force to be ignored. I know there is nothing as flimsy as a shared life without sex.

She goes from crawling to walking on her wobbly legs. She watches everything we do with those startling eyes. She can speak only a few words, but she points with her tiny finger at every new thing that catches her eye—the flowers, the birds above, a tiny spot on the linoleum. She is like a spy in our world, watching and seeing everything. I feel as if she understands everything. But she gives no information about where she comes from, the secret place she has left. We teach her about our world, thinking it important, thinking ourselves important. But the mystery is, where did she come from? She can't tell us. The cosmic joke abides; the mystery protects itself.

When she cries, she wrings her little hands, twisting them in the most heartbreakingly helpless way, as if around invisible objects. There is something graceful in this motion of grief. It makes me adore this child who has come unexpectedly among us.

When Daniel is home, he's a good dad. He is sweet and generous and patient. He knows when she's tired. He packs snacks, water, blankies, wet wipes—the whole range of possibilities. He loves her completely. He reads her stories before she can understand them, and she is silent just listening to his voice. I see the bond growing between them.

When she bawls, he carries her around the house or puts her in the car and drives miles until she falls asleep. We go to the park and I sit on a blanket in the grass and watch them. He pushes her high on a swing into the sparkling sky. I hear the squeal of her laughter, see her dress fluttering like bird's wings, her legs kicking the wind. My heart too kicks in happiness. This is all I ever wanted. These two people, one large and one small. They are my tribe. I belong to them only. When I can't stand it anymore, I go to them. I grab her off the swing and squish her small face against mine. She looks into my eyes, deep and long as if she can read secrets there, as if she sees entirely how I am and loves me anyway.

A photograph from this time: I'm holding her over my shoulder and he is bending to kiss her high-sloped forehead. Her face is turned toward the camera while we are in profile. He has tucked a small white daisy behind her minuscule ear. It mirrors the perfect purity of her face, the softness of her skin. She is beatific, her mouth an open *oh*, her eyes wide and amazed to find herself held in so much love.

She is one and a half and we go to the zoo. We watch her eyes grow wide at these far-fetched creatures, the strutting emu, the plodding giant tortoise. She makes us consider the impossibility of the giraffe, its head teetering on that ridiculous neck; the painted symmetry of the zebra. We laugh at her clear consternation, the way her eyebrows rise, and you can see her thinking *What* are *those things? What are they?* She flaps her arms toward the animals and says, "Bow-wow, bow-wow," the sound that dogs make in picture books. This is her word for all animals—some logic here, some rendering all creatures into a kingdom of their own.

We stop in front of the elephants and she won't let us leave. We must stay here and *look* at these creatures, their gray bulk, those strange flat feet with the familiar toenails, the intelligence in their small lashed eyes as they sway back and forth and back and forth with that slow, lumbering grace.

A lost afternoon blooms around me. Humidity and that scent of home, lush and green. I am small, watching the elephants walk up Kandy road, my hand tight in my father's. There are a line of them ambling up the mountain road, coming from all parts of the island for the annual procession, enormous loads of grass balanced on their backs. "They are carrying their lunch," my father says. I can feel him tall and straight next to me, the rub of his fingers over mine. His presence true and unshakable, but some menace also there. I shake my head to clear him away; my adult body comes back to me, and I am again with him and her in the kingdom of animals.

He says, "Shouldn't she be talking more by now?"

I say, "She's fine. She'll talk when she's ready, won't you, sweetness?" kissing her, that sweet scent of baby girl, the perfect curve of forehead under my lips.

Thinking, *Maybe for me it is better that she doesn't talk.* Not yet at least; that it is strange, of course, but maybe also convenient. There are so many secrets we share. So much I don't want her telling her daddy.

When he's gone she watches me with those great brown eyes. Every bit of her attuned to my mood, my state. I am her deity. She knows how I feel and adjusts her mood to mine as if I am her weather. She knows my anxieties, my terrors, and my dangers, and she accommodates herself to them. This is something not noted or commented upon: the gentleness with which they approach us. We who are not gentle with their small, delicate selves. In this way they know us in a way that we do not ever know them.

She comes to me where I lie on the old gold couch, staring into the occluded sunlight that falls through the window. She puts one small hand on either side of my face, pulls my clouded face close to her own bright one, dispels the images, says, "Mama sad?"

And I, startled to be seen so clearly, say, "I'm not sad, baby. I'm fine . . . I'm good. I'm just very tired." I flash the brightest smile in my repertoire, know that it comes off like a shark spotting something seal-shaped in the water above. Her face works as she assimilates this, the evidence of her own eyes at odds with my words. I see her coming to the inevitable conclusion that she must be wrong, that her reading is mistaken, that mommies can lie on the couch not talking, not moving, barely breathing, tears rolling silently over the planes of their faces, and still be happy. I see it as it happens, the first time she knows she can't trust her own feelings, that they are unreliable. It is perhaps the cruelest moment, but I can't do what was required, which is to say, "Yes, Mommy is very sad. But it's okay. I'll be okay soon." She rests her forehead against mine, little and confused, wanting to understand.

I come to myself. I am in the shower, the water tepid, running to cold. He is banging a fist on the door, shouting. I turn off the water with trembling, wrinkled fingers. How long has it been? Where did I leave her? I grab a towel and open the door and he is there, huge and blocking the light, his hair in lifted tufts as if he has raked his fingers through it. "What the hell are you doing?"

"Where is she?"

"In her room. How long did you leave her?"

"Not long." My voice like something coming from far under-ground.

He leans close, grabs my upper arms, his eyes slitted, glacial blue. "I don't believe you. I think you left her for a long, long time. Her diaper was filthy." He pushes me from him so I smash into the basin with my hip, sink to the floor sobbing, the towel fallen around my feet.

He says, "Just don't infect her with your disease. Whatever that is." He turns away and his footsteps are loud as drumbeats.

I nod into my hands. Yes, it is a disease. Yes, I am infected. Yes, I need to keep it away from her. She is too fragile to hold the weight. Even on perfect days, there is something under my skin. Some beast that moves below the surface. I can keep it at bay, mostly. But every now and then, it awakes and unfurls in jerky movements. It is the minotaur in the maze of my body. It wakes up and howls and wants to be seen, wants to show its broken face that is also mine. It asks for sympathy or perhaps for love. It screams that it too was a child once and it was hurt. It asks why it cannot have these things: love, belonging, ease. When it emerges, it has no pity, no mercy. His presence is the antidote. It keeps the beast away.

He's gone into her room, holding her to his chest, the one place I want to be. The place she has taken. I reach for the sink and pull myself up slowly. My hip feels disjointed, already a bruise ris-ing like paint swirled on my skin from the inside. I limp into the bedroom, pull aside the covers, and sink into the bed. I'm still wet, so the sheets stick to me, sucking away moisture, my hair on the pillow like a mermaid's.

I remember that time before she came. I remember rolling around in Golden Gate Park, his body over mine, breathless for each other. I remember that a group of bicyclists had yelled and hollered, cheering on our passion. And we, shy but also ecstatic, had risen to look and wave at them. I remember when he wanted me so badly he ground his teeth at me in desire and groaned when he touched me. I remember when I wanted him so badly it felt like hunger, like thirst.

I burn alone until morning.

twenty

My little girl never darkens. She is milk with the slightest splash of tea, golden headed as if birthed from him and a much paler woman. On the streets they stare at us, this dark woman and this fair little girl. They say, "Look at her. So pretty. So cute." South Asian mothers come up to me and say, "My goodness, she's so fair. Your husband must be American, no?" Their eyes are covetous, appraising. They like these gifts of whiteness. Where am I in her blood? I had read somewhere that young children most often look like their fathers. It's a way to ensure that a man knows who his children are, that he will not kill them because he suspects they are not his. Here is biology in action, her pale skin and yellow curls. Only her staring, watchful eyes, darkening to chocolate, are like mine.

• • •

I take her to the city, a park in Noe Valley where her father used to live in those other fairy-tale days. I sit on a bench and watch her toddle around, drag her blanket behind her to the sandbox, stumble over the edge, sit down. She runs her fingers though the sand, holds her hands out to see the sand fall through her tiny fingers. I watch her like a hawk, always. You never know what could happen to a girl. A woman comes and sits next to me. There is a sort of peace. The day is bright and airy. Clouds speed high overhead so that we are in light, then shadow, and then bright sunlight again.

The woman next to me makes a gesture, her hand rising to shade her eyes. I can tell she wants to chat. I straighten my back, curve away from her so that she will know my solitude must not be breached. But she cannot abide this turning away. We are one tribe, after all, the community of mommy. She leans toward me, says, "Hola. Cómo estas?" I realize that we are not in fact one tribe. Instead, she has confused me with one of the Latina nannies that run around after white charges in this wealthy neighborhood. She has read me as one of those women who have abandoned their own children in some faraway place to look after these American offspring. It is an old role she has found for me, the children of this country for so long brought up by women with dark skin, black skin.

Now Bodhi comes up to me, clutches my knees, pushes between my legs, flings her head and arms out, and reaches up to me. I grab her and lift her into my arms, stand up and kiss her cheeks, my dark hand in her lit curls.

The woman says, "Wow. She's really attached to you, isn't she?"

I turn around and stare at her. My eyes are slitted; the blood is slow in my veins. "Why wouldn't she be?"

The color jumps into her cheeks, two spots like a painted doll's rouge. "Oh, I just meant that . . . you know . . ."

"Yes, I know what you mean. I'm not the nanny. I'm not the babysitter. This is *my* child."

"Oh I'm so sorry. I didn't mean . . ."

I want to say, "Fuck you, you racist piece of shit." The words slide down my throat, thick, unspeakable. Tears springing in my eyes, I turn on my heel and walk away with my girl draped over my shoulder, leaving behind us the woman's unslapped face.

She is always quiet, always meek, and it reminds me of my mother saying, "You used to sit so quietly. We would leave you sitting in a room by yourself, and if we came back much later you were still sitting there. You didn't move. You weren't rowdy like the other children. Our friends' children."

Bodhi has inherited my childhood stillness. But unlike my mother, I am not fooled. This is not obedience. When a baby bird falls out of the nest, it does not chirp to alert the slinking cat. The kittens in their turn are silent when left by their mother. They are aware of the shadow of the owl. No matter how long she is gone, they will not call out. Only at the edge of starvation, weeks later, will they cry out, desperate for salvation.

My girl's stillness is likewise a certain careful gauging, a waiting to see how things will unfold. She is watching to see from
which direction danger comes. My mother had thought it was
some inherent goodness in me. Instead it was an act of survival.

At the playground I sit on a bench while Bodhi plays and smoke
cigarettes to the bitter stub, trying to suck down enough nicotine
to get me through the long evenings ahead, the sleepless nights.
I sit on the edge of the bench, my knees jiggling high, and smoke
and try not to slip into the bottomless pit.

Before Daniel came, my soul had been cloistered. I had been
reconciled to isolation, and in this, there had been a kind of con-
tentment. But I had let him inside and I had swallowed happiness. I had feasted on his flesh; I had dwelt within it. I had fallen
into the arms of this country that was first his. Then she had come
and my world had swelled with love, but had also shrunk down
to the size of a pinhead. There is the sensation of a shroud dropped
over my head, no more air to breathe. I don't like this, I realize. I
don't like being the mommy. I love my child, but I don't like
motherhood. Motherhood is the constancy of a pair of eyes seek-
ing you out, wanting you, needing you. It is the feeling that there
is no darkness, no private place, no escape from those small but
piercing eyes. I had not thought that a child could intrude so completely into one's solitude. I see now that she does not share my
serenity but rather disrupts and shatters it. Now wherever I go,
her eyes track me like a hunter's.

I remember the trip Daniel and I had taken once, that deep

mountain lake. All those corpses he had claimed lay at the bottom of the freezing depths. The sun is shining, but I can't feel it on my skin anymore. The water has reached out once again and dipped its pointed finger into my jugular. I feel what it would be like to fall through miles of dark water, the horror of coming to bed in the mud surrounded by smashed, water-torn bodies.

A sharp cry, and I look up to see that Bodhi has fallen, her knee skinned. She looks at me with tears trembling unshed from her eyes. We have an important and silent conversation then. Her asking for succor and my replying, "I am not the one to come to. I will not help you. This is the nature of my maternity."

"Who should I go to, then?" her eyes ask, and mine reply, "No one. There is no one in the world to go to." I look away, I take a drag, and when I look back she has brushed off the bruised place and already turned away. I don't think she will ask again. I'm teaching her to be tough, to be strong. No one else can teach her like I can. There are people in the world who can hurt her like they hurt me. But if she is as strong as iron, if she can lock up that inside place where no hands can reach, then she will survive the world of men as I have survived.

When he's gone, sometimes I'm wound so tight, so much is bursting under my skin, I can't stand it. I want to scream and rage and fight, and there is no one to do this with. There are no adults in my world. So instead I grasp the glasses in our kitchen one by one and throw them as hard as I can against the wall. The cataclysmic smash of each glass exploding, a necessary shattering. A crashing like sea surf against a cliff. I smash and smash until finally there is release.

In my skin is a buried chest that came forth on the tide with her birth. A chest I have lost the key to, and this crashing is the only way to break into it. Inside are unspoken names, bruises I cannot look at, flesh torn like a piece of paper. These things burst loose from between my bones, go crashing through the walls of our house, rise into the air, and are pulled into the sky, far away from us.

When I come back, the kitchen is like the inside of a glass cave, sparking ice on every surface, dancing prisms of light as in the aftermath of a storm. I sink to my knees, put my forehead on the floor, and sob in great gaping breaths, hair dredged over my face, shoulders shaking.

In her bedroom, Bodhi is huddled into a ball, her Winnie the Pooh blanket tight in her fist, a corner of it stuck between her lips, sucked clean. Her eyes are huge, tracking me as I approach. I push my hair behind my ears, smooth down my shirt, and say, "Mama had an accident. I'm going to clean it up and then we'll go shopping. You can help me get new glasses. Okay?" I am bright again. She stares, no babble issues from her mouth. The child must be dumb, stupid even. I clench my fists to stop them from grabbing. An image of a child thrown into the ice cave in the kitchen. Bare skin touching a thousand icicles and turning frozen. No, no, I cannot. I turn away.

A few minutes later the kitchen is swept clean, a sense of relief, newness. The knowledge that everything ugly and shattered can be swept away so there is no hint of disorder left.

twenty-one

I had longed for normalcy. I had wanted only these things—a marriage, a shared place, the serenity of a long-lived love. But normalcy is a miracle, not granted to all who ask.

I call him at the studio and he picks up and says, "Yes, what is it?" I can hear the rasp of annoyance in his voice. He pretends to listen, but I know that his eyes are snagged on the latest canvas, that assessments about color and form are being made. I shake my head as if he can see. I say, "Nothing. I just . . . *I miss you.*" The words leave my mouth in the tone of a petulant child. I cringe. When did I become this other person? He sighs. "I'll be home soon. I told you."

"You promise?"

He says, "Yes. *I promise.*"

Midnight comes and goes. I lie awake, watching the night pass through the room. Framed in the window, a high sickle moon watches, waiting with me. In the other room Bodhi twists and murmurs as if she can sense my rage.

Then sleep, and with it, Samson slipping quiet from behind the door. I have been running from him for so long. But I'm tired and now he's here. He has found me even in this far place. His hair is plastered to his dripping temples; my father's cast-off trousers are wrapped soaking around his legs. He smiles like something amphibious, comes closer, stands over the bed, teeth glinting.

My heart thuds against the walls of its cage. My mouth will not open, but the words come anyway.

"Samson. You disappeared. You died. You cannot be here."

His lips don't move, but I can hear his voice in my head. "No, Baby Madame, not dead. Samson has looked so long and everywhere for you and now has found you." He leans over me, river water falling on my face like tears. His face comes closer. My heart will leap out of my throat. I will asphyxiate. I cannot tell if he will kiss me or bite me. He says my name, and again, louder and louder like a shouting, and I am being shaken and it is Daniel yelling my name into my face, shaking me by the shoulders, and I am awake and he is holding me tight to him and I am sobbing and he is kissing my face and wiping away tears and holding me to him.

He holds me for a long time. And then he says, "Will you tell me what it is?" I am stiff suddenly. Ice cold. He pulls away, looks into my eyes, says, "Tell me. Whatever happened, we can figure it out together. You have to trust me." I cannot move; I cannot speak.

He sighs, settles both of us into bed, body to body beneath the blankets. His lips against my hair, moving. "If you won't tell me, I can't help." I stay as still as I can, daring only to breathe. If I am quiet, the danger will pass. He hugs me close and kisses me on the forehead. It is the closest we've been in months. I inhale him. I cling to him, ready to love him more, ready to try harder, to be good. We fall asleep and it is the dreamless rest of paradise.

I wake to bright sun the next day. The sky is a perfectly uniform cobalt bowl, with every cloud banished. The cherry trees on our lane are bursting into pink fluffy blossom. I take Bodhi to the park and she toddles around searching for dandelions and buttercups, her fingers reaching down and pulling at them until the plant releases them. She brings them to me one by one, drops them into my lap until a small pile has formed. I know this is a coronation; she is claiming me as her queen. I show her how the exuberance of the dandelion is different from the concise precision of the buttercup despite their common color. She is intent on these lessons, these moments when she has all my attention. I put the flowers in the fall of my hair, where they glimmer like gems. She sits on my lap and holds her little fist out for me while I lace the minuscule stems together to make her a bracelet. She is in love with me and with these tiny bright flowers, these almost metallic drops of life.

I stand and swing her up on my hip to walk home. I point out a plant with small, downturned white blossoms. Bees are humming, disappearing into the hanging flowers, making them bounce up and down in giant arcs as if the insects are joyriding. When they emerge they are fat with pollen and fly homeward, fuzzy with their golden treasure. "Look, baby," I say, "the bees are buzzing in the trees. To make some honey just for us." She laughs and claps her hands in delight. I hold her small, hot, alive body against mine.

We go home and I peel and mash a banana for her. She sits on her booster chair, swings her feet in a wide arc, makes her various words at me.

Then everything is alive in my body, like a sparking of electricity. The sense of being watched, of being sighted by someone and held there like a pinned insect, rises. As if my body is a target and secret eyes are homing in. I lift my head to listen, my hackles rising. I push a hand against my mouth. I will not scream. I will not frighten the child. I go to the window, tug the curtain open a sliver. Across the street a man is waiting. He is dripping wet, a pool forming beneath his feet, shiny as knives. He raises his eyes to me; he smiles with jagged teeth. I swirl around, grab my child, run with her to my bedroom. We have to hide. He has come again. He has come. He has truly found me this time. I am sobbing in terror.

In a corner of the dark bedroom, the terrified child held tight against me, I fumble in my pocket for my phone. Daniel's voice. I gasp, "He's found me. Please help. Please. Come."

My hands are shaking so hard I drop the phone, must sweep fingers along the ground for it, saying to the child all along,

"Shh . . . baby, shh . . . we have to be quiet. Or he will hear us." In the dark, her terror-stricken eyes gleam, but she does not cry. When I find the phone, he is saying, "What? What's happened?"

"He's come. He's here. Help me. Please."

"Slow down. Who? Who's come?"

I can't believe he doesn't know. "Samson," I whisper. "He's here outside."

"Who?"

I drop the phone into my lap. Remember that I have never told him. He doesn't know. I have kept the secrets locked up inside me. No one knows. I raise the phone to my ear. He is saying, "Are you okay? Is Bodhi okay? What happened? Who is Samson?"

"It's okay. It's okay. He's nobody. Nothing. I imagined things. I thought I saw someone outside, but it's fine. We're fine." I force a settled tone into my voice. I make myself sure and steady. If he comes, he will ask questions. He will want to know who Samson is. More than I want to see him, I do not want to open the locked chest of my body.

"Pull yourself together. You're going to freak out the kid. Give her the phone. I want to make sure you haven't scared her to death."

I put my little girl on the floor, leave her babbling with her father. I crawl to the window, stick up just the tip of my head. I flick the curtain. The street below me is empty.

In the corner Bodhi puts the phone on the ground, comes over to me, and falls into my lap. She reaches her hands up to my face. I nuzzle her cheek.

. . .

When he comes home a half hour later, Bodhi is in her room, I am in bed. This time he shakes me awake but doesn't hold me. His eyes are ice hard. He runs fingers through his hair and says, "What the hell happened? What was that? You said someone was here."

"I'm sorry, Daniel. I'm sorry. It was nothing. No one was here."

He stands up and paces the room. "No, it's not enough. This isn't working. I'm worried about Bodhi. I can't have you around her like this. You need some time. Just to figure things out. Whatever's bothering you."

Panic clutches my throat. "Daniel. What are you doing?"

"We're going to go and live somewhere else. Bodhi and I. Just for part of the time. You can see her, but she'll stay with me. Until you feel better."

"What? Are you leaving me?"

"No, no. It's just for a while. Just to give you some time. I've found a nice place for us. My parents are coming. They've always wanted to spend some time with Bodhi, and now they have it. They'll look after her in the daytime and I'll be home more now that this show is over." He passes a hand over his face. "And then you can relax for a while. Just a few weeks. Okay? It'll be good for us. You'll have a break and then we can be together. Yes?"

They are leaving me. Of course they are leaving me. A lesson I learned young: Everyone leaves.

"Why are you doing this?"

He turns and looks at me as if taking me in, as if seeing past me to everything I hide. "I can't be around you right now. The way you are."

"What way? What way am I?"

"Like your mother. Everything you told me about her. The locking herself up when you were little and leaving you outside, falling asleep for hours. It's exactly the same. I can't have that around Bodhi right now. Get yourself together and we'll be together, I promise. But not now, not for a while."

The words hit me between the eyes. I sink back into the bed, lie there curled up as he walks away. Evening sun pours down through the window and over me like water. It feels like when Samson used to bathe me at the well. I remember the liquid spilling over my head, the chill and shock of it.

He leaves two weeks later, taking her with him. I've begged and begged, but nothing will change his mind. I lie in bed and listen as he packs, taking his clothes from the closet, from the drawers, dumping them into a big duffel bag. In other rooms, he makes decisions about essentials—her stroller, her toys, her jars of food. He is packing them up, taking them to the car. He is pulling these things out of our marriage like pieces of a jigsaw puzzle. How does a jigsaw make sense with half its pieces gone? It is only jumbled chaos, bits of colored nonsense.

He has gutted me like a fish. He has slid a large knife along my skin's seam and slit me from throat to groin. He is removing the organs from my body. My kidneys, my gallbladder, my heart—things hugely important to the workings of my whole. He is wrenching each one out of its place in my chest and abdomen, snipping the blood cords that bind it in place, fitting them all into one of his cardboard packing boxes, the bottom slowly splotching red.

His feet walk back to me; he holds a box of my organs in one arm, my baby in the other. He says from miles above me, "We're going now. Mama doesn't feel well, so we're going to let her rest. Bodhi, do you wanna say bye-bye?" He puts her down and her arms wrap hard around my neck, her small face against mine. She kisses my nose, my cheek. A flurry of small, fierce kisses before he reaches down and grabs her again. She is crying when he walks out.

I whisper, "Please. Don't. You don't love her like I do. *I'm her mother.*"

The front door opens and slams shut. They are gone. They have taken every part of me. Only an empty husk is left, the sort of thing an insect climbs out of and leaves behind on a windowsill.

twenty-two

Now I am that desolate thing, an abandoned woman left by her man, without her child. I remember my mother and her friends talking about a woman left like this. They spoke of her in whispers; they dropped pity like acid. She had lost her looks overnight, she had stopped eating, she had had to move back into her parents' house. They had gone to visit and she had seen them and tried to pretend everything was all right. But how could everything be all right? Even back then in girlhood, I knew this was the worst fate, to be left by a man.

Daniel calls often. To make sure that I am okay, he says. I realize that his leaving is more constructed than I had thought. This is no last-minute decision, this is a plan with well-thought-out architecture. He has rented a house a few miles from this one. His parents are there. He says, "It's just for a little while. Just till you get yourself up and about. How are you?"

I say, "I'm good, Daniel. I'm good." I exhale and ask the only question on my mind. "When are you coming home?" We both ignore the jagged edge in my voice.

"Soon, baby, soon. Just give it a little time, okay?" His voice is so tender, I tear up. I can see him, worrying his eyebrow as he does when the wheels are turning deeply. He says, "Just take a little time to feel better. Maybe see someone . . ."

"See who?"

"A professional. Those nightmares of yours, they're so fierce. I think you need to talk them out. Maybe something happened when you were little. When you were Bodhi's age. Sometimes having a kid can bring up buried memories, you know."

A dark door inches open.

"Daniel! I don't need someone professional. *Nothing* happened to me. What I need is you and my little girl back."

His voice is different, sadder than I've ever heard it before. "Okay. We'll talk soon. I love you."

I want to reach through the phone to his body, his presence and scent. These things would save me.

A quiet click in my ear.

This is what I know will happen: she will disappear into his world; she will be brought up by people who never speak of me. The fairness of her skin, the light in her hair will ensure it. She will fit in in a way I never had. She will go to school with girls who look like her, who speak like her. There will be no memory of me. I will be erased. Our marriage would mean nothing. My motherhood would mean nothing. The way I loved them both would mean nothing.

And then someday this will happen: a woman will come. A woman with light skin and hair like the two of them, and then the three of them will be together. I can see her, the green-eyed siren woman, her silver tail transmuted to human legs by some dangerous-won magic. She will entice him away from me with her eyes and her supple skin, her breasts and her sex. She will erase every memory of us, every promise he has made, every kiss on my skin. The mark on my face that was his to kiss burns like a wound.

The worst of it, the thing that tastes like broken glass, is that in time she will become the mother. She will cajole my child and spoil her. She will be affectionate and entertaining. She will be the good mother. I can see them hand in hand. People seeing them will bend over Bodhi to say, "What a lovely mama you have." To the water-woman, they will say, "What a beautiful daughter you have."

After a time it will be the truth. It will be as simple as a mother, a father, and a child, that holy trinity. Somewhere far in the distance, there will be a ghost wearing my skin.

In my worst moments I know this is what will happen, but not yet, not yet, not yet. There is still time to fight, still time to reclaim my place. Daniel calls and invites me to the house. I go with my heart in my mouth, but his mother opens the door and pulls me into her arms and then Bodhi comes toddling up, yelling in delight, and latches onto me. The old father grins at us from the living room. I pick up my daughter, kiss and cuddle her. I can come anytime, they say. They are only here so I can rest a bit, regain myself. We eat dinner together. Daniel is at the studio. I will come every day. When I say goodbye, she clings to me, won't let me go. They have to pull her away. My heart is cracking asunder, but also there is some deep knowledge that they are right. I do need some time. Just to pull the pieces of myself together, just long enough for this dizziness and fog to lift. I walk to the car and feel a sort of peace. The dusk sky above is drenched in late golden light; the giant blowsy scarlet roses in the neighbor's yard are swaying. The wind is pulling petals off them like a lover's clothing and flinging them about. My hair unravels like one more set of petals. I let the evening dance around me and my blood slows its relentless race.

I wake up and the day stretches before me. There is time now. For myself. Precious time and freedom. What can I do? *Anything.* A quick leap of joy in my pulse. I drive across the long, low-slung bridge into the city, that familiar skyline sparking in the sunshine. I cross the familiar streets to my old haunt, the dahlia garden. I had forgotten what it meant to be among these mad, bursting blossoms.

I use my expired volunteer card to enter, and there are the flowers like old and beloved friends. I sink fingers into the dirt, hold it in my hands, this holy fragrant soil. I pull off dead leaves and check for parasites. The flowers around me nod in time to the breeze, whisper among themselves.

I realize they talk to each other all the time, a long and quiet conversation. I have just never been allowed to hear it before. I bend closer to listen. I can't make out what they are saying, but I can hear my name. I take a huge red flower in my palms. It is as wide as my two cupped hands. I bend my face to it. The petals pull at me like the furred, furrowed legs of insects, deep inward toward the hidden heart, a loving grip. It is like sipping magenta, like tasting crimson. I let the flower bounce away. I promise myself that I will be better, that I will love Daniel more. I will pull myself together and make it all work. I will make Bodhi a life. I will be that other thing: a good mother. The flowers, they make it possible to imagine this.

It is a good day. They've let me have my baby for an afternoon. We are in my living room on the couch. I have bought stargazer lilies and their perfume tints the room, a small threaded offering of golden pollen dripping down onto the green vase. Her small, curved feet nestle in my lap. She reaches up and spins the globe that has always rested on the side table. She says, "Mama." Her finger lands exactly as I have taught her on the island, a green speck of land in that mass of blue water.

I say, "Do you want to go there?" I have shown her pictures of the island. Pictures of myself at her age, in front of that old white house, held by my mother and flanked by my father, who stands behind us, his hands held behind his back. I've shown her pictures of temples and lotus flowers and school kids in white uniforms. All the beautiful parts. She nods, big eyed and serious.

Maybe it is possible. Maybe one day she and I and Daniel will be there, in the land of my birth. Sitting at a table with Amma, eating and laughing while the ceiling fan far above stirs the thick air. I think about being surrounded by my first language, about dipping my fingers into food made by old women. I think of the smash of a river against my stomach, the slipping under to let the current take me while downstream women beat clothes on rocks and work suds into the folds, about the riotous calling of birds in the morning, about the sudden heat of the day saturating everything, making the sweat stand and glide on skin. Bodhi and Daniel. They would love it.

The thought blooms through me, makes my skin crackle in a sort of excitement. Yes, why not? I could show them this place I came from. It would be homecoming.

I fold the idea carefully away into a drawer in my mind to be taken out when the time is right. Now I read *Alice in Wonderland* to her. Both of us reveling in the tiny bottles, the unreliable cakes that swell or shrink Alice from giant to ant-sized and back. I remember being small and reading these stories, feeling the uncertain and fluid parameters of my child's body. I read her the exploits of the Queen of Hearts screaming for blood, shouting for heads to roll, issuing commandments that change the very color of the roses.

The power to have the flowers painted a color you desire, this is a mother's tyranny over the child. The white roses dripping red, the red roses dripping white. I feel her body vibrate next to mine. I wonder if she feels the same recognition I do. I hug her to me, inhale deeply; this is the scent of the sacred. She is my greatest treasure. I know this on days when I am not pulled under by despair or rage.

On a day in May, I pick her up and we take the subway to the ferry pier. It is a place populated by seabirds, gulls, strange small squat birds with jauntily hat-like feathers. By the ocean's frothy edge she reaches into the bag into which I have collected the heels of loaves. I hold her as she opens her palm and a whirl of squawking birds are drawn to us as if by magnetism. There is a sudden loudness when before there had been quiet gray water, wispy clouds. Thrilled, she wants to be put down into the center, where she throws her arms up into the frenzy of winged creatures. Now there is a greater gathering of wings and beating of feathers. She runs back to nestle between my legs and we watch the small, flighted dinosaurs with their balanced tails and cruel beaks peck and squabble over our offering. I kiss the tender curve of her flower-soft cheek. This perfect, small person belongs to me.

The sea smashes below us. The tourists come to lean over the railing and exclaim at the span of the bridge arcing overhead. They turn to face the weakened sun. It is hidden behind such billowed and racing clouds that it looks like the full moon. They pose for pictures with their arms about each other. They smile and gawk; they look out into the mist and point out Alcatraz, beyond that Marin, the magic hills of Sausalito. They are right, the beauty of this place is astounding.

I gather my child closer to me. We go home spent, her hand in mine, holding tight. The skin of her palm against mine. The heat of it, the tenderness of it, I could not have imagined before I was a mother.

twenty-three

His mother calls. We chat sometimes. About Bodhi mostly, but this time I can tell she's trying to tell me something. She hedges for a while and then says, "You should call Daniel. You know he misses you, right?"

A silence. My pulse thumping. "Really?"

"Yes, child. I know my son. He loves you. He goes around here like a zombie. He barely eats or sleeps. The universal signs of a broken heart. You need to be together."

"But . . . he's the one who left."

"Couples go through these little things all the time. But you're married. You should be together. It's the best thing for the baby too. Call him."

. . .

Hope runs through me. Is it possible? My life, can I get it all back? Can it be as it was? All of my lost paradise? Perhaps! Why not?

I pace through the house rehearsing conversations, hoping, praying, begging whatever invisible deities rule over reuniting broken lovers, promising them my fealty and anything else they demand. If I have him back, they can have all my treasure.

I gather myself and call him. He picks up immediately. "What's wrong?"

"Nothing. I just wanted to . . ."

"What?"

"Say hi."

"Okay." Strained exasperation I can hear over the line.

I plunge in. "Listen, would you like to come for dinner?"

"What?" Incredulity in his voice.

"There's no reason we shouldn't have a friendly dinner."

A pause. I picture him contemplating this, running a hand through that tawny mop.

He says, "What's this about?"

"Nothing . . . I've just been thinking. There's no reason for us to be unpleasant, is there? What if you just came for dinner tomorrow? No big deal."

Another pause and I can feel him sighing, releasing. He says, "Will you make pol sambol?"

I laugh, delighted. "Yes if you like, and also string hoppers and watalappam."

"My god, what did I do to deserve this?"

"Nothing whatsoever. I've just decided to be magnanimous."

"Okay, I need to talk to you anyway. Discuss a few things."

The flamboyant bird of hope flapping its wings across my chest.

I clean the house until every surface gleams and shows me my own delighted face. I place Bodhi's toys in the empty spaces on the bookshelf where his books used to live. For hours I sweat in the kitchen like I used to do in those first breathtaking years when it was just us two. I chop vegetables, put the chicken in its bed of spices and coconut milk, let it soak into tenderness. I know what he loves.

What is an appropriate outfit to seduce back a husband? I throw off my sweatshirt and jeans and look at my body. I haven't looked at it in months, and lo and behold, sadness has carved the flesh off me. I'm thin as a model, all angles and elegance. So this is what is needed, I think, misery and loneliness, that's what they should sell as a post-baby diet. Nothing else works as well.

I pull piles of fabrics on the bed. I try on everything I own. Is it okay to wear my wedding dress? It's so beautiful. He bought it for me, loved the way the silver straps made my shoulders shine. Can I wear it? No, that would be too mad! I slip on a gray sheath that has always been just a bit too snug. It fits beautifully. I paint my eyes and my lips, and then he is at the door looking at me and his eyebrows rise and he says, "Wow . . ." and I am in heaven.

He walks in and we are awkward. Neither of us sure how this works. We sit and eat. He exclaims over the food, his fingers working through it. He says, "My god, I didn't realize how much

I missed all this. It is incredible." I open a bottle of red wine, like the blood of a gorgon. It used to be our favorite. He says, "No, really, I shouldn't."

I say, "Suit yourself," and pour my own fat goblet, and he must be surprised at my good mood because soon he takes a glass. He drinks, I drink. We finish a bottle. I pull out another.

It is magic, all of it. The way the wine pours, a crimson fire filling the bellies of the glasses we had gotten for our wedding, the way it roars down my throat. We settle on our couch. The one we bought together a lifetime ago. The closeness of him. The scent emanating from his skin. I know this man. It is easy because the thing we'd had had never gone away, not fully. Love, it was always there. Deep-down love. In a way that we *both* know. No one else can ever understand us like this. The depth of it, the pull of it—the old jokes, the shared years—bringing us ever closer, so that laughing, giggling, we make our way across the acres of the couch until our fingers are only inches apart and then he says, "My god." The breath catches in his throat. I can see the pulse jumping in his jaw. The moment of decision has arrived and he is torn about whether to fall into this thing that is still there or not and I reach out and pull his head to mine and taste his lips.

Our bodies lock as if no time has passed, as if unknown to us, these bodies have been in communion the entire evening, waiting for this moment to fall against each other. I pull his hips into mine. Kissing and rolling, we fall heavily on the ground, gasp, laugh, and then are on each other.

His lips are in my hair, kissing the heavy strands, breathing in deeply, and I know he has missed me desperately. I know he has always loved me. He has never stopped. He is still mine. He will always be mine. My gray dress is lost somewhere. Kisses on bare skin, by the ear and the edge of my eye, where a tear dangles and his tongue shoots out and tastes it. His body against mine. The sweetest of homecomings.

After, we lie entangled. My head against the curve of his chest. My ear to his heart, so I can hear its frenzied thud slowing down. Our legs intertwined, so it feels like from below the waist we are one animal. These legs rising into two torsos, a many-limbed, one-bodied creature. He has come back to me. I want to get up and dance around the room. I want to jump up and sing, but I can't bear to pull myself away from his skin. There's so much to do. We have to make space for his things again. We have to hire a moving van. We have to go and pick up our girl. Even now she might be waiting for us to come for her. I force myself to breathe deeply. To savor this moment when all my dreams have again come true.

My lips warm with the heat of him, I whisper against his throat, "I love you so much."

The silence thunders. I wait, and with every passing moment, my skin is flayed.

He sighs and shifts. "I have to tell you something."

"What? It can't be that important. Nothing is that important. Don't tell me . . . shh." I press myself against him. Willing him to be silent, to stay here with me.

He gets up, carefully disentangling himself from my limbs, so that I'm left in a slump on the floor.

He says, "I have to go."

"What?"

He's buttoning his shirt with trembling fingers, pulling on his jeans.

I grab his calf. "What's happening? Why are you going? We'll be together now right?"

He starts walking and I have to let go of him.

"I'll call you," he says as he walks out the door.

I lie on the floor and try to understand what has happened.

I call his cell phone over and over. He doesn't pick up. I pace and smoke until the room is clouded. I listen to his voice telling me he isn't available right now. But it's okay, it's going to be fine. We are back together. Even the thought of sleep is impossible. Outside, the slivered moon is high, glaring into the room like an intruder. I jerk the curtains shut. I can't bear that searing light. My phone clicks, a message from him. "Can I come back? We have to talk."

He walks in looking terrible. His hair is raised in stiff quills, his face pale as if he has been walking the cold streets since he left. I will time to reverse, taking us both back to that beautiful place a few hours ago.

He takes a deep breath and says, "I'm sorry. About what just happened. About everything. I shouldn't have. But you know it doesn't really change anything. We just aren't suited. You must know that, right? We're too different. Different worlds. It just isn't working."

Some terrible thing is happening inside me. Over the ruins of the world, the dark waterweed is unfurling, the minotaur is awakening. I feel its shadow; it has grown tenfold. It shudders along every passage in my body, crawls along the inside, so I am dark green rotted, bull faced.

And then I know. I say, "Is there anything else?"

He looks like he's going to cry. He says, "No, what else could there be?"

"You've met someone, haven't you? Another woman."

"No. I knew you'd say that. I haven't met someone. I just can't be with you anymore. This isn't working. You know that."

"Liar!" I throw the word at him and turn to stagger blindly down the hall. He says, "Wait! Are you all right?" He comes after me. I slash at his face, drawing bloody streaks along his cheek. He grabs my wrists, pulls me hard against him, says, "Stop it. Calm down." I wrench away from him and run into the bathroom, lock the door, turn on the scalding water. I plug up the tub, get in, lay against the curved bottom shivering, my arms clutched around my knees. Hot water pools around me, floods my clothes. The rush of water in my ears. Outside, he is calling my name, slamming his palm and then his fist against the wood. "Please, just talk to me . . . just come out for a minute, just . . . I didn't mean it. Why do you always do this? I just want to talk to you. Please."

I lie in the rushing, burning water. After a while, I hear him slump down to the floor, rest his back against the door. I roll in the water. Like returning to the womb. I am a fetus again, warm and safe inside my mother. No man has reached in yet to hurt me. Hours later, I hear him call out from very far away. "Okay, I'm going now. I'm sorry. I never ever meant to hurt you." I stay silent and he says, "Okay, I'll call you tomorrow. It'll be fine. We'll work something out." And then he is gone.

I float, weightless, thinking of a different time. A time when I was the container and she swam inside me. When she was only a squirm of life, the bulge of eyes to be, the stubs of limbs, the entirety of her coming into being inside me. I had given him this. I had created her. The greatest gift I could give. And now he might deny it, but I know the truth: the siren-woman has come to steal everything. Screaming voices, rage, pain ripping through my whole body. I gasp and shudder and sink underwater, open my eyes, my mouth, scream into liquid.

It's much later. The water has grown cold. I stand up in the tub, pull off my sodden clothes, and drop them into the water. I walk into the bedroom, dripping puddles. I open drawers and put on heavy clothes, a gray sweatshirt that he has forgotten, sweat pants. My hair is stuck to my face, water soaking through the fabric across my breasts like a new mother's milk.

There's only one person I want to talk to. The clock reads three in the morning; it is daytime on the other side of the planet. I dial my mother's number. She picks up right away, and the sound of her voice has me choking broken sounds down my throat.

Her voice rises. "Darling, is that you? What is it? What has happened?"

"Amma." The word is a plea.

"Sweetheart, what is it? Is the baby okay?"

"Yes, Amma." I can hear her breathe again.

I say, "But Daniel . . ."

"What? What's happened to him?"

"He's leaving me, Amma."

A shocked little "Oh." I can see her mouth making the sound.

"He's leaving, Amma. He's going. He'll take Bodhi with him. I'll be alone." A flood of tears, and then the words rushing out of my mouth. "Amma, I think something's wrong with me. I don't know what it is. I feel like something is wrong with me. Something really, really bad. That's why he's going."

A silence.

"Amma, what is it?"

She sighs. "It's all my fault."

"What?"

"It's my fault. I was trying to protect you. So we never talked about it. I thought you couldn't remember. What happened with you when you were small. I should have stopped it. I'm so sorry. It's all my fault. I didn't know any better."

The door is opening. She will swing it open. I want to hear her say it. I want to hear her voice saying the words. I need to hear it.

"You mean what happened with Samson?"

"Samson?"

"Yes . . ." I will her to speak the words.

Her voice is gentle and heartbroken. "No, baby. It wasn't Samson. He didn't do anything to you. Samson always tried to protect you." She says, "He died trying. Don't you know that?"

"What? No, Amma, how can you say that? I was hurt. He hurt me. He touched me. I remember his hands. For years."

"No, baby. It wasn't Samson. If it had been him, it would have been easy. He was a servant. I could have had him thrown out at any moment. It would have been easy." Her voice is cracking wide as if a river will flow out of the crack in her soul. Her words are sinking inch by inch into the strata of my brain.

"Amma, it happened. All the time. When you weren't there. In the dark and in the corners."

"Yes, baby. I know that. I tried to protect you. But I wasn't strong enough. I was just a village girl. If I had said anything, you and I would have been thrown out. No one would have believed me. No one would have taken us in. They would have thought I was making up stories. Things like that didn't happen back then. Or if they did, no one believed it. No one talked about it. But it wasn't Samson."

My chest is shattered open, memories flying out like bits of torn paper with the truth written on them. A maelstrom of words flying around my face, a heaving, swirling snowstorm of memory. I'm in the house. It rises up all around me. Dark passages and empty hallways. I'm small again and running from someone whose footsteps thud just behind my fleeing body. But not Samson. Someone else. A hand landing huge and heavy on my shoulder, spinning me around weightless as a top, a blast of arrack in my face. A gasping shudder from deep inside me. My body naming its perpetrator.

Amma is talking. "He touched you. But he never raped you. You know that, right? It was only some touching. I'm sorry. I tried to protect you. So did Samson that night, and then your father went out with the gun and . . . I'm so sorry. I thought you knew. And now you are the mother of a daughter. I didn't want to bring up these terrible memories. I was trying to protect you."

Everything is quiet inside my head. The storm of words and visions subsides into a single point that pierces my chest, reenters. There are no more tears. I force my voice to be calm. "Amma, it's okay. I have to go, okay? I'll call you later. I promise."

And she, lulled by this tone, says, "Okay, baby. I'm sorry. I love you." I hang up and all my life falls into a different pattern than it had been in before. Everything is shaken and reconfigured at grotesque, unnatural angles. Voices whisper what must be done, what is the only thing. I listen; I am attentive. They make me remember. All those times Daniel hugged Bodhi to him. All those times he went to comfort her and left me alone. It all falls into a different pattern now. I must save her. The way Amma never saved me. But I can save my little girl.

I go to the kitchen and find the pills. Sleeping pills I stored up for all those nights when Samson threatened to come. Their whiteness as pure as the underside of a sea gull's belly, pills to give me wings, to make me fly. I shake the capsules, one two three four five six seven eight nine ten eleven twelve thirteen fourteen fifteen sixteen, seventeen, eighteen, nineteen, twenty into the wooden mortar.

Unbidden, the memory of the last Kandyan noble woman comes. She who with her torn ears gushing down onto her sari blouse crushed her children's heads in a mortar like this one. With a pestle that she had to raise and slam down onto their skulls.

Their dulled eyes watched her, their broken mouths did not protest. What had fractured in her, then? Did some crack in her soul reach down through the ages, through the bloodlines of those born in that place, and touch me here now?

I go into her old bedroom and get her sippy cup, come back to the kitchen and fill it with apple juice. I reach for my own water bottle, unscrew the lid, pour in juice. I upturn the mortar into the golden liquid. Two chalices. One for the queen, one for the child. Then I go to the bathroom, wash my face. My eyes in the mirror are clear, are focused. I change into jeans and a sweater; I brush my hair. Purpose is important. It's the only way I will save her.

There are a thousand demons in the room. I can feel their wings brush my skin, their shadows settling in my hair. They are shrieking in my ear, wrapping themselves in my skin. I put the chalices with their golden liquid in my bag, wrap myself in my big black coat, and walk out into a dawn just lit in gold.

I knock until the old couple, sleep-faced and in their pajamas, open the door. Daniel's mom say, "Oh, hi. We didn't expect you so early. Daniel came in late last night. Shall I wake him?"

I say, "Oh no. I just wanted to get Bodhi. We're making breakfast at my place. Pancakes." I'm smiling hard so they don't see the great gashed tear in me.

The old man says, "But it's just dawn. Poor child. She's fast asleep. Maybe it's better if you get her in a few hours."

"No, I *promised*. She'll be sad if I'm not there when she wakes up." I push gently past him. I walk through the house and into the room, bend over to kiss her, and she wakes, wraps her arms and legs around me, and says, "Mama?"

"We have to go, okay?"

She nods, reaches down to grasp her Pooh blanket.

The old lady, standing in the door, breaks in. "Are you sure everything is fine?"

"Yes. Everything is completely all right. We just have to go."

Her heavy little body is in my arms. She is barefoot and in her pink fleece pajamas. I push past their worried faces, out the door, down the stairs into the honeyed light. I walk to the car and strap her tight into the car seat, cover her in the blanket, the yellow bear smiling at me. I tuck the corners in around her knees. Her eyes rake my face, taking in everything, and she knows she's safe now. I am taking her away from people who could hurt her. Because you never know who could hurt a little girl. Sometimes it's the ones you trust most. She pulls on a corner of the blanket, feels it between her finger pads, sucks it into her mouth. I say, "We're going for a ride, okay?" I kiss her temple, inhale her sweet scent. I get into the front seat, start the car, and drive fast across the Bay Bridge; it's too early for traffic. I'm heading toward the city.

Somewhere in the maze of the city she asks, "Daddy?"

It might have been different if she hadn't said *this* word. We might have driven home, the long way perhaps, the scenic way past the Bay. We might have turned around and gone back home. I might have carried her back into the house, put her in her bed. We might have made our way through the world.

But the thing is, she said this word. And it opened a rip in me, some hidden wound that was already hemorrhaging blood. It killed me, this word. It spoke of trust and betrayal. She was asking for her daddy. I was picturing another father and what had been done to me. Her daddy would take her from me. He would call in the evening and say he was filing. He would steal himself out of my life; he would steal her away, forever out of my reach. And she would be a little girl in the world with no one to protect her. Just as I had once been.

I reach into my bag and then back, say, "Here, baby, apple juice." My shaking fingers hand her the sippy cup. She grasps it with both hands like a squirrel. She doesn't ask about her daddy again. Maybe she is used to disappointment already. Maybe she's too small yet to know that love can kill.

I am calm. The pace of the world is slowed, the traffic is easy. A certain grace fills the air. I unscrew my water bottle, raise it to my lips, and then set it down untouched in the cup holder. I will do this awake. Aware. The morning bursts through the sky with ribbons of pink, catching the world on fire. Sunlight slants across the window, strokes my face like a lover's hand. On the other side of the sky, a bitten moon lingers. I roll the window down as we stop at a light; the birds have started their symphony.

She says, "Mama," and tries to hand me the sippy cup.

"What? How's that, my love? It's just your juice."

"Icky. Don't wan it."

"No, baby, it's just your juice. Drink up. It's good for you." And she, wanting to please, ready to do what Mommy said because Mommy is the sun and she is the smallest flower, listens. This is the bane of childhood, isn't it? That the small person is entirely powerless, entirely dependent on the large person despite whatever grace the larger might or might not possess.

I watch her face in my mirror, the eyelids fluttering, the color changing, the sippy cup slipping out of her fingers, the lid coming off. I hear what's left glug onto the carpet. In the rear mirror I see these things: her head lolling, her body twitching and shaking, a milky froth spilling out of the corner of her mouth, her eyes rolling upward once twice thrice, and then her face settling against her shoulder. She is cradled in the car seat like a nut inside its shell.

I don't look in the mirror anymore. I drive along the smooth avenues, past the park. I remember the bison there, trapped in their meadow. Once not long ago they had thundered across this land in the millions; they had been the monarchs of this continent, unrivaled in strength and number. Seeing them cover the earth, in their day, you would have found it impossible to imagine an end to them. Now there are only these few shaggy outcasts in a far field like deposed kings in exile. We had visited them once. We had stood hand in hand and looked at these lone survivors. We had felt sad for all they had lost, but then we had kissed and were again reminded of luck and love. We had felt blessed. I had not known then how happy I was. Now I know. Now I know exactly how happy I had been in that moment.

I drive across the span to the other side. This is the place that has been waiting for me all along. I pull the car into the parking lot. At this time, it is not crowded. Later there will be tourists, but for now they are all tucked into their various hotels dreaming of the sights they have seen in this most beautiful of cities. I almost cry out when I open the back door and see how her head leans, her moon-silvered eyes. I unbuckle the car seat, pull her out of it, her blanket wrapped so very tight around her. I have to hold her close, so very close. She's like a big doll now. I walk with her head cradled in my palm, held tight and steady against my breast, her sunlit curls bursting forth between my fingers, pulled this way and that by the playful wind.

There are a few people about. The famous red-orange span flies overhead, the tossed sea is below. I linger. On my left, the wide ocean flows. Asia lies that way. Asia like a beckoning glow, far, far over the curve of the earth. The water is full of ghosts; they could claim me and show me how to catch the currents all the way home. All the way to childhood, before cohesion was broken, before skin was split.

One-handed, I pull myself up and clamber across the barrier. We sit on the rim, against the edge of the world; the abyss opens under my feet, the void gapes its toothed maw and cackles. The ocean plays in the sparkling early light. There are voices behind me. I turn and look at suspicious, uneasy faces, unsure whether they are seeing what they think they are seeing, but none coming too close, none bold enough to try and catch me and risk my slipping away from between their fingers. One has pulled out her phone. But there can be no help now.

Samson is here. Looking at me with those eyes, that sad smile. But he means something else now. He's not the one I have to run from. He nods, I turn away.

It is like being an ant on the side of a mountain. The drop beneath my feet makes my nerves tingle. The wind is pulling at her Winnie the Pooh blanket like a dog nipping and tugging at a bone. I let it go and people gasp as it sails away on the currents of the sky, dipping and rising like a kite, fondled and played with by the affectionate streams of air before it's swallowed by the smashing waters. I look down and cry out to see her face slumped against my skin, slightly smashed at the edges, her mouth open.

A man is coming closer, trying to talk to me, trying to tell me it is okay, and I know he will soon try to grab at me. So there is nothing to do but release my arm and let her go tumbling toward the waves and then I step out like my father before me, one hand still holding on, everything else bent toward the open sky, and I unclench my hand and am instantly falling, unable to breathe, a panicked sensation of nothing under my feet, no solidity anywhere, just rushing air and the wind thrusting like needles into my skin. The water below churns like heated oil. I am sobbing and gasping against the wind.

What have I done what have I done what have I done?

The black coat billows around me like the wings of the angel of death that used to sit on the roof of our hospital waiting for the souls streaming out of our windows, and now I am streaming down, down toward the rushing, roiling water. Dear god, what have I done? I have killed her.

I am sobbing and gasping against the wind, pain like a bomb through my chest, and the water is rushing up closer and closer and I will hit soon and then I smash through liquid like hitting a brick wall and it is in my nose and mouth and I am screaming and struggling and fighting and flailing and then suddenly silence explodes in my ears, all around me. The waterweed that has existed in my body sucks me down, pulls at every limb in slow motion. I am suspended, all is silence. I open my eyes and see the yellow blanket undulating so close to my grasping hands. And if it is here, then where is she? I turn my head and see my baby girl. She is just inches away from me, her eyes open and staring, their chocolate brown transmuted into deep green in this place, her fair hair streaming, so much longer now, the curls unwound, reach out as if they would twine about me, pull me to her like golden spider webs, but they don't reach, they only kiss the sides of my face. I stretch my hands out to catch her, but she is just out of reach. She undulates like shimmering ink spilled into water, a gorgeous slow ballet of limbs and movement. She is dancing away from me. There are other forces that want her. They suck her away slowly until she is only a tiny thing so very far away. Then she is gone. I struggle and thrash to follow, but they do not want me.

I am alone.

All around is a viscous, uncanny silence. The hum I have heard all my life, that awful echo is gone. It is all gone: light, sound, pain, time, familiarity. I lie on a bed made of darkness. I have fallen into some other realm, unknown, unseen, and felt only in dream. I float as if I am in amniotic fluid. The void opens around me. I have leapt from the planet. Now there are only fires in the distance, stars burning, silent galaxies slowly, serenely twisting and forming. I am in the grasp of the sacred. I am beyond the reach of my species.

Sunlight drops through the darkness, illuminates thin columns of water like blades come to touch my skin. It gathers about me. The sun god is calling, is claiming, is pulling me up and out of the silence. I don't want this. I need to stay in the abyss. Instead, the water around me too is churning me upward. I am sucked toward light, and above me there is movement, chaos, noise, and then like a cork popping, I break into air and am surrounded by smashing waves and the implosion of my internals, excruciating, panting terror. I am thrown like a toy through the breaks and then a boat comes and men jump into the water, reach for me, haul me onboard. I am shattered, and one of them leaning over me in his huge white suit, looking down at me with tears in his eyes as he cuts away my clothes, asks, "Why?" and darkness wraps midnight around my head.

part five

epilogue
twenty-four

I had wanted to die. I had jumped and the water was supposed to take me. But for its own and secret reasons the water did not want me, and so I lived on.

I wake up in a hospital bed, a guard at the door, people coming and going, needles thrust into my arm. The nurse is not gentle. I keep trying to tell her that she is hurting me, but then I realize that she is doing it on purpose. She wants to hurt me. My brain muddled on sedatives swims up to the surface. Why would she do that? What have I done to warrant this? And this question "What have I done?" leads to a room of such horror that I can't open the door. It is so much easier to sleep. To lie in this slim bed between these cool, clean sheets and sleep.

. . .

Through the drugs there is something gnawing at me. My mind is like a vulture circling; it spots the red ragged thing in the center, but is not able to swoop down and grasp the relevant facts.

In the midst of these days, his face. My love. My lost beloved. He screams and fights. His ravaged frame barely recognizable—the caverns beneath his eyes, the flesh worn, all that solid flesh, all that gleaming muscle has melted away in anguish. This is a wraith of the man I knew.

They have to hold him away from me. "Why! Why? Why'd you do this?" he shouts and sobs. Tears running down his face, he howls, "How could you?" His fists hurl out, itching to make satisfying thuds against my skin. The cops pull him away. They will not give him the pleasure. But they wish for it themselves, to smash my soft face, to let loose a cascade of my teeth, to break my bones. Their job is to pull him away, so they do it, all the while patting him on the back, saying, "It's okay, man. It's okay."

But none of this matters now. The worst thing has already happened.

I spend a long time in that bed. They tell me I am "lucky," with their eyes averted. No one will ever look me in the eyes again. They say that I hit the water at exactly the right angle, feetfirst, as if I was sitting. A nurse says, "It's the only position that wouldn't have broken you into bits." They say I survived what ninety-eight percent of those who jump don't. Human bodies are shattered by that fall. They hit the water with the force of a truck hitting a brick wall. It causes an implosion; organs smash loose from their moorings, ruptured by the jagged edges of broken bones. It is almost always a devastation. And beyond that there are the currents that rip a body miles away in minutes.

What they don't ever want to talk about: my little girl. She was pulled away by the water. They never found her. She was taken far away from me, from everything she knew. I knew as soon as I jumped that I was wrong. That everything I had thought was wrong. I had been given the gift that exceeded all gifts, the gift of a life had been entrusted into my hands, but I had flung this gift from me into the freezing depths. When the drugs lift and I remember this, I am the most anguished soul in the world. I turn my face to the wall and howl.

They take the picture from the frame that sat next to our couch. Her head tilted to the side, two tumbles of blond-brown curls, the pink T-shirt, the tiny denim jacket. I remember dressing her that morning. Toweling off her wet limbs, combing her hair into these two fluffy ponytails. We had laughed that day. It had been a good day. We had loved each other. All these things no one else can know. She was only mine then. Now this picture is everywhere. Now she belongs to the world.

Outside the trial there are a blur of faces, open mouths, screaming voices. People have brought blown-up posters of me with her on my lap, the word *Murderer!* scrawled across our faces. A child

holds a poster that asks, "How could you kill a baby like me?"
Her mother grips her arm. A man waves a sign that reads, *Justice
for Bodhi Anne!* Everywhere my girl's face, her eyes, her lips, that
pink T-shirt and denim jacket. The policemen drag me, my toes
stumbling against the steps. I think, *Look, Bodhi girl, look, they've
come for you because they love you. So many of them. They love
you.* I have to smile and hear a hail of clicking cameras. They'll
publish these pictures with captions that read "Baby-Killer Mom
Shows No Remorse; Smiles Outside Trial." I don't care. It doesn't
matter now.

As the lawyers talk, I study my hands. The oval moons of my
nails. I turn my hand over and look at the lines on my palm. Wonder that nothing there says, "Child-killer. Baby-killer. Medea."

I sit in the courtroom. I let them say what they want. I can see
that they are chilled when my eyes sweep their way. It is laugh-
able. I want to lean forward and say boo. I want to make them
shudder with my murderous breath.

They put up pictures of her. I keep my gaze steady. I refuse to
cry. None of them will ever know the depth of my sorrow, the
sights I see in the night. My pain will be a secret wound blooming just under my skin, filling the whole space of my body.

Fifteen years. It has been fifteen years since it happened,
since I have been inside this place from where I speak to you.

It hasn't been as bad as you would think. I have found a comfort in the institutionalization of life, the measuring out of hours one after the other into these long years, a security in being in one locked place on the planet, a comfort in being given my due.

I think about her every day. She who will always be two and a half but never three years old. Her small body as it was then, before I did what I did.

In dreams I stand on the bank and watch and know that far below the surface, someone is drowning. The air is leaving their lungs through their wide-open mouth. Oxygen is fleeing that dying body in a stream of silver bubbles that catches the light and dances all the way up to the surface of that dark water. Silver bubbles rising in a stream like a twisting ribbon. Whose body? My father's? My daughter's? Samson's? Impossible to tell. All distinction is lost under liquid.

Sometimes she comes to visit me. She's always a different age. She comes as the older child, the teenager, the young woman, as if she were merely somewhere else, in some other far country but able to visit me here inside these cement walls as easily as a thought. We sit on my narrow bed in this small white cell and talk like old friends. It's very easy, very cozy. She laughs often. I drink in her luminescent face, her carved features, the smooth skin. She shakes her hair that falls in a tangle of long corkscrews. It has darkened; her face too has darkened. She looks more like me now, I realize. The planes of my face are apparent in her now. This is my daughter. This is my girl, all grown up.

She says, "Remember how you used to read to me?"

I remember our two bodies pressed together, the whisper of pages. Those nights when I was good.

I nod.

She says, "I really liked that, Mommy. It was nice. You were such a good mama."

I hug her to me. I'll never let her go.

Other times she is harder to please. She asks, "Why?"

My heart clenches. I say, "They were going to take you. I couldn't keep you. They would have taken you."

"Who?"

"Them. Your father and his people. You would have grown up without me."

"So you did this thing instead?"

"I didn't mean to."

"It hurt! When I fell into the cold, it was so painful. I was just a little girl. I was so small."

Her lips are suddenly blue, her eyes bloodshot, her hair dripping. The cell fills with the rush and roar of seawater. It smashes past my ankles and then my knees. I am flailing, thigh-high in the churn of an angry ocean. The water is reaching higher. It will rise above my head soon. She comes to grasp me in her drenched embrace, the scent of brine reaching deep into my head. She smiles her siren smile and her eyes are emerald again, her silver tail flashes. I must wrench myself away from her with a cry, and then I am again alone in my small bed.

. . .

I have committed the unimaginable sin. I am the one who makes all other mothers *good* mothers. In America, to be a mother is to be crucified in a million ways. There is no way to do this job perfectly. Each decision will be derided or decried. Beyond all that, I am the madwoman in the house, I am the maternal nightmare. But also consider this: this is a place that devours its young. Here there are so many other little ones destroyed by these who should love them most.

But I'll say this also. If you had looked closely enough, you would have seen. Most of us were damaged long ago, hurt in some tender place long, long before we were mothers. Wounded flowers, bruised even in their tight closed bud, bear bitter fruit. The prisons are full of us.

My mother writes often. She begs for permission to come to America, to see me. I never answer her letters. I am coming to some sort of understanding. It had not been Samson, as she had revealed in that fateful phone call. It was that other that I still cannot bear to name. It had been too hard for my mother to see or speak the truth, and I had been the sacrifice.

And in turn, this is my inheritance: silence and shame. A silence around the body so complete that the idea of breaking it was worse than the specter of death. A shame so deep that it needed to be buried. And the soil this secret would be buried in, my flesh. I wonder what it would have meant if I could have spoken up in childhood. What would it have meant if I knew I would have been believed? This is not a justification. This is only my truth.

They say that family is the place of safety. But sometimes this is the greatest lie; family is not sanctuary, it is not safety and succor. For some of us, it is the secret wound. Sooner or later we pay for the woundings of our ancestors. This was the truth for me and for my beautiful bright-faced child.

People talk of forgiveness. They say that it's merciful to forgive, that entire religions were founded on the concept. They say that I should be forgiven. They forget that I don't want this. I should be locked in this cell for life.

If this was a fair world, the old machines that enacted retribution would be employed. The rack, the scavenger's daughter, that coffin-like box you stepped into with long spikes that pierced your organs so that you bled out slowly over days. They used to burn witches and pull the hags half alive out of the flames, so that all could see the weight of justice before plunging them back into the flames.

On the island, the Kandyan kings used elephants. They secured the prisoner spread-eagled on the ground, then drove the elephant to plunge a thousand pounds onto his back. You could probably hear the snap of the man's spine, the pop of his skin, the hissing escape of his blood. This is what I deserve; these are the retributions I long for.

• • •

In all the years I have been here, there have been few visitors. I have refused to see almost all who have asked. But when she writes, I can only say yes. When she sits on the other side of the thick glass, I see that she's grown older, of course, more staid. There's a wing of white at each temple, but she is still tiny, and I can still see the imprint of features I loved in a different time. I say in my raspy, unused voice, "Dharshi?" and she nods and smiles, and instantly I remember how we were then when we were only girls and before so much happened. She says, "How are you?" I wave it away. My days have been the same for so many years that the question has no meaning.

We are awkward with each other. She tells me about her life. She's an architect, as she always wanted to be. She's created a life she likes. We talk about those long-lost days when we lived in her room, those two beds just feet away from each other. We remember those long walks after school, the hours watching TV, our feet resting on each other. She reminds me: "When you came you were such a scraggly thing. Like an alien from another world. You didn't even know how to shave your legs. Do you remember?" I think of her showing me, of her sliding the razor along my skin. The way we had been, that kingdom of girlhood. We laugh a little shyly, aware of the sound bouncing around these walls. Her face here in this place is a blessing. I had never expected to see her again. Never expected to hear the sound of her voice. She is a dispatch from the world of the living.

It's almost time to leave when she says she wants to show me something. She reaches into her pocket and the guard in the corner shifts, but she pulls out a photo and lays it against the glass facing me and he calms down. The picture is of her and Roshan, with two tall boys who tower over them and a pretty girl. They all have their arms around one another, their heads tilted together. They are laughing, and the love between them is alive, beating. She smiles and says, "You have to meet the kids. Their names are Dinesh and Dhumal. My girl is Asha. I'll bring them to see you sometime."

I say, "They're beautiful." Determined not to cry. No one has shown me such love in years. I don't deserve it.

Another gift comes. Something I had never dared imagine. A postcard bearing a single red dahlia bursting off its surface. I run my fingers along its surface every day. I know its hues so well that I can close my eyes and see every folded petal. I imagine the live blossom in my hands, its wild exuberance lighting up this dark place. He must know that I miss flowers. Flowers and the scent of him. His writing. It says, "I'll never forgive you. I'll always love you." It says his name. And this is everything.

There is one last thing I must reveal. You know my story and now you must know my name. My name is Ganga. Amma named me after the River Goddess. In the ancient Hindu epics, the Goddess Ganga flows down all the way from the frozen Himalayas across the immense stretch of the subcontinent and into the welcoming Ocean. She is birthed out of the purest snowmelt. In the cities they burn their dead upon her bosom, they fertilize their fields with her, they bathe and drink from her endless flow. And yet the water is always sacred, always pure, an elixir of life. I bear the name of flowing water. A name that reminds us that all liquid is connected. In this way, each of us is bound, one to the other.

I am here now alone, except for my beloved dead.

acknowledgments

My profound gratitude to the following:

Jennifer Weis, my editor at St. Martin's Press. This book is all the better for your careful work on it.

Dori Weintraub, my publicist at St. Martin's Press, for all your dedication to this book.

Ellen Levine, my wonderful agent. Thank you for being my champion.

Sylvan Creekmore at St. Martin's Press, for always responding to my smallest concern.

Lauren Cerand, for taking on this book.

My mother, Upamali Munaweera, whose love for her daughters and granddaughter is fierce and true.

My father, Neil Munaweera, who sees more than we know and whose gift of storytelling has entered my blood.

My sister and brother-in-law, Namal Tantula and Shehan Tantula, for their sweet presence in my life. To Miss Taylor Tantula, who brought the sunshine. I'm glad you were born after I was pretty much done with this book. I couldn't have written it after I saw your tiny face.

My in-laws, Kathy and Daniel Missildine, who remind me that marriage can be blissful and that a shared life of the mind is the best possibility.

The early readers, who are also family and dear friends: Nat Missildine, Ayesha Mattu, and Yosmay Del Mazo.

Candi Martinez, the girl who survived and kept on doing so, so much love to you.

Phiroozeh Romer, so many days writing this book in cafés next to you. Thank you for being there and listening to me work out life and writing.

Yosmay Del Mazo, in gratitude for the many walks and talks on the days when writing this book was just too painful. You inspire me in all ways.

Keenan Norris, our friendship over the years is a beautiful part of my life. No one I'd rather talk writing and books with than you.

Master Melissa McPeters and Gustavo El Diablo Sandi, deep and long friendship. (Gus, if I mention you here, will you read this book? ;)

Ian Brownlee, thank you for so many things, including allowing me to steal your day job, and for your incredible paintings and your talent. All paintings and murals described in this book belong to Ian Brownlee and can be viewed at www.ianbrownlee.com.

Dinesh Rajawasan, you've been my partner in crime from the crib. Here's to so many more adventures together.

Reetika Vazirani, I never met you and I was deep into the writing of this book when I heard your story, but your voice was there all along. Your poetry endures.

If it takes a village to raise a writer, here are my villagers: Raj Ponniah and the Ponniah family, Dhumal Aturaliye, Muthoni Kiarie, Melissa Rae Sipin-Gabon, Sandip Roy, Shyam Selvadurai, Kathryn Shanks, Alina Moloney, Yael Martinez, Nathanael F. Trimboli, Susan Ruth, Faith Adiele, Janet Fitch, Jen Cat Kwong, Ajesh Shah, Hector Coronado, Meow Mix, Tara Dorabji, Cecile and Julie and Louise Missildine, Kavya and Saakya Rajawasan, Nina and Matt Missildine, Neelanjana Bannerjee, Nawaaz Ahmed, Serena Wong and Nick Van Eyck, Jolan Brogan and Scott

Martinez, and the St. Martin's de Porres House of Hospitality Tuesday Crew.

The various writing programs that have supported me: VONA Voices, Kearny Street Workshop's IWL, Litquake, Write to Reconcile, and the Squaw Valley Community of Writers.